FATSO GIONINNI, THE SALTY SAILOR OF *NOW, HEAR THIS!* IS AT IT AGAIN!

"It would take half the page to do justice to this ferociously funny novel. . . . The imperturbable malice Admiral Gallery uses to spoof everything from the way the Navy is run to the poverty program is an exercise in risible ingenuity. This is one of the most hilarious sugarcoatings over a hard core of fact I have read and if it isn't made into a movie or serves as the nucleus for a TV series, there is no justice!"

—*Jefferson Parish Times*, Metairie, La.

"Fatso has the best of weapons—luck, a contagious sense of humor, and an ingenuity which turns sows ears into silk purses."   —*William J. Lederer*

"Walter Mitty in a sailor suit."
—*Admiral Arleigh Burke, U.S.N. (Ret.)*

"The U.S. Navy doesn't need a whole fleet in the Mediterranean. All it needs is a 70-foot motorized barge—LCU-1124—commanded by a resourceful boatswain's Mate First Class like Fatso Gioninni."
—*The New York Times Book Review*

Daniel V. Gallery
Rear Admiral, U.S.N. (Ret.)
CAP'N FATSO

PAPERBACK LIBRARY

New York

PAPERBACK LIBRARY EDITION

First Printing: August, 1970

Copyright © 1969 by Daniel V. Gallery

All rights reserved

Library of Congress Catalog Card Number: 73-83751

This Paperback Library Edition is published by arrangement with
W. W. Norton & Company, Inc.

Contents

FOREWORD

It is unfair to struggling authors to lend books.

If you like this one, after you have read it, lock it up in a safe place or burn it. Then tell your friends about it, and direct them to the nearest reputable book shop.

D.V.G.

Chapter One

Away All Boats

THE SIXTH FLEET is our country's instrument of national policy in the Mediterranean. It has ships, planes, and submarines for spreading peace and good will on, over, and under the seas. It also has Marines to put ashore wherever needed to help their co-workers in the Peace Corps. In case small countries around the Med take any ill-advised action, these Leathernecks are always ready to land, beat the hell out of the local inhabitants, and restore peace and good will.

This morning in May 1967 the fleet was off the west end of Crete practicing the all-hands drill of landing the Marines.

Seizing a hostile beachhead is quite a job, involving every arm of the fleet. This shore line was supposed to be heavily defended, so the whole power of the fleet was zeroed in on it.

An armada of amphibious ships and mine sweeps was hove to a mile off shore. Further out, heavy cruisers steamed back and forth pretending to blast the shore defenses with eight-inch guns. Overhead a stream of snarling jet aircraft from carriers just beyond the horizon "strafed" the shoreline fore and aft and athwartships. Melambo Beach would have been a bad place that morning for natives unfriendly to the Marines.

Sniffing around the edges of the fleet, and sometimes barging right into the middle of it, were a pair of Russian destroyers. This is SOP in the Med these days. Each task force of the Sixth Fleet has a Russian escort wherever it goes. Some of these muzhiks have fairly good sea manners and keep out of the way. Others behave exactly as you would expect, if you have read any Russian naval history—and can hardly get out of their own way.

The beach was now cluttered with small landing craft that had put the first assault wave ashore. A dozen sat with their bow ramps down on the dry sand and the waves washing up half way around them. Others had coasted in on big waves and were high and dry. Some had broached and swamped. At one end of the beach, dwarfing all the small craft, an LST, with its bow ramp up on the sand, was disgorging tanks.

Things were a bit disorganized at the present moment, as they always are right after you land on a hostile shore, even in peacetime. The beach master and his helpers were roaring up and down the strand in jeeps, cursing, swearing, and sweating blood, trying to convert utter chaos into mere confusion.

A battalion of Marines had already stormed ashore, seized the beach head, and were pursuing the fleeing make-believe enemy inland. In another day or so the situation would be well enough in hand for the Army to come ashore and take over.

The second assault wave was now nearing the beach. These were larger boats carrying vehicles and the tons of gear that Marines like to take along to set up housekeeping on shores where the natives are hostile. Bowling along in the middle of this wave with a great bone in her teeth was LCU 1124, Boatswains Mate First Class "Fatso" Gioninni commanding.

Fatso was in his glory this morning. He liked to be where the action is. And there's action enough for anybody in the second wave of an amphibious landing, even when you're just pretending. Fatso stood on the bridge squinting into the wind, his feet braced apart, his hat on the back of his head, and a big cigar in his face.

He had been in real landings at Tarawa, Iwo Jima, and Inchon . . . had two Purple Hearts to show for it. This assault against make-believe bullets was kindergarten stuff for him. But it was fine training for the six young students of naval warfare in his crew.

With one hand on the wheel and the other on the throttles, Fatso handled that two-hundred-ton LCU the way Pablo Casals plays his cello. His popeyed crew studied every move the maestro made. Next time, one of them would have to do it. Whoever got the job would either have to do it almost as well as Fatso did, or else wind up pushing a swab back on the mother ship.

Fatso cocked an eye over the bow gate and lined up his spot on the beach between two LCM's. He allowed a

8

little this way for the wind and that way for the tide. If you had asked him, "How much?" he would have answered, "Just enough."

Fifty yards offshore he bellowed, "Let go kedge anchor." A sailor clouted a pelican hook with a maul, and the kedge plopped into the water. Another lad keeping a loose turn on the winch paid out line to it as they plowed inshore.

Looking back over his shoulder and sizing up the incoming waves, Fatso diddled with his throttles a little bit. He slowed down and let one wave sweep past him. Then he gave her the gun and rode in on the forward slope of the next one. You couldn't call it surfboarding—not with a two-hundred-ton LCU. But it was the next thing to it.

At the last second, Fatso whacked off his throttles and yelled, "Heigh-yo Silver. Ride 'em cowboy!" The LCU slid up on the beach with a crunch. The lad at the winch set taut on the kedge line and took an easy strain. LCU 1124 was beached right smack where she belonged, her bow high and dry and her stern in deep enough water to use her rudder and engines freely.

General MacArthur himself couldn't have done it much better.

"Down ramp. Disembark," roared Fatso. The big bow gate plopped down on the sand, and a platoon of yelling Marines swarmed ashore followed by four snorting jeeps.

"Not bad if I do say so myself," observed Fatso to his admiring crew. "Two feet further up would be better. But this will do."

Fatso was nearing the end of a long and distinguished naval career. He was a veteran of thirty years more or less faithful service. It had been very faithful indeed whenever bombs, shells, or torpedoes were bursting around him. But no more faithful than necessary in peacetime. On his dress blues he wore an array of ribbons headed by a Navy Cross with a gold star for a second one in it. You see very few sailors with one Navy Cross. Two was a record.

He had swum away from two ships that got sunk under him by the Japs. He figured he was now living on borrowed time and intended to live the full life until the loan was called.

He took a rather hardnose view of the Navy Regulations. He felt that they were absolutely necessary—for those left-handed swab handles who wouldn't know what to do unless it was all spelled out for them in a book. But regulations had nothing to do with old-timers like him. He was perfectly willing to die for his country in wartime. But he didn't propose to put up with any horsefeathers for it in peacetime.

This tolerant attitude toward regulations had sometimes got Fatso involved in legal proceedings instigated by young postwar officers who had never seen a shot fired in anger. But whenever he took his seat in the prisoner's dock, wearing all those ribbons and those two Navy Crosses, the government always had a hard time getting a fair hearing for its case. Older officers on the court martial were inclined to badger the prosecution's witnesses.

Fatso had served in all types of ships from nuclear-powered carriers to mine sweeps. He was one of those all-around seafaring men who are fast disappearing from this modern mechanized navy. If you needed someone to program a computer or to tinker with the insides of a black box, you would get some long-haired youngster to do it. But if you had to lower a whale boat in a rough sea, put a mooring swivel on the great bow anchor chain, or do any other job requiring a seaman's eye and knowledge of the wind and wave—Fatso was your man.

This job in which he was winding up his naval career was one of his own choosing. It had always been his ambition to command a ship of his own. This, of course, is impossible for a first class petty officer. But skipper of an LCU is close to it.

True, an LCU is not a commissioned ship. Its status is that of a ship's boat belonging to a bigger vessel. But it is the grandaddy of all boats—bigger than most steam yachts.

It is a flat-bottomed bargelike craft seventy feet long with a thirty-foot beam, with blunt bow and stern. It has two diesel engines which can drive it at fifteen knots. It is designed to carry heavy equipment ashore and deliver it right on the beach. The engine rooms and crew's quarters are aft, extending clear across the craft. Above them are the bridge and charthouse. Everything forward of this is just a big empty compartment with a ramp at the bow which can be lowered when they're on the beach. All that empty space forward and the deckhouse aft makes it look like a craft that can't make up its mind whether it is a barge or a houseboat.

An LCU can just barely fit in the belly of its mother ship—the Landing Ship Dock. The LSD is a strange craft, too. It is a self-propelled, seagoing, floating dry dock of fifteen thousand tons. It can't beach itself like an LST. But in its big well deck, which is flooded when the stern gates are open, it carries a flotilla of small amphibious craft that do beach themselves. The largest of these is the LCU, and each LSD has one of these.

The crew of an LCU live on board their craft even when she is in the hold of the mother ship, although they are actually in the crew of the LSD. They eat in the mess of the big ship, go to its movies, and buy stuff in its canteen and geedunk shops. Their pay accounts and records are carried on the mother ship. But they hang out on their own craft, work and sleep there. They have a tight little navy all their own, and when you've got a good skipper, it's nice work if you can get it.

Fatso was a good skipper. He ran a taut ship. But there was only one Navy Regulation on board—"Do your job." There was no more chicken shit than was absolutely necessary. When there was nothing to do, you could do it any way you damn pleased. When there was a job to be done, working hours were from midnight until the job got done.

The high brass often judge a ship by her outer appearance. So LCU 1124 was always shined up like the inside of a five-inch twin turret. The Admiral could take one squint at her shipshape topside, her gleaming bright work, and her clean, smartly uniformed crew, and feel that here was a craft that was run by the book. Obviously, on inspections, there was no need to waste time snooping around below decks on *her*.

This was good, because certain things not visible to the naked eye might have caused unfavorable comment by a narrow-minded inspecting officer. Among them were a well-stocked bar and enough gambling equipment to open a joint in Las Vegas.

11

As the last jeep roared down the ramp that morning, Fatso said, "Aw right now. Secure and set the watch. We may sit here two, three days. . . . With all that cargo ashore, we may be a little loose at high tide. That's why I said we could of run her up a couple of feet higher." He then adjourned below to the crew's lounge to await orders from higher authority.

The crew's lounge of an LCU is also the messroom, bunkroom and galley, all rolled into one. There are folding bunks along the bulkheads, a mess table in the center, a small galley range at one end, and radio and TV sets at the other. Outside on the well deck are lockers, the head, and washroom.

As Fatso entered the lounge he was greeted by Scuttlebutt Grogan, Engine Man First Class, and Chief Engineer of LCU 1124.

"We gonna set up shop tonight, skipper?" asked Scuttlebutt.

"Yeah," said Fatso. "Right after chow. There must be a hundred Marines in the beach party. They sure can't spend any money ashore here. We might as well give them some action for it."

"Okay," said Scuttlebutt. "I'll pass the word to them."

Scuttlebutt and Fatso were old pals who had gotten in and out of many jams together, both in peace and in war. Although Fatso was in the deck force and Scuttlebutt the black gang, they were both the same mark and mode of sailor man. Their outlook on life, liberty, and the pursuit of happiness was the same. They demanded their full allowance of each.

Fatso regarded Scuttlebutt as a seagoing version of Thomas Edison. He often said Scut must have been born with a monkey wrench in one hand and a pair of pliers in the other. Using nothing but those two tools, a screw driver, a roll of tape, and some baling wire, he could fix any piece of balky machinery so it would operate as designed.

Between them, he and Fatso were masters of all the arts needed to run a ship—until ships became floating electronic labs. The six young sailors in their crew were picked to supply the special skills needed to sail the seas in the atomic age. They were specially screened for im-

12

agination, coolness in a jam, and the ability to figure odds and to shoot the works when the price was right. They were an improbable crew who might have served with distinction under Captain Kidd. The only thing they had in common was a somewhat lukewarm respect for higher authority.

The reader may already suspect this from what has been said about her skipper and chief engineer. The six other lads all hoped that if they avoided the rocks and shoals, they might someday be like these two. But they had a long way to go.

A certain attitude toward life on this earth and the authorities in charge of it can only be acquired by hearing enough pieces of jagged metal whiz past you at high speed. Fatso and Scuttlebutt had heard plenty. None of the other lads had ever been shot at.

That didn't matter too much with Fatso. He knew you can never tell ahead of time how people will act when they hear those kinds of noises. If it disconcerts them too much, you just have to be sorry and get rid of them. If they take it in stride, that's nothing to really brag about—that's what U.S. Navy sailors are supposed to do.

Fatso favored lads who spoke softly but could swing a haymaker in close quarters if the situation called for it. What he looked for in his men was the ability to participate in enterprises not exactly authorized by the regulations and while so engaged to give all outward appearance of being Sea Scouts intent on doing their daily good turn.

Enlisted men who possess the strength of character and initiative to do this naturally gravitate to positions of responsibility and trust in a military organization. Although presently in minor jobs on LCU 1124, Fatso's boys were destined for bigger and better things later on. All regarded Fatso as a modern John Paul Jones.

"Jughaid" Jordan was a hillbilly from Tennessee. He was a dropout from sixth grade who might have been an Einstein if his education hadn't been cut short because his pappy needed a helper on his still. Jughaid claimed he had two dead revenuers to his credit—"Made 'em run so hard trying to catch me they dropped daid."

Henry Cabot Worthington was a spoiled brat from a wealthy New England family. He was a sort of a dropout too, but from MIT in his second year of a PG course

13

in atomic physics. He got into a hassle with his old man over a chorus gal they were both chasing and simply walked out and joined the Navy. Naturally, he was known on LCU 1124 as "the Professor."

"Judge" Frawley came by his nickname because he had attended Columbia Law School. He was a kickout rather than a dropout. He had been a brilliant student until the faculty as well as the local police began nosing into some of his extra-curricular activities. When this happened his legal training, incomplete though it was, convinced him he had better leave town. He was the legal authority on board, and although the Supreme Court might have dissented from some of his opinions, Fatso had great respect for them.

Abe Ginsberg was an ex-newspaper photographer from Brooklyn. He had been drafted just when his fellow newsmen were about to kick him out of their union for violating their professional ethics. They claimed he was giving their trade a bad name by sticking his nose into places where it didn't belong, riding roughshod over the public's rights of privacy, and making bums of his colleagues by getting pictures no one else could.

Webfoot Foley had been a steeple jack and a sky diver before going to sea. He had served three years in the Navy with the UDT boys as one of the bomb disposal men who swim under water to enemy mines and take the fuses out. This is a tough way to make a living, and no one has yet retired from that profession on a pension. Webfoot was one of the best in the business. But he was persuaded to give up that line of work by teammates to whom he owed money.

Finally, there was Satchmo Armstrong. Satch was one of our Disadvantaged Citizens, although it never occurred to him that he was. He was darker than eight bells on the midwatch of an overcast night. Inside a blacked-out clothes closet, he would loom up as a dark area.

He was a jack of all trades, good at everything he put his hand to. He could have been one of the head cooks at the Waldorf but preferred the galley of LCU 1124. He was a good signalman, fine helmsman, blew a hot trumpet, and was an expert at rolling dice. If you had asked him if he could fly, he might well have said, "Ah dunno, Cap'n— I ain't never tried."

Discipline was no problem on LCU 1124. Its crew, when on board the mother ship, were, of course, subject to the same rigors of military law as any other sailors. But aboard LCU 1124, Fatso was the law. If your conduct was such as to incur his wrath, there was only one punishment —a cruel and unusual one. You got kicked off.

Everyone on board pooled their skills to help the ship fulfill its military mission. It did this so well it had won the coveted gold E for excellence among all amphibious craft three years in a row. Everyone, when he first came aboard, also pooled his money in the ship's "welfare fund," thus buying into the bank which ran the bar and casino.

This bank was run as a nonprofit enterprise—although I doubt if Internal Revenue would ever certify it as such. At any rate, it didn't keep money out of circulation long. Each pay day, when other sailors were drawing their money from the government, Fatso and his boys whacked up the surplus in the bank. This left their regular pay on the books and available to the Treasurer of the United States. In this way, the bank helped ease the dollar shortage and was really a patriotic service.

Chapter Two

Happy Hour

A HALF HOUR after LCU 1124 came ashore, a Marine jeep whisked down the beach and slid to a halt in the sand at the end of the ramp. A VIP disembarked from the rear seat, said a curt word to the driver, and strode up the ramp to the well deck.

The visitor was a lanky, weather-beaten character, big enough to be a line backer for the Green Bay Packers but a little too old. He had piercing eagle eyes and the easy air of final authority that comes from years of being the boss man wherever you go. He was obviously either a Supreme Court judge, a Big League umpire, or a Marine top sergeant.

"Take me to your skipper," he growled at Satchmo, who met him at the head of the ramp.

"Yes, SIR!" said Satchmo. "Follow me, SIR," and he led the way to the mess room.

Fatso was seated at the table finishing a cup of coffee.

"Gent'man to see you, skipper," said Satchmo, as the top sergeant followed him in, ducking his head to get through the door.

Characters like Fatso and the Marine don't fiddle around with protocol when they first meet. Such men know a kindred spirit by instinct, developed only by long years of military service keeping just barely within the limits set by the Articles of War. Fatso and the top sergeant passed each other's inspection at first glance.

"Har ya, Cap'n?" said the Marine.

"Hello, Sarge," said Fatso. "Have a seat."

"Nice craft ya got here," said the Marine, peering around the messroom as he sat down.

"It'll do," said Fatso. "We take our bunks and our mess table along wherever we go. That's more than you guys do sometimes."

"You're telling *me*," said the Marine. . . . "I hear you're having a sort of happy hour aboard for my boys tonight."

16

"Yeah," said Fatso. "We figure there ain't much for them to do on this here beach, so we thought we would have a little party for them tonight. It'll do 'em good to relax a little."

"Uh huh," observed the Marine, lighting up a cigarette. The hand that held the match shook almost as if it had a dice box in it. "It'll do *you* some good, too, from what I hear. What kind of action are you going to have?"

"Roulette, craps, blackjack—which do you like?"

"Personally, I ain't a gambling man, myself," said the Marine. "I figure I used up all my luck at Iwo Jima."

"Iwo?" said Fatso. "I was there too. Funny we missed each other."

"Well, I didn't stay long," said the Marine. "In fact you might say I just barely got there—with the seat of my pants blown off."

"How come?"

"Our boat got blowed up just before we got to the beach. I was lucky to get ashore at all with a handful of shrapnel where the seat of my pants should of been. I always say that landing gave me the worst pain in the ass of all I've ever been in."

"What beach was that on?" asked Fatso.

"Charlie One."

"Which wave?"

"The first one."

"I'll be damn," said Fatso. "I was in the first wave on Charlie One. We almost got it too. One of our own fly boys planted a bomb in the boat right next to us."

"Hah! That musta been the one I was in," said the Marine. "That goddam aviator claimed afterwards his bomb got hung up and fell off when he was on his way home, just as he crossed the beach."

"Imagine that," said Fatso. "In the boat right next to me at Iwo! It's a small world—ain't it? That was tough luck, all right."

"I dunno," replied the Marine philosophically. "If it hadn't of been for that I might still be on Iwo. But here I am now in Crete, doing my last hitch on thirty years."

"Would you like a little snifter?" asked Fatso.

"Don't mind if I do," said the Marine.

"Let's go to my cabin," said Fatso, getting up and leading the way.

"Cabin" is a bit of an overstatement for Fatso's pad. It was little more than a king-sized swab locker. It had a bunk, a small desk, a clothes locker, a washstand, and a porthole. But it did provide Fatso with privacy, which is the skipper's traditional right on any ship.

"Have a chair, Sarge," said Fatso, indicating the bunk while he seated himself at the desk, pulled out the bottom drawer, and produced a bottle of Old Granddad. He placed a shot glass alongside it, filled a tumbler half full of water, uncorked the bottle, and shoved it toward the Marine.

"Help yourself," he said.

The Marine, his hand still shaking, filled the shot glass to the brim and set the bottle down. Then he picked up the shot glass, held it up toward the port and squinted at it judiciously, his hand now as steady as a concrete block. He took a small sip from it, swallowed it slowly with a studious look, and then tossed off the rest. Then he dumped the water out of the tumbler in the wash basin, filled the glass half full of whiskey and took a swig from it that left no more than three or four shot glasses full in the tumbler.

"Not bad," he announced, smacking his lips.

Fatso corked up the bottle and put it back in the bottom drawer. "Yeah?" he said. "They claim it's pretty good stuff. This is the hundred proof version of it."

"I *thought* it tasted a little sharp," observed the Marine. "I guess that's why. . . . Now, let's talk business."

"Okay. What's on your mind?"

"This action tonight. I want a piece of it."

"You can have all you want of it," said Fatso, as if he didn't get what the Marine meant. "We got a ten-buck limit on the wheel, fifty on the crap game, and twenty-five on the blackjack. You can get pretty fast action in any of them."

"That ain't what I mean," said the Marine. "I want a cut on the house's percentage."

"Well, now," said Fatso. "I hadn't given that much thought. Just how big a cut did you have in mind?"

"Fifty-fifty," said the Marine.

"I wouldn't hardly think it oughta be that much," said Fatso. "After all, we provide the layout, run the whole show, and give each guy his first can of beer free. We

18

wouldn't even clear the nut on the joint if we split right down the middle with you."

"Yeah—I see what you mean," said the Marine. "But, of course, if none of my boys come to the party, there won't be nothin' at all to split."

"You got a point there, all right," said Fatso. "But another thing to think about is that when we're playing with outsiders like the Army or sailors off the big flat tops, both zeros on the wheel go for the house. Playing with the amphibs or Marines, we don't count the double zero."

"That's mighty fair of you," conceded the Marine. "But if you count both zeros tonight, then you could give me my cut and your take would still be the same as if you were only using one zero."

"Yeah," said Fatso. "But there's another angle you got to consider, Sarge. When we make a one-night stand somewheres and we're gonna leave the next day, then it's smart to jack up the house cut as high as you can. But if you're going to be somewhere for a week, then it's smart to cut down the percentage and prolong the action. You wind up with the same amount of dough either way. There's just so much to be had out of a crowd like yours, and when you get it, the action is over. You can take it all the first night or string it out over several nights. I like to string it out. It gives the boys something to do and keeps 'em out of trouble. . . . Tell you what I'll do, Sarge. I'll pay you a flat fifty bucks instead of a percentage. How about that?"

The Marine tossed off the rest of the glass, deliberated a moment, and then said, "Let's do it this way. I'll take either a flat fifty bucks or a quarter of your net after the last night—whichever is the biggest."

"Okay," said Fatso.

"See you tonight," said the Marine, getting up off the bunk. "Thanks for the snifter."

At dinner that evening, Scuttlebutt said to Fatso, "you know who that Marine was that come aboard this afternoon?"

"Well, I guess you might say I met him," said Fatso. "But I never did get his name."

"That was old Shaky Stokes," said Scuttlebutt.

"Shaky Stokes?" said Fatso. "I been hearing about him for years. Used to be a famous pistol shot, didn't he?"

"One of the best in the country," declared Scuttlebutt. "And to watch him shoot, you wouldn't think he could hit a elephant at ten paces. I've seen him at a pistol match hold that gun up in the air waiting his turn with his hand shaking like a leaf. When his turn came, he'd draw down, still shaking until the target came in his sights. Then he'd freeze, and squeeze off a shot drilling the bull's-eye at fifty yards."

"I noticed his hand shook a little," said Fatso.

"He used to drink quite a lot," observed Scuttlebutt.

"*Used* to?" snorted Fatso. "If he's tapering off now, I'm glad I never offered him a snifter when he was working at it."

Scuttlebutt got a gleam in his eye as old sailors always do when they are about to tell a tale. "The Marines tell a story about him taking his annual physical some years ago," he said. "At the end of it, the doctor asked him about the shakes. He says, 'I guess maybe I'm smoking a little too much, doc.' 'How much do you smoke?' says the doc. 'Oh, I dunno—maybe three or four packs a day,' says Shaky. The doc tells him 'Yeah, you ought to cut down a little'—and then he says, 'It takes more than smoking to make you shake the way you do—how about liquor?' So Shaky says, 'Yeah—I guess maybe I drink a little too much, too.' 'How much do you drink?' asks the doc. 'Oh, I dunno,' says Shaky; 'I don't keep track of it.' 'Can't you give me *some* idea?' says the doc. 'Is it as much as, say, a quart a day?' 'Aw hell, doctor,' says Shaky, 'I *spill* more than that.'"

Later that evening, the happy hour was in full swing on the well deck. Lights were discreetly shaded to shine downward, and the bow ramp was up so nothing was visible from the beach. A hundred or so Marines divided their play about equally among the roulette wheel, crap game, and blackjack table. Fatso's boys were professionals so the action was brisk, and the gaming was just as orderly as that at Monte Carlo. Except, of course, for the language.

Most of these Marines were pink-cheeked lads just out of boot camp. At boot camp, for reasons known only to the Marines, the first thing they teach the recruits is how to inject a word rhyming with "duck," with proper blasphemous modifiers and amplifying phrases, into every declarative statement they make, except when speaking to military superiors directly. It may be that this is done to safeguard the boys' morals. Such language is apt to get you thrown out of any well-run whorehouse in the western world, and most of these lads are too young to be patronizing such places.

Fatso also thought they were too young to drink hard liquor. So all he sold them on LCU 1124 was beer. Scuttlebutt tended the bar at one end of the mess hall, where beer was ten cents a can after the first one on the house.

Fatso and Shaky Stokes were seated at the other end of the messroom surrounded by a group of spellbound admirers. On the table between them there was a Gordon Gin bottle. Fatso wasn't about to put his Old Granddad bottle within reach of Shaky again. Matter of fact, the gin bottle contained a mixture of medical alcohol and water, which of course looks the same as gin. After a snifter or so, it tastes about the same, too.

Fatso and Shaky were swapping lies about what they had done in the war, with their young fans listening in popeyed amazement.

After a while they got around to the characters they had served with in the old days. Some of them were dillies. Any ordinary citizen listening in on these sagas would wonder how in the world we managed to win World War II with such oddballs in high command posts. We probably *wouldn't* have won it, except, of course, we had Fatso and Shaky on our side too.

"I was in old Thirty-Knot Dugan's tin-can division for a while after the *Lexington* got sunk," said Fatso. *"There* was a character for you. Never a dull moment in his outfit. We used to call ourselves 'Dugan's Johnny Busters.' We was based in Espiritu and the channel to the lagoon where we anchored ran right close to the beach for about a mile. The Army built a big camp right along that beach and to save themselves the trouble of digging latrines, they had a row of a couple of dozen privies sitting on beams that stuck out over the water. After they got them built, every time old Dugan took us out of that lagoon he'd bend on

21

about thirty knots. Of course we would drag a stern wave behind us about six feet high, and the beams those privies sat on were only about two feet above the water. When our wake hit that row of privies it would knock 'em over like ten pins. Funniest sight I've ever seen was all them shit houses popping up in the air one after another with soldiers scrambling out of them hauling their pants up as they ran. Old Dugan used to look back at 'em and say, "The Army must be feeding the boys those Mexican jumping beans again." The General was in one of 'em when it got klobbered, and he had a hell of a time getting out. Damn near got drownded. There was hell to pay about that. It got all the way up to Admiral Nimitz, and he made old Dugan knock it off. The Army was going to take it clear up to the Joint Chiefs if he hadn't."

"Speaking of shit houses," said Shaky, with an I-can-top-that-one gleam in his eye, "when we were in Noumea getting ready to land on Guadalcanal, old Grandma Gillis was our division commander. How he ever got two stars I'll never know—except this was early in the war, and he was one of those peacetime soldiers who used to make it just by outliving everybody else. They got rid of him just before the invasion, and it's a damn good thing they did. Otherwise, the Japs would of wound up in Australia. Old Grandma was the most indecisive guy I've ever known. Never could make up his mind about anything. It used to take him ten minutes each morning at breakfast to decide whether he wanted his eggs fried straight up or turned over. Anyway, when we were building the camp, Grandma wanted a special privy of his own right near his Quonset hut. He told his Chief of Staff he wanted a two-holer, with green and yellow stripes on it, a field telephone to HQ in it, and a wind vane on top. The COS told the top sergeant, and the top told me. I had to build it. Our top was old Squarehead Bates, and he couldn't stand people who hemmed and hawed about deciding things. His mind was made up about everything the day he was born, and he never changed it. When old Squarehead had told me what to build, he said a one-holer, and that's what I did. When I got it finished, stripes, battle phone, wind vane, and all, Squarehead brought the COS around to inspect it. The Colonel said, 'What the hell—I told you I wanted a two-holer.' Squarehead says, 'Yessir, Colonel, but I figure if we gave the old gentleman a two-holer, while he was making up his mind which hole to use, he'd crap in his pants.' "

When the whoops over that yarn subsided, Fatso shook his head and said, "I wonder what's become of all the old characters we used to have?"

Shaky took a studious swig of "gin" and observed, "I dunno. But we sure don't have 'em like that any more."

One of the young listeners nudged the guy sitting next to him and said, under his breath, "Get a load of those two balmy old (suitably modified) bastards saying there ain't no more characters in this outfit."

When the party broke up that evening, the sergeant said to Fatso, "Okay, Cap'n—see you tomorrow night."

"Righto," said Fatso. "Same time."

There had been quite a redistribution of wealth among the Marines that night. But it was only Marine money that changed hands. Fatso and his boys never gambled—they just ran the games, handled the money, and took the usual cut for the house.

When they closed up that night there were three hundred and fifty new dollars in the bank. This wasn't bad, considering that when playing against the Marines, Fatso would not allow the house to use certain dice that were not exactly in dynamic balance or cards you could read just as well from either side, when you knew how.

"Pretty good night," announced Scuttlebutt, when he finished counting the dough. "This brings the welfare fund up to just over a thousand dollars."

"Yeah," said Fatso. "We'll do just as good tomorrow night, too. We gotta declare a dividend pretty soon."

Chapter Three

Change of Plans

WHILE FATSO and his lads were entertaining the Marines, the skipper of their mother ship, the USS *Alamo,* had the Commodore of the squadron in his cabin for dinner. Over their coffee they were reviewing recent events of global significance.

"I almost hit that goddam Russian cruiser the other night," said the skipper.

"Yeah. I saw that," replied the Commodore. "For a minute I thought you *were* going to hit him."

"It was mighty close," said the Captain. "I think he was trying to get hit. He spent an hour getting into position where he could suddenly cut across my bow showing me his red light. I had to go hard right and back full to miss him. What the hell are they trying to prove, anyway?"

"There's no use trying to make sense out of what they do," observed the Commodore. "They're just out to stir up trouble. If they can get hit when they've got the legal right of way, they may think they can make something out of it."

"What do you think would happen if I hit him next time?"

"As long as the Navy handled it, you'd have no trouble at all. In fact, the Admiral might feel like slipping you a medal under the table. He's burned up about the Roosians. But of course, a thing like this becomes an international incident, and gawd knows what the naval strategists in the State Department would do."

"Y'know, Commodore," observed the skipper; "in a way, I think it's a Good Thing to have these Russian snoopers hanging around."

"How the hell do you figure that?"

"Well, . . . when they get back home, there's only one thing in the world they can report—those guys are big leaguers, and they're damn good."

"Maybe you've got something there," laughed the Commodore. "I'll tell that to the Admiral next time I see him. He'll get a kick out of it."

"By the way," said the skipper, "I see by the radio press news where the amphibs are getting into the Vietnam war in a big way. It looks like they'll be in it more and more from now on."

"Yeah. I saw that item in the press. They're cooking up a regular gunboat navy for the river war out there. The amphibs are going to be in it up to their ears from now on. By God, that's where I'd like to be—instead of fooling around here playing games. I'd swap this commodore job right now for command of a ship out there on the firing line."

"I'd rather be out there, too," said the skipper. "These make-believe battles around here don't get you any combat stars in your service ribbon. But I see by the dispatches where there's trouble brewing between the Israelis and the Arabs. We'll be right in the middle of it if that breaks."

"Nothing will come of that," said the Commodore pontifically. "Nasser has got all the Arabs lined up behind him now. I see where Jordan and Syria just fell in line. He's got pretty near forty million Arabs on his side against two and a half million Israelis. Those Jews have got a pretty good little army and air force. But they're too smart to start a shooting war against odds like that."

"I guess you're right, Commodore," said the skipper. "I. . . ."

At this point a messenger entered and handed a dispatch board to the Captain. The Captain scanned the message, initialed it, and handed it to the Commodore.

"Change in our supply schedule," he observed. "The *Sylvania* is being diverted. Instead of coming here she's going back to the States. She has fifty tons of stores for us that she's going to leave in Malta. We can pick it up after our visit to Athens."

"Hell," growled the Commodore, "Some of that stuff is for me. And I want it before we go to Athens. My official car is in it. I've been pulling wires to get that car for six months, and I want to have it in Athens. Those two deep-freeze lockers they mention are for me, too . . . special stuff for my mess, including six dozen king crabs that old

Blubber Ass Davis is sending all the way from Sitka. . . . Nuts!"

The skipper saw a chance to make character for himself with the Commodore—as up and coming skippers are always alert to do. "I can get that stuff here for you, Commodore, before we go to Athens," he said.

"I will consider you a great naval strategist if you do," said the Commodore. "How?"

"This little game we're playing here is going to last a week. My LCU has nothing to do but just sit there on the beach till we take the troops back aboard. She can make it to Malta and back in five days and can easily handle fifty tons—I can send her off tomorrow, if you say so."

"Sa-a-a-ay! That's an idea," said the Commodore. "You sure she can make it there and back? After all, those LCU's aren't meant to get out of sight of their own ship."

"This one is special, Commodore. Her skipper is that boatswains mate with two Navy Crosses—the same one that got us that letter of commendation for helping to get the A-bomb off the bottom near Spain. I'll bet he could take her clear to Norfolk and back if you told him to."

"Hunh!" observed the Commodore, skeptically. "Well, Columbus made it over and back in a bucket only half as big. After all, it's your LCU. If you say he can do it—it's okay with me."

Soon a blinker message went in from the *Alamo* to the Marine signal station on the beach. An orderly took it down the beach to LCU 1124 and handed it to Fatso, just as they finished counting the swag from the evening's work. It said, COME ALONGSIDE 0600 TOMORROW.

"Okay," announced Fatso. "Plan of the Day for tomorrow is—Reveille 0530. Underway 0545. We will get breakfast on the *Alamo*."

Next morning, came the dawn and found Melambo Beach as peaceful as a country churchyard. The eternal stars still peered down quietly from the west as the golden glow of the sun began lighting up the east. The new day spreading west across the world found no sign of the turmoil and trouble that afflict this earth. Nobody was up yet.

A few early birds flapped lazily along the shoreline.

Perhaps they were doves, confident that no hawks would molest them here.

The peace and quiet was broken only by the gentle swish of small swells washing ashore—and by the snores of the Marine sentries asleep at their posts, their weapons loaded, cocked, and ready.

At 0530 the anchor watch on LCU 1124 made three bells. He did this by tapping twice on the ship's bell, waiting two seconds, hitting one more lick. Then he flipped a switch. The silence of Melambo Beach was shattered by Toscanini's symphony orchestra blasting out *Stars and Stripes Forever* on Fatso's hi-fi record player with the volume turned up to war emergency power.

This was regular daily routine on LCU 1124 when they were not embarked in the mother ship. For a short while it had been on the mother ship too—until the Captain made Fatso knock it off. Even though the officers' quarters are forward and the LCU berthed aft, the *Alamo*'s officers claimed it blasted them right out of their bunks.

Martial music was Fatso's idea of how to start the day off right. It also helped him to check on the military character of new men trying out for his crew. Any sailor who could stay in his bunk while Toscanini was belting out *Stars and Stripes* obviously was not the sort of man that Fatso wanted to take into battle with him.

At 0545, with a seaman at the wheel and Fatso looking on, LCU 1124 took a strain on the kedge line, backed full, and came off the beach. Ten minutes later she eased into the well deck of the *Alamo* with only a foot to spare on each side, and tied up.

A few minutes later, Fatso was in the cabin getting his orders from the Captain.

"Gioninni," said the skipper, "I want you to go to Malta and pick up some freight." He handed Fatso the message from the *Sylvania*.

"Malta?" said Fatso. "Aye aye, sir. No strain."

"You can draw any charts you need from the navigator."

"Don't need any, Cap'n. I've got a complete set of the whole Med—just in case."

"Okay," said the Captain. "We're due to leave here a

week from today for Athens. I'll expect you back in five days."

The first few days of LCU 1124's voyage to Malta were quiet and uneventful. That is, they were for LCU 1124. But they were far from it for the Middle East.

The Arab-Israeli hassle suddenly went critical and threatened to fission. Nasser said "Boo" to the United Nations, which promptly yanked its peace-keeping force out of the Gaza Strip. The Arabs and Israelis rushed troops up to the border to fill the void. Nasser blockaded the Gulf of Aqaba. The Israelis made belligerent noises about this. In Jerusalem and Cairo, derogatory comments were voiced about each other's armies, and each side officially notified the other that if they didn't watch out, they would get their goddam block knocked off. Nasser got ready to close the Suez Canal.

While these international courtesies were being exchanged, Commander Sixth Fleet got an urgent message from CNO. It said that more amphibious craft were needed in Vietnam, and those in the Sixth Fleet could get there quicker than any others as long as Suez was open. So CNO directed Sixth Fleet to send most of their amphibious forces to Vietnam, *right now*.

This, of course, stopped the landing exercise. There was a mad scramble to get the Marines and their gear off the beach and get the ships started on their way to war in Vietnam.

On the *Alamo*, the skipper and Commodore had their heads together.

The skipper was saying, "We can't possibly get our LCU back in less than seventy-two hours, Commodore. We can't reach him by radio. We'd have to send a message to Malta, and it would take at least three days to get him back."

"All right," said the Commodore. "We've got to leave him behind. They need these ships real bad in Vietnam, and I'm not going to miss a chance to get in that war by having the canal closed on us while we're waiting. They've probably got plenty of LCU's out there anyway. Send word to Malta to have your man go up to Naples and check in with HQ there."

28

"Aye aye, sir," said the skipper. "There's a whirlybird coming in soon from one of the carriers to pick up the mail. I'll put the records and pay accounts of the crew aboard with a letter to the Carrier Division Commander asking him to have Malta send her up to Naples."

"Okay," said the Commodore. "That ought to take care of it."

It would have, too. Except that on the way back to the carrier that morning a little thing-um-a-jig in the transmission joint of the whirlybird's rotor began working loose. A mile from the carrier, it came off altogether. This caused one rotor blade to fly off and dumped the whirlybird into the drink with a hell of a splash.

The pilot and his two crewmen were lucky to get out of it and got picked up by the plane guard destroyer. The whirlybird, and the mail, of course, wound up on the bottom in a thousand fathoms of water.

Meantime, the USS *Alamo* and others were high-tailing it for Suez, and LCU 1124 was plugging along toward Malta.

Soon after Fatso's interview with the Captain of the *Alamo*, LCU 1124 squared away on her course to Malta and set the cruising watch. The watch consisted of the Officer of the Deck, the helmsman, the lookout, boatswain's mate, signalman, and OOD's messenger. They were all the same guy, of course. With only six men in the crew you have to stretch duties a bit.

As skipper Fatso was, of course, on duty at all times. So was Scuttlebutt, although he didn't spend much time below in his engine room. If anything started to go wrong down there, Scuttlebutt knew it before the engines did. His ears told him how his engines were running just as well as an array of gauges could. And he felt any strange vibration the way a seismograph picks up a small earthquake thousands of miles away.

As Crete dropped below the horizon astern, Fatso and Scuttlebutt were leaning on the rail of the bridge discussing matters that interest seafaring men.

"You got any good numbers in Athens?" asked Scuttlebutt.

29

"Sure," said Fatso. "What kind you want—blondes or brunettes?"

"Friendly ones."

"They're all as friendly as you want, so long as your money holds out . . . some of 'em even after that, if you're polite to them," said Fatso reminiscently. "I remember. . . ."

"Sail ho! Cap'n," came a hail from Satchmo, who was at the wheel.

"Where away?" demanded Fatso.

"Two points faw-ahd of de port beam," intoned Satchmo.

"Can you make her out," yelled Fatso.

"Jes a mast on de horizon, Cap'n."

This ritual for a sighting by the lookout goes back to the days of sail. It is fast being forgotten now that radar dishes are replacing the Mark I eyeball of the lookouts. But Fatso insisted on keeping it alive on his ship.

Fatso and Scuttlebutt swung their glasses around to the bearing indicated and found the top of a mast sticking up over the horizon.

"That's what I call eagle eyes," observed Scuttlebutt.

"Good work, Satchmo!" called Fatso.

Five minutes later more of the ship's upper works, including the tops of two smokestacks, had come up over the horizon. The bearing remained unchanged.

"She's comin' up fast," observed Scuttlebutt. "Must be a destroyer."

"Yeah," said Fatso. "Bearing isn't changing, so we'll pass close aboard and get a good look at her."

For the next five minutes, more and more of the ship came into sight, and finally the bow wave broke over the horizon and you could see the whole ship.

"It's a Russian," observed Scuttlebutt. "Must be making about thirty knots."

"Yeah," said Fatso. "Bearing hasn't changed a bit. . . . What are you gonna do about that guy?" yelled Fatso at the pilot house.

"Ah ain't gonna do nuthin', Cap'n," replied Satchmo. "Ah's got de right of way, so I must hold mah course and speed."

"Right," replied Fatso. "He should be changing course any minute now to pass astern of you."

"I'll bet he don't," said Scuttlebutt.

Fatso walked into the charthouse and came out a minute later with a Very's pistol. The range was down to three miles now and closing rapidly.

Fatso yelled at the pilot house, "If he doesn't make his move in another minute, give him one long blast."

"Aye aye, Cap'n," replied Satchmo, his hand on the whistle control.

"Looks like he wants to play a game of chicken with you," observed Scuttlebutt.

"Uh huh," said Fatso. "And he's got us over a barrel if he does. We ain't allowed to change course or speed until just before it's too late."

Pretty soon Satchmo let out one long blast on his whistle. Fatso and Scuttlebutt focused their glasses on the destroyer's forward stack to watch for the answering whistle blast confirming that the rules of the road would be observed. You can see the plume of steam from a whistle before you can hear it. Another minute went by with no sign from the destroyer that she had heard Satchmo's blast or that she saw the LCU or intended to avoid it.

Fatso raised the Very's pistol and fired a red star up in the air. Still nothing happened. When the range got down to one mile, Fatso strode into the pilot house, took station behind Satchmo, and said, "Okay, Satch—I've got the conn."

By now the destroyer was looming up fast, and it was clear that if neither ship did anything there would be a collision. Fatso held on to the last possible instant. Had he kept going, he would have hit the destroyer smack amidships. The big bow wave of the destroyer swept by and tossed the LCU in the air as it rolled past. The small craft came down behind it with a great splash.

"All engines back full speed," said Fatso.

As Satchmo threw his engines in reverse, Fatso blew a series of sharp blasts on the whistle—as required by the rules of the road when the ship with the right of way changes course or speed.

"Left full rudder," said Fatso.

Satchmo threw the wheel hard over and LCU 1124 swung left and paralleled the destroyer on opposite course. The big ship swept past at express train speed, towering over the little one only twenty feet away. The Russians ignored the small ship, except for a short fat little officer who leaned over the rail of the bridge and focused his binoculars on her. Three gold stripes on his sleeve showed that he was the skipper.

Fatso ran over to the starboard wing of the bridge, shaking his fist at the Russian's bridge, and cut loose with a string of free-wheeling opinions about her skipper. The Chief of Naval Operations might have deplored his choice of words in spots. His language was not the kind usually employed in international intercourse. It was a blast of purple obscenity that would have shocked even a bunch of boot Marines.

By this time, all hands in Fatso's crew were on deck. Fatso yelled at a signalman, "Put your light on them and see if they answer."

The signalman swung his searchlight around and started blinking A-A-A at the Russian. Soon answering blinks came back.

"Okay," said Fatso. "Now just send them one word— Z-V-O-L-O-C-H."

The signalman started blinking the letters.

"What the hell does that mean?" asked Scuttlebutt.

"I dunno," said Fatso. "But it must be pretty awful. I learned it from a Russian countess. She said it's an insult and a curse rolled into one, and there's no such word in English. She said it's the worst thing you can call a Russian."

"How come a countess was teaching you words like that?"

"She ran the biggest cat house in Hong Kong," said Fatso. "And I heard her call it to a Russian sailor after he tried to rape one of her gals."

"Rape? In a cat house?" asked Scuttlebutt, incredulously.

"Well," said Fatso, "she caught him trying to sneak out without paying, and she claimed it was the same thing. Anyway, the guy she called it to was a stinking louse, but he got awful insulted about it."

"Message sent, Cap'n," yelled the signalman. "No reply—and they didn't receipt for it, either."

"I wonder where the hell he's going in such a hurry,"

said Scuttlebutt, as the Russian was dropping under the horizon to the north.

"From the way he's heading, I'd say he's bound for the Gulf of Laconia at the south end of Greece," said Fatso.

"What's up there?" asked Scuttlebutt.

"They got a sort of half-assed fleet base there," said Fatso. "They keep a couple of supply ships, tenders, and tankers anchored all the time, just outside the Greek territorial waters where they're in pretty good lee. Their cruisers, destroyers, and submarines go in there for supplies and for repair jobs that a tender can do. There's always a bunch of them in there. It saves them a long trip back to their regular bases in the Black Sea."

That evening one item in the radio news made Fatso prick up his ears and take notice. It said that Rear Admiral Hughes had just been promoted to Vice Admiral.

"Well I'll be damn," said Fatso. "Old 'Hotshot' Hughes gets three stars! Whaddya know?"

"You know him?" asked the Professor.

"Well—sort of," said Fatso. "We first met about twenty years ago, the day the *Lexington* got sunk. He was a brand new ensign in the air group then. I drug him out of a burning plane on the flight deck and swum around holding him up for a couple of hours after the ship went down. He was real nice about it afterwards. Claimed I saved him from drowning and recommended me for a Navy Cross. Admiral Halsey just loved to hand out medals—so he gave it to me."

"I guess you're entitled to say you know him," conceded the Professor. "Ever serve with him later?"

"Yeah. A couple of times. Once he was head of a general court that tried me for bustin' an MP in the nose."

"Hah!" said the Judge. "According to law he should of disqualified himself. What did he do?"

"Well, naturally, he didn't believe none of the witnesses the government dredged up. I was acquitted."

The Judge shook his head sadly over this flagrant breach of legal ethics. "In civil life," he said, "Only big-shot politicians and other judges can get away with things like that."

"And a couple of years ago I served in a big carrier, the *Guadalcanal,* when he was skipper."

"That musta been pretty nice," said the Professor. "What was your job? Honorary commodore of the starboard anchor or something?"

"No. I was captain of the incinerator."

"That's a hell of a job for a first class petty officer," declared the Professor. "You musta had some angle."

"Hunh! I never work no angles," said Fatso, piously. "I just do my duty whatever my job is. . . . But we had a pretty good arrangement on that ship. He let me run the incinerator the way I wanted to, and he took care of all the rest of the ship."

"I've heard some wild tales about what used to go on down in that incinerator compartment," observed the Judge.*

"Don't you believe a damn word of them," said Fatso. "There *were* rumors got started around the ship now and then when some of the junior officers misunderstood some of the things that happened down there. But the Cap'n always straightened them out."

* Note: See *Now, Hear This* by Rear Admiral D. V. Gallery (Paperback Library)

Chapter Four

The Gathering Storm

NEXT DAY LCU 1124 tied up at the Naval Station, Valetta, Malta. Had she been a commissioned ship her commanding officer would, of course, have put on his sword and cocked hat and paid the usual courtesy call on the Senior Naval Officer, Malta. On such a call he might have learned about recent events affecting naval strategy in the Med—including the redeployment of the amphibious forces to the Far East.

But Fatso's contacts were on a lower level, with Supply Department types. Their interest in global strategy was confined to vouchers, requisitions, invoices, and receipts. They simply produced the stuff that the strategists put in for, and they didn't give a damn what became of it as long as the paperwork was straight.

In the fighting forces, a round of ammunition isn't expended until somebody pulls the trigger on it in the heat of battle, with bombs bursting all around him. But for the supply types, it is expended as soon as they get a proper signature for it.

When Fatso checked in with the Supply Officer's chief yeoman, that worthy said, "Yeah. The *Sylvania* invoiced a lot of stuff to us for the *Alamo*—and some for the Marines, too. It's all ready. All you gotta do is sign the papers. There's about a hundred tons of it. Can you handle that much?"

"No strain," said Fatso. "I can take two hundred if I have to. I wanna get loaded and start back this afternoon."

"Can do," said the Chief. "There's some special stuff for the Commodore, too—an official car, two deep freezes, and a fancy little motorboat."

"Okay," said Fatso. "We'll take good care of it."

"You'd better," said the Chief. "The Commodore has been bugging us about this stuff for a month."

Early that afternoon the loading was finished. The last item to come aboard was a light tank for the Marines, mounting a 90 mm. gun. When that was secured, LCU 1124 cast off and headed back for Crete.

On a small craft like an LCU, there isn't much to do in your spare time at sea. Standing one watch in six, as they did, it meant that everyone put in a four-hour trick at the wheel each day and had all the rest of the day to live it up.

A large part of the time was put in caulking off— Navy lingo for boresighting your bunk. The term originates from the fact that in the old days, to caulk a ship's bottom when she was beached and hove down, you had to lie flat on your back. So now, when you assume the same position for rest and relaxation, you are "caulking off."

The rest of the time off watch is put in eating and lounging around the messroom shooting the breeze or playing acey-deucey.

Improbable tales are told during these bull sessions and acey-deucey games. Many of them concerning adventures in previous ports of call are not only improbable, they are damn lies. But with a group like Fatso's, the fact that some saga of adventure told as a fact hadn't happened yet didn't matter too much. All hands knew it could easily happen in the next port.

After dinner this evening, the Judge was telling a pop-eyed group about Polly Adler's famous whorehouse in New York. "I used to know the old gal pretty well when I was in Columbia Law School," he said.

"Expensive joint for a college boy, wasn't it?" asked the Professor.

"Not for *me*," said the Judge proudly. "It was on the house whenever I went there."

"Even if that was so, I wouldn't believe it," said the Professor. "They tell me you couldn't get out of that joint for less than a hundred bucks even if all you did was pinch a gal's (biblical beast of burden)."

"Maybe she stuck it on my old man's bill. He was one of her best customers," said the Judge. "When *I* went there, there was nothing commercial about it. Everything was on a purely social basis—until I ran into my old man there one day. He started to bawl me out for hanging around whorehouses and Polly got insulted and had

36

us both thrown out. The old man said it was the most humiliating thing ever happened to him—thrown out of Polly Adler's! It got into Winchell's column, and he was afraid he might get kicked out of the Harvard Club. But actually, about a dozen members asked him to introduce them to Polly."

After the bull session, an acey-deucey game got going. Acey-deucey is the seagoing version of backgammon and has been popular in the Navy since the days of sail. It is about 90% luck and 10% skill. Tradition says that John Paul Jones was the first all-Navy champ at it, and that he claimed he played a scientific game, and his opponents were just shot full of luck. Everyone who has served in the Navy since then has claimed the title, too, and made similar statements about his own and his opponents' game.

A kibitzer at the acey-deucey game remarked, "We sure took aboard a lot of stuff today."

"That's what we sure took aboard a lot of," replied another. "All sorts of radio gear, infra-red snoopers, sideband radars—we got enough to fit out a regular spy ship."

"There's a lot of stuff for the UDT boys, too," said another. ". . . Scubas, underwater demolition charges, underwater telephones. And a lot of guns and hand grenades for the Marines, too."

"Speaking of hand grenades," said the first, "Have you heard about the new atomic hand grenade they're working on?"

"An *atomic* hand grenade," said several, incredulously.

"Yeah. They've got it down to about the size of a softball. It blows a hole in the ground about a huhnert yards in diameter. But they're having a hell of a time testing it —because you can only throw it about forty feet. . . . But speaking of new stuff, what's all that stack of curved pipes we took aboard? I never seen nothing like that before."

"That's what they call a geodetic frame," said Scuttlebutt. "When you fit all those pipes together, they make a frame that's like a slice off the top of a great big ball. There's sections of tarpoleum that come with it. You stretch them over the framework and you get something that looks like an Eskimo's igloo. It makes a nice roomy

HQ for the General, that keeps the wind and rain out. And if you gotta move, you can take it down in ten minutes."

While Fatso and the Sixth Fleet were maintaining our control of the seas in the Mediterranean, the government was trying to maintain control of the streets at home. It does this through a system called the Great Society. In this system, most of the citizens who don't want to work get jobs with the government. Those who won't work for anybody draw relief checks, conduct riots, and burn down obsolete buildings. The rest of the citizens try to earn enough money to stay out of jail for not paying their taxes. This enables the government to make relief payments, to protect the rioters from the police, and to defend our freedoms from foreign aggressors (and our allies) who would like to do to us what only our own underprivileged citizens are allowed to do.

To run the domestic affairs of the country, there are ten government departments, the Supreme Court, and the Media. Each department tries to protect the citizens from the other nine. The Supreme Court's job is to uphold the constitutional rights of the rioters and to liberate any citizens who get in trouble with the cops. Riding herd over all other agencies are the Media—Press, Radio, and TV. They devote most of their efforts to telling the citizens that Freedom of the Press is what enables the sun to rise each morning. Their other duties are to raise hell about everything, keep the citizens stirred up and angry, and to sell advertising.

The branches of the government that protect us from foreign "adversaries" (and also from friendly foreign allies) are the State and Defense Departments and the Executive Office of the President.

The Defense Department works the same way as the rest of the government. It consists of the Army, Navy, Air Force, the Joint Chiefs of Staff, the whiz Kids, and the Marines. The function of each of these is to protect the country from the other five.

The Joint Chiefs of Staff are the top military officers in the Defense Department. They are supposed to correct the mistakes of our delegates to the United Nations. When our statesmen and diplomats get us into wars, the

JCS's job is to restore peace and good will in the world with high explosives. In peacetime, they try to educate the Whiz Kids and prevent them from setting their computers in such a way as to put the armed forces out of business. They also try to keep the State Department from butting into private fights all over the world and committing so many of our soldiers to keeping the peace in far-away jungles that we won't have enough at home to make the citizens conduct their riots in an orderly manner.

For some months before the Arab-Israeli misunderstanding, life had gone on as usual in the U.S.A. The White Sox were in first place (it was only May), the teamsters, steel workers, teachers, and garbage men were out on strike, and J. Edgar Hoover had just issued a report saying rape and murder were skyrocketing faster than wages. There were a few civil-rights rallies here and there where fires and looters got out of hand for a while, until the Army moved in to stop rioting without a license. But in general, things were pretty dull.

It was at this point in world history that the UN bugged out of the Gaza Strip, and the Arabs and Israelis rushed troops there to preserve order in the empty desert they left behind.

In Washington, the President was trying to cut down on the National Debt. So the lights went out early in the White House that night. But they burned late in the Pentagon, as chicken colonels and four-stripe captains prepared briefs for the Joint Chiefs of Staff on the order of battle of the Near East nations. The cold figures on infantry divisions, tanks, artillery, and air wings made it obvious to any expert on military strategy that the Israelis would be overwhelmed in a few days if war broke out.

A Marine captain aviator who had just returned from Israel briefed the briefers on the Israeli air force. He said that if war started, the Israelis would win it in a week, because their flyers were real professionals who would knock every Arab airplane out of the sky.

This young man got orders to a squadron bound for Vietnam the next morning. Were it not for the fact that he had political influence, the orders would have been to St. Elizabeth's.

That same morning, the Joint Chiefs met in their inner

sanctum on the E ring of the Pentagon. Everyone seated around the broad table had three or four stars on his shoulder and a dozen rows of ribbons on his chest. This is where the fate of nations and the course of history would be decided—if the statesmen paid any attention to the advice of the Joint Chiefs which, of course, they don't.

Nearby was the Situation Room, with great vertical display maps of the world dotted with magnetic markers of many colors and shapes, showing the latest order of battle for all possible adversaries and the up-to-the-minute deployment of our own fleets, armies, and air forces. Hot lines and side-band radios enabled the Chiefs to talk via satellite relays to four-star admirals in their HQ on the other side of the world, or to first lieutenants in front line fox holes in Vietnam. Even the matchbooks in this area are "top secret—eyes only," and the runner for the daily Pentagon numbers game has a Q clearance and a background check by the FBI.

When the briefers finished their presentation to the Chiefs there was a thoughtful silence around the table for a few moments. Then the Chairman said, "This thing is going to blow over after a lot of huffing and puffing. There won't be any real war. The Israelis aren't crazy enough to take on forty million Arabs."

All heads around the table nodded gravely.

"I'm keeping the Sixth Fleet back to this side of Crete," said the Chief of Naval Operations. "Just in case war *does* break out. That will keep all our ships five hundred miles away from the scene of action . . . and something else you all have an interest in—I'm sending the amphibious forces from the Sixth Fleet out to Vietnam. It is possible Nasser may close the canal, and we are in urgent need of more amphibious forces in the Far East. Suez is the quickest way to get them there."

"Now, just a minute," said the Army Chief of Staff. "Suppose I have to put troops ashore in the Near East. How am I going to it with no amphibious craft?"

"Don't worry about that, Joe," said the Air Force Chief of Staff, smugly. "MATS can airlift a whole division for you overnight."

"Hunh," snorted the Commandant of the Marine Corps. "What good will that do you unless somebody has captured a beachhead for you?"

40

"The Marines aren't the *only* ones who can capture beachheads," bristled the Army COS. "We've got the Green Berets. You've heard of them, I hope."

"Hunh!" reiterated the Marine.

"We've got more Marines and amphibious craft ready to sail from Norfolk for the Med right now," said the CNO. "They'll be there in another ten days—so you——"

"Okay, okay," interrupted the chairman. "Let's not get into any hassle about that. I think the Med will be safe for ten days, even with no Marines in it. Now . . . I think we all agree that an actual war between the Jews and Arabs is very unlikely. If one should break out, I think we also agree that no matter where our sympathy lies, we've got to stay out of it. We are over-extended now in the Far East. But remember—the Israelis have powerful friends in this country. If war does start, they may persuade the State Department we've got to pull the Israelis' chestnuts out of the fire for them. So we've got to keep our forces alert and ready in case we are ordered to butt in by our own—er—global strategists."

"Of course," said the Air Force COS, "If war should break out, the outcome will depend on who gets control of the air. The Arabs are almost sure to, with all their Russian MIG's and ground-to-air missiles. But the Israelis have got a good little Air Force. If they caught the Arabs on the ground with their first attack, they might have a battling chance—for a while, anyway."

"I can't see any possibility of that happening," said the Chairman. "With all the ballyhoo and bluster that's going on now, they will both be on round-the-clock alerts. There's no chance whatever that a sneak attack would get through. That's absurd."

"I said *if* they caught the Arabs on the ground," said the airman.

The Marine Commandant leaned over and said in an aside to the CNO sitting next to him, "Sure. And if his aunt had balls, she'd be his uncle."

"I didn't catch that, General," said the Chairman.

"The General said," replied the CNO, "That he considers this possibility to be extremely remote."

Later that day, the Security Council met in the Cabinet Room of the White House. By special invitation, Mr.

Goldberg, U.S. Ambassador to the UN, was present.

To open the meeting, the President said to the head of CIA, "All right, George. What top secret stuff have you got for us today that hasn't been in Drew Pearson's column yet?"

For the next ten minutes, the CIA took the assembled VIPs on a trip around the world, peeking in on secret meetings held behind closed doors and drawn blinds; listening to bugged and taped conversations between kings, presidents, sheiks, and commissars; and watching over the shoulders of ambassadors decoding secret ciphers. No one around the table was naïve enough to ask questions about how we came by all this red-hot dope. Obviously cloaks and often daggers had been involved in getting it.

The last item discussed was the Near East Crisis.

"Gentlemen," said our Chief Gum Shoe, "the Arabs have finally closed ranks behind Nasser, and the Russians are committed to giving them all-out help. This could be the end of Israel. If we try to help the Israelis, we will be backing a lost cause. We will have nothing to gain, and maybe a lot to lose."

"Now just a minute," said Ambassador Goldberg. "We're involved whether we like it or not."

"Why?" demanded the President.

"Israel is the homeland of the Jewish people. Their title to it is over two thousand years old, and they've had a long struggle winning it back. We must defend justice and freedom. We can't just stand idly by and see the Jews thrown out of a country that belonged to them originally."

"Wa-a-al, now. I dunno that I buy that argument," said the President. "If Ah did, some goddam Indian in a crummy blanket might paddle up the Pedernales River some day, knock on mah door and say—mah great-grandfather used to own this place only two hundred years ago. Git out."

"Harrumph," said the Ambassador. "I. . . ."

"Let's not get involved in that kind of argument," said the Secretary of State. "This isn't a Sunday School Class, where things are run by the Golden Rule. This is high-level international politics, where gentlemen settle their differences on the basis of who's got the biggest club. But

42

unfortunately, we are committed by solemn treaty obligations to prevent Israel from being overwhelmed. I don't see how we can get out of it. And the danger is that if either the Arabs or the Jews go off half-cocked, it could get us and Russia into an atomic war."

Everyone around the table squirmed uncomfortably and studied his fingertips as if the Secretary had accidentally let out a sonorous belch. "Atomic war" is an obscene expression seldom used at Security Council meetings.

"That couldn't happen unless we and the Russians are both crazy," said the President. "If it comes to a showdown between letting the Jews and the Arabs tear each other up or having a . . . er . . . confrontation with Russia, we don't have to hold any Gallup poll to find out what to do."

Then, fixing his eye on Mr. Goldberg, he continued: "Can't the UN do something about this? After all, that's what they are for—to prevent wars, big or little."

"Yes, indeed," said the Ambassador. "I can get the Security Council or the Assembly to appoint a commission to . . ."

"The UN can't do a damn thing in a crisis like this," interrupted the Secretary of State. "Except provide a forum for wild-eyed oratory where nations most of us never heard of before can threaten to throw their weight one way or the other. The UN brought on this crisis by suddenly pulling out of the Gaza Strip, where their forces had kept an uneasy peace for ten years. They won't get back in the picture again till it's all settled. Meantime, we and the Russians have got to work things out between us and then tell the Israelis, the Arabs, and the UN—this is the way it *is*. You've got to take it and like it. Then the UN can go back to cutting out paper dolls again."

Ambassador Goldberg rumbled and cleared his throat, but before he could speak, the President asked the Secretary of State, "Do you think it's possible for us to agree with Russia on a thing of this kind?"

"It *has* to be," said the Secretary. "The Russians don't want to blow the world apart any more than we do. That's what can happen if we *don't* agree."

On that comforting note, the meeting adjourned.

Chapter Five

High Level Snafu

THE NIGHT before LCU 1124 got back to Crete, the Armed Forces Radio broadcast said that although the situation in the Near East was still critical, the State Department was now confident that there would be no war.

"Hoo boy," said the Professor. "Here we go again. I'll bet it busts out tomorrow morning."

"The Security Council of the UN," continued the broadcast, "today passed a resolution urging both sides to remain calm."

"By gawd that'll make 'em stop and think," observed the Judge.

"Both sides are fully mobilized now," the broadcast went on; "and Nasser today warned the Israelis that if they make a false move, retaliation will be swift and terrible."

"Hah!" snorted Ginsberg. "The Arabs are going to get beat worse this time than they did the last."

"Look, Abie," said the Professor; "last time they were only fighting Egypt. Now they got the whole A-rab world lined up against them and the Russians besides. Hell, they haven't got a chance."

Next morning, as they neared Crete, all hands were on deck. The absence of air activity was noticeable, and the cruisers were not in their usual place. A spit of land obscured the beach where the amphibs had been moored. But it never occurred to anyone that their ship wasn't behind it.

As they cleared the headland and the beach came in sight, all hands got an eye-popping surprise. Except for a couple of Greek fishermen, the bay was as empty as a vacant lot.

"Well, I'll be dipped in luke-warm gook," observed Scuttlebutt. "They ain't here!"

"That's exactly where they ain't," conceded Fatso.

"They musta gone somewhere else," declared Scuttle-butt, after a moment's thought.

"I'll betcha that's right where they went," said Fatso. "But you'd think they might of left a note for us, or something."

"Yeah," said Scuttlebutt. "Maybe they put it in a bottle and thrun it overboard," he added—coming closer to the truth than he knew.

"We-e-e-ll," said Fatso. "The last thing the skipper told me was that they were going to Athens from here. So, . . . I guess the smart thing for us to do is go up there."

That evening, during the acey-deucey game, one of the lads at the table was reading a copy of the *Navy Times* he had picked up in Malta. Suddenly he let out a whoop and held up the paper, pointing to a headline: "Snafu in the Army."

"Hey! Look at this," he said.

"What's so funny about that?" demanded another. "Things are always screwed up in the Army."

"But not as good as this," said the reader. "This guy finishes boot camp and is sent home on leave to await orders. Somehow or another, they got his records fouled up and forgot about him. He had an allotment, so his pay kept coming home. He sits around for two years, waiting for orders, and then he goes to the nearest Army post, tells them his time is up, and he wants his discharge."

"Well—what's the matter with that?" demanded Web-foot. "If they hadn't of lost track of him they would of had him sitting on his ass in some Army post for two years. He sits on it at home instead, and I don't see nothing wrong with that. It saved the gummint the cost of feeding him."

"Yeah. But the paper says the Army don't know what the hell to do about the guy, now. Some of their legal beagles say they gotta discharge him and some claim he still owes them two years, and others want to court martial him. The Joint Chiefs of Staff will prob'ly have to settle it. Anyway—that's something that couldn't happen in the Navy. We keep track of things better than that."

45

"Oh yeah?" said Fatso. "When I was on the *Enterprise,* we had a guy who was lost on board ship for three weeks."

"How the hell could that happen?"

"He was just out of boot camp too and came aboard with a big draft of new men just before we sailed for the Med. He didn't hear his name called when they were mustering the draft in on the hangar deck. When the draft fell out, he wasn't assigned to any division, so he just took his bag and wandered around till he found an empty bunk back in the messboys' compartment, and moved in there. The ship reported him missing from the draft and sent his records back to boot camp. We sailed for the Med next day, and there he was, not assigned to any division, no battle station, . . . nothing. He had sense enough to find his way from the chow line to the head and back to his bunk again, and for three weeks he was just a sight-seeing tourist on board. Might of made the whole cruise that way, except he tried to go on liberty in Naples, and they nailed him for not having a liberty card."

"What did they do to him?" asked the Judge.

"They brought him up to mast with a string of charges a mile long. But the Old Man wouldn't have it. He said if the Master at Arms force had been on the job they would of found the guy in a day or two. He made the kid his orderly, because he'd done so much rubbernecking he knew his way around on the ship better than lots of other guys who had been aboard working in the same place the whole cruise. . . . So don't kid yourself. We can get things screwed up just as bad as the Army."

"Yeah," said Scuttlebutt. "We lost a whole big ship for quite a while at the end of the war. The *Indianapolis.* She was sunk and all her guys were in the water for damn near a week before anybody missed her."

When Fatso and the boys gathered around the mess table at lunch that day, the Armed Forces Radio Newscast came on. It said Washington was gravely concerned over the possibility of war in the Middle East. It said the U.S. was calling for an emergency session of the UN because a war in which the Israelis were overwhelmed could

46

easily produce a confrontation between the U.S. and Russia.

"Nuts," observed Fatso. "This raises hell with my ops plans for the next couple of weeks. I was going to visit Beirut, Tel Aviv, and Alexandria if we don't find the *Alamo* in Athens. But now we can't."

"If war does break out, it'll be over in a couple of weeks at the most," observed Scuttlebutt. "The Israelis can't possibly hold out any longer than that against all them A-rabs."

Ginsberg did not concur with this Estimate of the Situation. "The hell you say," he observed. "You guys just watch. Them crummy Arabs are going to find out they tangled with a buzz saw. The Israelis will give them the bum's rush right into the Red Sea."

"Abie," said Fatso tolerantly, "we all know how you feel. And we'd all like to see the Israelis clobber the A-rabs, too. I was talking to Izzy Goldberg on the *Alamo*. He spent a month in Israel last year, and he says they've got a nice little country started there, with a good army and even a pretty good little air force. But hell, there's just too damn many A-rabs. They wouldn't have a chance. Too bad."

All heads around the table nodded grave agreement.

"You just wait and see," said Ginsberg. "They beat the hell out of the Arabs a few years ago. They can do it again."

"Okay, Abie," said Fatso, tolerantly. "But while we're waiting for that to happen, we gotta figure out something to do. I think maybe we can have some fun getting in the Russians' hair."

Next morning, LCU 1124 anchored in Piraeus, the seaport of Athens. The only American warship present was the USS *Pillsbury,* a destroyer. No sign of the *Alamo*. This posed a problem for Fatso. What should he do now?

Fatso prided himself on being able to carry out any orders he received from higher authority without having to break out the Regulations Book to find out how. But now he found himself without any orders and apparently abandoned by higher authority.

Had Fatso been a graduate of the Naval War College,

47

he would, of course, have made an Estimate of the Situation. Starting from the Navy's major mission of controlling the seas, and, making due allowance for all local conditions, he could then have derived a logical Course of Action for himself. But Fatso's knowledge of global strategy and tactics had been acquired in waterfront barrooms, and did not include how to make a formal Estimate of the Situation.

So he and Scuttlebutt thumbed through the regulations till they came to the article about the Senior Officer Present Afloat. This article, a leftover from the preradio days of sail, confers far-reaching powers upon the SOPA. This officer, whatever his rank, represents the Navy Department to all juniors within visual signal distance. When problems come up which they can't settle, they simply refer them to him. Since SOPA, in Piraeus at the moment was the *Pillsbury*, Fatso put on his best blue uniform, put the Commodore's gig in the water, and went over to the *Pillsbury* to call officially on SOPA and present his problem.

This stirred up quite a flap aboard the *Pillsbury*. When the young ensign OOD saw the Commodore's gig approaching, he hit the panic button and got the skipper— a Lieutenant Commander—up on deck to greet the visiting VIP at the head of the gangway. This was a bad goof. It was aggravated by the fact that the skipper was recovering from a hard week at sea and an even harder night ashore among the fleshpots of Athens, and the young ensign's alarm about a visiting flag officer had routed him out of his bunk.

When the bleary-eyed skipper saw a rather portly first class petty officer disembark from the gig and come up the gangway, he thought for a moment that perhaps he was still asleep and having strange dreams from that last nightcap. When Fatso saluted and said, "Boatswains Mate First Class Gioninni coming aboard to report to the Senior Officer Present Afloat," he found himself confronting a rather irate SOPA.

There is no need to repeat here what the skipper said to the red-faced ensign before turning on his heel and marching back to his cabin, leaving Fatso with his mouth agape and his troubles untold.

Back on LCU 1124, Fatso and Scuttlebutt held another

council of war. They decided that Fatso had carried out the orders of his own skipper, had complied with the regulations by reporting to SOPA when those orders ran out, and was now his own boss and could write his own ticket. The first item on the ticket was to put the Commodore's car ashore so the two of them would have proper transportation while showing the flag and representing the United States in Athens. That afternoon, LCU 1124 moved in to the beach, let down the bow ramp, and the car was driven ashore by Satchmo, with Fatso and Scuttlebutt ensconced in the stern sheets, all wearing their best liberty blues and grins like three cats full of canaries.

They made the Grand Tour of Athens that afternoon, during which they picked up Sparky Wright, radioman 1/C from the *Pillsbury* and an old pal of Fatso's and Scuttlebutt's. From him they learned of the *Alamo*'s hasty departure for Vietnam before Nasser closed the Canal.

"Vietnam, for gawd's sake," said Fatso. "With the canal closed, my thirty years would be up before we could make it out there. That sort of leaves me on detached duty—almost like being marooned. What the hell am I supposed to do now?"

"If I was you I'd report to SOPA and let him figure it out," said Sparky.

"I did that this morning," said Fatso. "He gave your young OOD an earful of good advice, but he didn't seem interested in hearing about my problems. . . . I wonder if *Alamo* sent any radio despatches about us. We don't keep a regular radio watch."

"No," said Sparky. "We copy everything on the FOX schedule, and I have to check the log every day. There's been nothing about you in the past week. They probably sent your records and stuff by mail to ComSixthFleet in Naples. You'll most likely hear from him when his staff gets around to it."

"Well, look," said Fatso. "You guard the Sixth Fleet FOX circuit, so if they put out anything about me, you'll copy it, won't you?"

"Sure. We copy the whole FOX schedule."

"Okay. After we leave Athens, suppose I give you a call each day at noon on 2580 KC's. If you've heard anything for me, you can pass it on to me then."

49

"Sure. We can do that."

"So—until I hear from you, I'm on my own. It's okay with me if it takes them a couple of months to get out orders. I can think of lots of things to do while I'm waiting."

Later that afternoon, while they were sightseeing around the Acropolis, a furtive character sidled up to them, looked both ways and said, "You like to see dirty post cards, meestaire?"

Fatso leered back at him and said, "Sure. What have you got?"

The peddler produced a pack of a dozen post cards and handed them to Fatso. They were a typical batch of uninhibited water-front art, showing men, women, and animals engaging in various unorthodox practices. I doubt if even the most long-haired liberals could have said they possessed artistic merit, social significance, or conformed to community standards—except, of course, the Supreme Court.

Fatso inspected them casually and handed them back.

"You no like?" asked the peddler.

"Sure—they're very good," said Fatso. "But I don't want any."

"Whatsa matter?" demanded the art dealer.

"I want something special from Athens to send my grandmother," said Fatso, "and she's got all those."

The peddler shrugged as if to say, "Americans are funny." He put the cards back in his pocket, leered sociably, and said, "You like to meet my seestaire?"

"Maybe," said Fatso. "What does she do?"

"Anything you want, sir," said the young man eagerly. "She ees very nice."

"With a brother like you she *must* be," observed Fatso. He bent over and touched the ground with his fingertips. Then he bent his knees till he was squatting on his heels and straightened up again a couple of times, keeping his fingertips on the ground. "How about that?" asked Fatso. "Can she do that?"

The young man looked puzzled, but said "Cer-tain-ly. She can do eet that way—if you *like*."

"Whoops," said Scuttlebutt, "You can learn something

new every day in this part of the world. I'd like to see it done that way."

"How about my friends here," asked Fatso, indicating Scuttlebutt, Sparky, and Satchmo.

The young man said, "But of course. She take care of all of you."

"Can she sew buttons on?" asked Fatso.

Their friend cocked his head to one side and said, "Soubuddonson? . . . I never heard of before. . . . Ees a new way, maybe?"

Fatso went through the motions of threading a needle and sewing a button on his sleeve.

A light seemed to dawn on the young man. He put two fingers of his right hand on his left wrist and pumped his thumb as if giving himself a shot in the arm. "Yes, SIR," he said. "I can get for you."

"This guy ought to go out to Berkeley," observed Scuttlebutt. "They might even make him a college professor out there."

"No-o-o," said Fatso, judiciously. "He'd be just a square out there. I don't think it's more than a week since he had a bath."

Later that afternoon they struck up an acquaintance with a wooden-legged seafaring gentleman who was trying to get drunk in a water-front barroom.

When strangers make friends in water-front barrooms, the first thing they do is explain their wooden legs.

"I was on sob-marine during the war," said the stranger. "We came up to shoot at merchant ship and our gun blow up."

"You were a U-boat sailor?" asked Fatso.

The stranger spat contemptuously on the floor. "Nyet," he said. "I was Rawshun Navy."

"Oh! A Russian," said Fatso. "Why did your gun blow up."

"The lieutenant was a *zvoloch*. He forgot to take out the mozzle plug."

"That'll do it, every time," observed Scuttlebutt.

"What ship are you from?" asked the Russian.

"The *George Washington*," said Fatso.

"What kind of ship is that?"

"It's one of our new Polaris submarines. You know what they are?" asked Fatso.

"Yass," said the Russian, beginning to sit up and take notice. "We have the same thing. Maybe better."

"Are you on a submarine now?" asked Sparky.

"No. I am on merchant ship *Volga*."

"What do you do?"

"I watch and listen."

Sparky looked puzzled. "What the hell," he said. "I didn't know they had sonar on their merchant ships."

"They don't," said Fatso. "But they have political commissars. I'll bet that's what he is. . . . You ashore all by yourself?" he asked, addressing the Russian.

"Yass. I don't go ashore with those peegs on the ship . . . 'ow many men you have in your crew?" he asked.

"Three hundred," said Fatso.

"Iss too many," said the Russian. "We only have one hundred on Rawshun sob-marines."

"But ours are very big ships."

" 'Ow big?"

"Twelve-thousand tons," said Fatso.

It was now obvious that the Russian thought he could find out something of interest from Fatso and his pals. Fatso was always alert to take advantage of a situation like this. "How about having dinner with us?" he asked.

"Hokay," said the Russian.

They dined at a swanky tourist night spot where everything was very informal and friendly, except the prices. When Sparky Wright picked up the menu and saw them, his eyes popped. But Scuttlebutt said, "Don't worry, pal—it won't cost you anything."

Their dinner would have satisfied Ivan the Terrible. They had canapes, soup, fish, and roast beef, washed down with red and white wine and champagne.

Fatso and Sparky regaled their Russian friend with wondrous tales about Polaris submarines, filling him up with data that may be top secret twenty years from now, but which is strictly science fiction today.

Scuttlebutt was ogling the cigarette gal before they even sat down. By the time soup came on, he had danced with her twice and had interesting plans laid out for the rest of the evening.

Satchmo made friends with the orchestra leader and

blasted out a few hot tunes on the trumpet between courses.

While waiting for dessert, Fatso tipped Scuttlebutt their private signal meaning, "Stand by to execute contingency plan number one." Scuttlebutt passed the word to Satchmo, who excused himself after dessert, went out, and got the car ready for a quick get away.

After they disposed of the dessert and ordered cordials, Scuttlebutt had a word with the cigarette gal and slipped her five bucks. The next time the orchestra struck up she came up to the table, smiled sweetly at the Russian, and said, "You dance with me?"

The Russian almost choked on his cognac. No good-looking gal had smiled at him since the battle of Stalingrad. He was soon clomping around the floor right briskly, wooden leg and all.

Fatso, Scuttlebutt, and Sparky withdrew toward the gent's can, slipped out a side door, popped into the car, and Satchmo took off.

"Boy oh boy," chuckled Sparky, as they picked up speed, "I'd sure like to see that Russian's face when he gets the bill. I'll bet it's over a hundred bucks. He may have to hock his wooden leg to pay it."

"Yeah," said Fatso. "Well, the Roosians can count it as part payment of what they owe us on Lend Lease."

Driving back to the ship in the wee small hours, Fatso remarked, "Boy oh boy! This is something I've wanted all my life. An independent command of my own—with a Commodore's gig and official car, yet! This is like being an Admiral. I can even write my own ticket and decide where I want to go."

"Yeah," said Sparky. "And speaking of Admirals, there's a new one taking over the Sixth Fleet tomorrow."

"Who?" asked Scuttlebutt.

"I dunno his name. But some of the guys on the *Pillsbury* who know him say he's a tough hombre. Four-stripe captains jump a foot in the air every time he farts."

"Well—he won't bother me none," said Fatso. "I'll give him a wide berth."

Chapter Six

USS *Turtle*

NEXT MORNING LCU 1124 got underway and stood out to sea. Fatso and Scuttlebutt were leaning on the rail of the bridge as the land dropped out of sight astern.

"Where we bound for, Cap'n?" asked Scuttlebutt. Up to now, all hands had addressed the hero of this tale either as "Fatso" or "skipper." Since LCU 1124 had now sort of acquired the status of a ship of the line in the U.S. Navy, a more formal mode of address seemed called for. So, by tacit agreement, they had all changed to "Captain."

"Haven't decided yet," said Fatso. "There's lots of good liberty ports we might visit around here—Istanbul—Smyrna—Beirut—Tel Aviv—Haifa. . . ."

"Sail ho!" came a hail from the pilothouse—followed by the regular ritual of queries and responses.

Fatso and Scuttlebutt swung their glasses around to the bearing indicated and picked up the upper works of a big Russian cruiser heading so as to pass about a mile abeam. At her main truck, a two-star admiral's flag was flying.

"Hah!" said Fatso. "I was hoping we would meet some big-shot Russian like this . . . . Hey!" he yelled at Jughaid, by the signal light, "What was the name of that Russian tin can that almost cut us in two on the way to Malta?"

"*Vosnik,* Cap'n," came back the answer.

"Okay," said Fatso. "Give this guy a call with your light. If he answers, I want to send him a message."

"Whatcha gonna do, Cap'n?" asked Scuttlebutt eagerly —knowing from the gleam in Fatso's eye that something was cooking.

"I'm gonna fix up our pal that almost ran us down."

"You gonna put him on the report to the Admiral for violating the rules of the road?" asked Scuttlebutt.

"Hell, no. But if this works the way I think it will, he may wish he had never left the farm."

"They're answering, Cap'n," called Jughaid. "I'm ready to send."

"The message is," said Fatso, " 'Please transmit following to Captain of *Vosnik:* Thank you very much for the vodka . . . enjoyed your visit . . . come aboard again any time.' "

"What the hell is that all about?" demanded Scuttlebutt, a puzzled look on his face as well as everyone else's within earshot.

"Can't you imagine," said Fatso, "what will happen when the Admiral sees that? This guy will probably spend the rest of his naval career trying to explain that it's a goddam lie and that he hasn't been playing footsie with the Americans when the Admiral wasn't looking."

All eyes popped, and admiring grins spread over all faces. "Ya-a-a-h," said Scuttlebutt. "Hell, they may even stand him up against a wall and shoot him."

"It'll be a good lesson to him if they do," observed Fatso. Then he called over to Jughaid, who was nearing the end of the message, "Add 'Good Luck' to the end of that. The poor son of a bitch may need it."

The cruiser receipted for the message as the ships were passing abeam. About ten minutes later she began blinking the general call A-A-A at them and then came through with the query, "What is the name of your ship?"

"Hah!" said Fatso. "The Admiral has seen it already! Answer them, USS *Turtle.*"

With those words a new ship of war was born and took its place among the battle fleets of the world. You won't find any USS *Turtle* in Janes's Fighting Ships, Brassey's Naval Annual, or on the roster of the U.S. Navy Department. But you can find her mentioned during the next month in the log books of various Russian, French, and Arab naval vessels, as well as in an exchange of diplomatic notes between the Kremlin, Cairo, and Washington.

All craft of the amphibious forces have their class letters and numbers painted on the bow in big white characters. That afternoon, Fatso's lads got busy with brushes and paint pots and painted out the "LC" and "124" on their bow, leaving only the U and the 1.

"That's fine," commented Fatso. "We are now the USS *Turtle*, U-1. U stands for unknown, unauthorized, or unassigned, and we're the first one of that class."

That was the morning that war broke out. What happened in the next five days will be studied in the War Colleges of the civilized world for many years. It is a classic example of how to negotiate when diplomacy fails.

The Israeli Air Force took off before reveille that morning, made a wide detour to sea, and came in from a direction in which the Arabs weren't looking. Matter of fact, the Arabs weren't looking anywhere at that time. They hadn't got up yet. The Israelis caught them in their bunks with their planes gassed and armed but unmanned and undispersed. They swooped in on the Arab airfields like a tornado hitting a shingle factory. They laid their bombs with pickle-barrel accuracy, shot up everything with incendiary bullets, and left a blazing shambles behind them. In a matter of minutes, the Egyptian airfields looked like American cities during a civil-rights rally, and Nasser had no air force.

After breakfast, the Israeli flyers were off again—to lend a hand to their army. It turned out the Arabs were running so fast and leaving such a cloud of dust behind them in the desert that even jet airplanes had trouble catching them.

Of course, all this was not known until days later. The Armed Forces Radio simply announced that war had broken out, there was heavy fighting everywhere, and both sides were claiming smashing victories.

"Well," said Fatso, when the broadcast was over, "There goes our plans for visiting any good liberty ports."

"Oh, I dunno," said Scuttlebutt. "This thing won't last more than a week. Maybe we can visit them after the Arabs take over."

"Maybe," said Fatso. "Meantime, we gotta figure out something else to do. . . . I think we can have some fun getting in the Russians' hair. So let's take a run down to their base at the Gulf of Laconia."

"If we ever run across the *Vosnik* again, after what you done to them this morning, I think we better give her a wide berth," chuckled the Judge.

"Hell, if we ever run across that bucket again she'll have a new skipper," said another.

"How do you figure we can get in the Russians' hair, Cap'n?" asked Scuttlebutt.

"Suppose we go down to the Gulf of Laconia and just hang around, watching what goes on at their base," said Fatso.

"I don't see why that should bother them much," said Scuttlebutt. "They're watching our ships all the time."

"Yeah. But they've never had anybody watching *them*. With all the talent we got on board here, maybe we can make them think we're doing a lot more than we really are. It might make them nervous."

"We're all listening, Cap'n," said Scuttlebutt, respectfully—knowing from long experience that when Fatso got a glint in his eye and started talking this way, strange things usually happened.

"I think we can convince them we're some kind of an electronic spy ship and maybe worry the hell out of them."

"It's kind of hard to make this bucket look like anything except just what she is," objected Scuttlebutt.

"Depends on how much imagination those Russians have got and how much we help it. Suppose we put something up forward that looked like a big radar dish and kept it pointed at them while we cruised back and forth. They might begin to wonder what the hell was coming off."

"Sure. But where we gonna get the big radar dish?"

"We already got it," declared Fatso. "That geodetic frame of the Marines. When you get that thing put together, there's only two things in this world it looks like. One is a geodetic frame for a Marine general's HQ— and hardly anybody but a Marine knows what that looks like. The other is a hell of a big radar dish. We can stand it up on its edge, and mount it on one of our fork-lift trucks so we can swing it around and point it anywheres we want to. Our high sides will hide the truck, and I'll bet anyone who sees it, except a goddam leatherneck, will swear it's the granddaddy of all radar dishes."

All eyes around the table were lighting up and heads nodding enthusiastically. The Professor, their radar technician, said, "By gawd, Cap'n, I think you're right. That's

57

exactly what I'd think if I seen something like that mounted on a ship."

"Okay," said Fatso. "If they fall for this, we may get them to do some foolish things. . . . I want to put that frame together this afternoon and mount it up near the bow. Then you guys get busy and dream up some ways of booby-trapping those Russian bastards into doing things that won't do them any good."

When you issue a directive like that to a group like Fatso's improbable things will probably happen. Soon the boys had assembled the geodetic frame, stood it on edge, and mounted it on a fork-lift truck. The truck could, of course, be easily swung around in any direction, and Scuttlebutt devised a way of tilting the dish so it could "look" nearly straight up as well as horizontally. The twenty-five foot frame towered over the boat, of course, but the high sides of the well deck concealed its mounting. By proper handling of the truck, it could put on a very convincing act of a big search radar scanning the surrounding sea and air.

Meantime, other projects were hatching. The stuff taken aboard in Malta proved to be a basket of golden eggs for the *Turtle*'s "dirty trick" department—aerology balloons, sonobuoys, walkie-talkies, Q-band radars, and many other pieces of scientific equipment designed to assist the U.S. Navy in maintaining control of the seas. With minor modifications by Fatso's ingenious boys they could also be fixed to do other things that might make the Russians rather curious to see what was inside them.

While the rest of the boys were assembling the "radar dish," the Professor and the Judge got a sonobuoy out of the Malta freight and a box of assorted spare parts for electronic sets. They lugged these up to the messroom and went to work.

A sonobuoy is a cylinder about the size of a golf bag that is full of electronic gear. It is used by airplanes hunting submarines. When a flyer suspects there is a submerged submarine nearby, he tosses it in the water. The buoy floats with just a few inches of one end sticking out of the water. When it hits the water, it lowers a microphone on a cable out of its bottom and shoves a whip antenna up out of the top. The mike picks up whatever noises there are in the water and feeds them into a radio transmitter that sends them up to the airplane. The flyer is thus able to eavesdrop on the surrounding ocean and to hear propeller noises if there is a submarine down there.

The Professor and Judge had the sonobuoy disassembled with its guts all over the table when Fatso came in. Fatso watched with interest for a few moments and then said, "Whatcha doin'?"

"We're making some changes in the circuits of this sonobuoy."

"What's it gonna do when you get through with it?" asked Fatso.

"Apt-so-lutely nothing," declared the Professor.

"Nothing?" said Fatso.

"Nossir. Not a gahdam thing. But it's going to *look* like it might do plenty."

"Yeah?" said Fatso, with interest.

"When we get this put back together, it's going to look like a perfectly good piece of equipment with a lot of extra circuits in it that ain't in our other sonobuoys they've picked up. Anybody who knows a little bit about electronics will take one squint at it and say, 'hey, we got something new here. This is worth looking into.' It's gonna take a half a dozen real experts to find out that it's as phoney as a rubber swab handle. They'll probably have to send it back to Russia before they find out."

Fatso grinned appreciatively. This was the sort of strategic thinking he liked to see among young sailors. "That's good," he said. "How ya gonna get the Russians interested in it?"

"We're gonna put it in the water where they can see it, and we're gonna put on an act with a walkie-talkie and an underwater phone that will make them think it's doing lots of things it ain't. They pick up pretty near anything we put in the water anyway—you remember that guy who was snooping on the landing drill even picked up a burned-out smoke float."

"Yup," said Fatso. "What kind of pitch you gonna give them?"

"We'll use our walkie-talkie to make out that we're talking to a submerged submarine. Their radio intercept guys will get their receivers on that pretty quick. We'll stick an underwater phone in the water and use that as if the submarine is answering. As soon as they think we got a sub down there, they'll man their sonars, and they'll be able to hear the sub talking underwater and being broadcast by the sonobuoy. We can make them think we got one of our Polaris subs hanging around poking up a periscope and peeking at them."

"That's damn good," said Fatso. "If it works, I'm gonna put both you guys up for second class. . . . We'll have a confab right after chow tonight and go over everything we're gonna do tomorrow."

That evening after chow all hands were listening to the radio news.

"Jerusalem: The Israeli high command has just announced that all the Egyptian air force was destroyed on the ground this morning. The Arab armies are in disorderly flight on all fronts. They are abandoning tanks, weapons, and even their shoes as they flee through the desert toward Suez."

"Holy Cow!" said Webfoot in an awed voice. "It's hard to believe."

"What the hell is hard to believe about it?" demanded Ginsberg. "I told you guys right from the start that's how it was going to be."

The radio continued:

"Cairo: Nasser announced that a treacherous sneak attack by the Israeli air force had been smashed, all the Israeli planes shot down, and many pilots captured. The Jewish armies had been routed on all fronts, and the victorious Arabs were racing on to Jerusalem, sweeping all before them."

"Ya see?" said Webfoot. "I *knew* that broadcast from Jerusalem was a phony."

Next morning at two bells of the forenoon watch (9 A.M. to landlubbers), the *Turtle* steamed into the Gulf of Laconia and began cruising back and forth a mile south of the group of Russians anchored there.

The big "radar dish" swung slowly so as to stay pointed

at the Russians. When the *Turtle* reversed course, the dish slewed around to the other side.

Meantime, Satchmo and the Professor were inflating an aerology balloon. When they got it blown up to its full five-foot diameter, they attached a small beeper radio and a smoke candle to it and turned it loose. Away it went, going *beep-beep-beep* and leaving a trail of brilliant yellow smoke behind it. The big dish immediately swung around and "locked" on the balloon.

"That oughta get them looking this way," observed Fatso.

"Yeah," said Scuttlebutt. "It's like the old story about the mule trainer who used to always start off by clouting the mule over the head with a two-by-four. He said the first thing you always gotta do is to attract the animal's attention."

"Same idea," agreed Fatso, putting his glass on the flagship.

Pretty soon he said, "Hah! They're manning their radars over there now. There they go swinging their dish around to get on the balloon."

so.

"Yeah," agreed Scuttlebutt. "Every ship over there has got their bridge spyglasses manned watching that thing."

Five minutes later, when they were sure all eyes in the fleet were on them, the *Turtle* hove to and put the gig in the water. The gig went off about a hundred yards, dropped the sonobuoy overboard, and returned.

"They see it," said Fatso as the gig was being hoisted in. "Half a dozen of 'em have got their glasses on it."

"You think they know what it's supposed to be?" asked Scuttlebutt.

"Sure," said Fatso. "Their snoopers have picked up dozens of our sonobuoys. They know all about 'em— and just what frequencies to tune in on."

Then the Professor and Judge went into a routine designed to make the Russians think they were talking to a Polaris submarine via the buoy. Using the sonobuoy frequency, the Professor said into his walkie-talkie mike, "One, two, three, four . . . four, three, two, one . . . *Turtle* testing . . . calling *Nautilus* . . . how do you hear . . . over."

He repeated this message a half a dozen times, as you would normally do when calling on a cold circuit. This gave the Russians time to fire up and get on the right frequency.

Judge, who was seated at a console nearby with phones clamped to his ears, said "I'm getting beeps and squawks all over the dial from snooper sets tuning in. I think they're about ready now."

"Okay," said the Professor. "Let's go with the underwater phone."

Judge pressed the button on the mike to his submerged phone and also to a walkie-talkie and said, *"Turtle, Turtle,* this is *Nautilus.* Hear you loud and clear . . . How me? . . . over."

"Turtle to *Nautilus.* Hear you five-by-five," was the reply. "What is your present position?"

"Nautilus to *Turtle.* My position one mile east of Russian ships. I am at periscope depth taking photographs."

For the next ten minutes there was a constant flow of "information" back and forth between *Nautilus* and *Turtle. Turtle* gave a report on the number and type of Russian ships present and on the state of the surface weather. *Turtle* informed her submerged friend she would remain in the area as long as needed. *Nautilus* came back and said she intended to stay here for the next week and would like to have *Turtle* stay, too.

The *Turtle* side of this conversation went out by walkie-talkie on the sonobuoy frequency. The *Nautilus* side came back simultaneously by underwater phone and radio, as if it were being sent by a submarine, picked up, and rebroadcast by the sonobuoy. The underwater part was, of course, picked up by several alert Russian sonar operators. A dozen radios were tuned in on the other part.

Soon Fatso said, "Hey! Look at the smoke pouring out of that tin can's stacks alongside the tender. I think they're lighting off more boilers to get underway."

"Yeah," agreed Scuttlebutt. "That's what they're doin', all right."

In a few minutes the destroyer confirmed this by casting off, backing clear of the tender, and heading east. A mile east of the group she began steaming slowly back and forth, pinging away on her sonar which was clearly audible in *Turtle*'s underwater phones.

"Get another position on *Nautilus*," yelled Fatso at Judge. "Put her three miles east of the fleet now, and take her down to three hundred feet."

Judge and the Professor went through their rigamorole and added the information from *Nautilus*, "We had to move on account of that destroyer."

By this time Judge had found the frequency of the Russian voice transmitters. He reported, "There's quite a hassle going on between that tin can and her tender . . . too bad we can't understand Russian."

"Hell, you don't have to speak Roosian to know what they're saying," observed Fatso. "The tin can is reporting there isn't a gahdam thing out there, and the tender is telling them they're stupid."

Soon a new voice came out of the loudspeaker with a blast of excited, emphatic language. "That's the Admiral," observed Fatso, "telling them to dig the crap out of their sonar operator's ears or the whole bunch of them will wind up in the salt mines."

After an hour of this, a motor launch was sighted coming out from the Russian fleet and heading for the sonobuoy.

"I think they're going to pick it up," said Fatso. "Go into your warning routine."

The Judge swung his signal searchlight around, pointed it at the boat, and started blinking the international danger signal. Flags fluttered up to the *Turtle*'s yardarm saying "Danger. Keep clear." Fatso fired a couple of Very's stars to draw attention to them. The Professor broadcast on the Russian frequency, "Danger. Keep clear of our buoy. Do not pick up the buoy. Danger."

The Russians paid no attention to his foolishness. Their boat proceeded direct to the buoy, picked it up, and returned to the ship.

The tin can continued its search to the east, gradually increasing the area as the day wore on.

Later, in the messroom, Fatso and the boys held a critique of the day's operations. "How long do you think it will be," he asked, "before they find out that buoy is a phony?"

"I don't think these guys here will *ever* find out," replied the Professor. "The circuits we rigged up in it all look real official, as if they *ought* to do *something*. If a thing like that was dumped in my lap it might take even me three or four days to find out that all those transistors, tubes, and stuff don't do a gahdam thing. I think their local experts will give up, and they'll have to send it back to Russia for the real longhairs to look at it."

"Okay," said Fatso. "Now. Whose job is it to rig up the one for tomorrow?"

"That's my department, Cap'n," said Webfoot, who was the Underwater Demolition expert.

"How big a charge are you gonna hang on it?" asked Fatso.

"Oh-h-h—I think about ten or fifteen pounds of TNT should be pretty near enough," said Webfoot judicially.

"And how are you gonna rig it?"

"I'm gonna hang it on a wire about thirty feet long from the bottom of the buoy. I got a hydrostatic fuse that will fire it when anybody pulls it up to a depth of ten feet."

"Ten feet?" said Fatso. "Sounds like that's too close to me. Hadn't you better hang it at fifty and make it go off at twenty-five? We don't want to blast the whole damn boat into orbit."

"Ten feet oughta be all right, Cap'n."

"Would *you* want to be in the boat picking it up?" demanded Fatso.

"Hell, no! But that's different. I can't stand being close to TNT when it goes off. Makes me nervous. But it won't really hurt those guys. It will ruin their boat. But the boat will absorb most of the blast. The boys in it will just get shook up a little."

"Okay," said Fatso. "We'll make a big try at warning 'em away again. And we'll have the gig ready to rescue them in case their boat sinks."

"It'll sink all right—after the pieces come down," said Webfoot.

All hands feathered their ears as the Armed Forces Radio came on with the news.

"Jerusalem: The high command announced today that so many Arabs are trying to surrender that Israel's

64

victorious armies have been forced to slow down. The plight of the defeated enemy soldiers is so pitiful that we cannot leave them in the desert, hungry, thirsty, and barefooted."

"I *told* you so!" gloated Ginsberg.

"Glory be," said Satchmo. "They beat 'em the way Joe Louis klobbered Schmeling! . . . in the *second* fight, I mean," he added.

The radio continued:

"Cairo: The Egyptians announced today that their air force had been treacherously attacked on the ground by U.S. Navy planes from the Sixth Fleet and the British RAF, which came sneaking in over the sea. President Gamal Nasser says, 'Our soldiers in the desert are fighting bravely against great odds and taking a heavy toll from the aggressors.' "

"Looks like some of them may not make it to Jerusalem," observed the Judge.

"A lot of 'em *will* get there," observed Ginsberg. "With their hands in the air and a bayonet prodding them in the ass."

"I wonder if our airplanes did help them," said Jughaid.

"They *must* of," declared Scuttlebutt. "How the hell else could the Israelis beat forty million Arabs unless they had outside help?"

"Hah!" snorted Ginsberg. "You just wait another day or so. They're going to capture Cairo the way Grant took Richmond."

Next morning at two bells they went through the business of putting another buoy in the water and tuning it on the *Nautilus* again. This time, the *Nautilus* claimed to be two miles west of the group. This stirred up a lot of chatter on the Russian frequencies, and the destroyer, which had been rooting around to the east all night, barged through the fleet heading west.

"I'm sure glad I ain't a sonar operator on *that* bucket," observed Scuttlebutt.

"Yeah," said Fatso. "They'll all be working for the

skipper of the *Vosnik* pretty soon in that salt mine out in Siberia."

Shortly after this, a motorboat with three sailors in it shoved off from the tender heading for the buoy. The *Turtle* made a great show of trying to warn the Russians of danger. They filled the yardarms with emergency flag signals; they fired a dozen red Very's stars; they blinked frantically with the searchlight. The Professor went on the air calling to the tender and warning them to have their boat keep clear. Fatso himself pointed a powerful loudspeaker at the buoy and kept yelling, *"Opastnost . . . Opastnost."* This was the closest he could come to pronouncing the Russian word for "danger," which they had looked up in their pocket dictionary.

The boat barged ahead, right up to the buoy; it hauled it aboard, and started heaving in on the wire attached to the bottom.

When they hauled in twenty feet of wire, Webfoot's fifteen pounds of TNT let go with a hell of a wham. A sledge-hammer blow split the bottom of the boat and little drops of water shot straight up in the air from an area twenty feet in diameter around the boat. A split second later the water bulged up and a geyser erupted, lifting the boat about five feet in the air.

"Just a l-e-e-etle bit on the strong side," observed Webfoot judicially. "Maybe ten pounds would of been enough."

When the boat hit the water again, it broke in two, leaving three dazed Russians paddling around in the mess of wreckage.

The *Turtle*'s gig had been standing by on the lee side, out of sight. It immediately darted out and boiled over to the scene of the disaster, hauled the stunned muzhiks aboard, and brought them to the *Turtle*.

As they were helped aboard, Scuttlebutt handed each a half tumbler of rye whiskey, which they tossed off almost at one gulp.

As soon as this took effect, the senior survivor, who spoke a little English, shook his head and said, "She's blow up. *Boom!"*

"That's probably what happened, all right," agreed Scuttlebutt solemnly. "We tried to warn you to keep clear."

In a few minutes another Russian boat came alongside, the rescued seamen were helped aboard, and they started back to their ship.

"I'll betcha the Admiral has them up in the cabin the minute they get aboard," observed Fatso.

Scuttlebutt was keeping his glass on the boat as she made her way back. Presently he began chuckling and shaking his head. "They'll never make it to the Admiral's cabin," he said. "In fact I doubt if they can hold out till they get aboard. All three are squirming already as if they had ants in their pants."

"How do you mean," demanded Fatso. "It didn't look to me like there was anything wrong when we got 'em aboard."

"There wasn't," said Scuttlebutt. "But I put a hell of a slug of physic in each one of them drinks . . . It's gonna take five more minutes to get to the ship. They'll never make it."

"Hmmmm!" said Fatso. "I think we better get out of here. Head south," he yelled at the pilot house. "Make turns for fifteen knots. There's apt to be a stink about this."

At that very moment, the USS *Santee* was entering the Straits of Gibraltar, eastbound to join the Fleet. The *Santee* was a brand-new supply ship on her maiden voyage after her shakedown cruise. As the Sixth Fleet would soon find out, there were a lot of things new and different about her.

Her job was to supply the fleet with everything it needed except fuel and explosives. Anything else: food, clothing, spare parts, paint, rope, canvas, monkey wrenches, transistors, anti-stink lotion, . . . you name it. The *Santee* had it.

Of course, most supply ships can produce at least one of nearly any article used aboard ship—if you give them time enough to rummage around in their holds and find it. But the *Santee* had a mechanical brain with memory circuits that kept track of everything on board—its catalogue number, what shelf it was stowed on, whether it had right- or left-hand threads, and anything else you wanted to know about it. She had the very latest cargo-handling gear for getting things out of the storerooms and up on deck. She had high-speed cargo winches, booms, and king posts to whip supplies over by high-line to a ship alongside at sea. She even had whirlybirds which could flutter over to an outlying destroyer in the screen and lower a whole cargo net full of stuff to the tin can's fantail.

During a replenishment operation, the skipper of a carrier could holler over at the captain of the *Santee* and say, "Hey, George, we need half a dozen twenty-four-volt sixty-cycle flip-flops for our XSQ radar. Have you got 'em?" The Captain would phone down to the supply office, the yeoman would punch a few buttons, and the mechanical brain would go *zoop-zoop-zoop.* Then a teletype would start chattering in the proper storeroom down below, and a fork-lift truck would appear at the door. In not much more than a minute, a cargo net would swoop down on the carrier's hangar deck with six twenty-four-volt flip-flops. It was the same story whether you wanted a crate of eggs, two tons of potatoes, or a dozen brown shoelaces.

The *Santee* was the naval version of a supermarket, Sears Roebuck's, and a shopping-center-drug-store all rolled into one, computerized, automated, and shined up like the President's yacht. All hands were proud of her.

Her skipper, Captain Gates, was a gung-ho type. He was, of course, a line officer, and had at times, when he commanded combatant ships, been burned up by supply department red tape in trying to draw stores that he needed to get on with his job. He wasn't going to have any of that kind of stuff on *this* ship. He announced the day the ship went into commission that the *Santee*'s motto would be SERVICE TO THE FLEET AND CAN DO. He was determined to make bums out of all the other supply ships in the Med, win the *Santee* the coveted gold E for efficiency, and maybe even a promotion for her skipper.

The Supply Officer went along with most of this too, although perhaps not quite as whole hog as the skipper did. He believed in cutting red tape. But not in heaving the whole damn ball of it overboard. After all, the supply officer is supposed to keep some kind of tabs on the government property entrusted to his care. If he loses track of too much of it, the Inspector General can get very stuffy about it. But he didn't look for any real trouble on that score. The battery of IBM's in his office could grind out invoices, requisitions, and vouchers almost as fast as the new winches on deck could handle freight.

Everybody from the Captain down to the Jack of the Dust was looking forward to their first replenishment job. They were bent on showing the Sixth Fleet that a new era had dawned in the prosaic business of supply.

So the USS *Santee* headed east for her first rendezvous with the fleet, full of piss, vinegar, and supplies of every kind you can think of.

Chapter Seven

Charley Noble

AS GREECE WAS dropping out of sight astern of the *Turtle*, a destroyer came boiling after with a great bone in her teeth.

"Oh-oh!" said Fatso. "This guy may be looking for trouble."

"Shall I unlimber the main battery, Cap'n?" asked the Professor.

"Whaddya mean, main battery? Those twenty millimeter machine guns we got?" demanded Fatso.

"No indeed," said the Professor. "That tank we got aboard has a 90 mm. gun and two hundred rounds of ammunition. I've been looking it over and can handle it without any trouble any time you say."

"That's fine," said Fatso. "That gives us a good ace in the hole. Let's keep it in the hole—for a while, anyways."

The destroyer came up about a hundred yards abeam of the *Turtle* and settled down there for a few minutes as if gaging her speed. Then she poured on the coal again and zigzagged several times close aboard, across the *Turtle*'s bow.

"Looks like they want to play chicken again," observed Scuttlebutt.

"Yeah," replied Fatso. "This puts us in a class with our big ships. They've done the same thing with some of our cruisers and carriers."

"We gonna do anything about it?" asked Scuttlebutt.

"Maybe. Let's see what else he does," said Fatso.

After a final zig across the bow on which the miss distance was too close for comfort, the Russian took station abeam to starboard again and came easing in till the sides of the two ships almost touched. She stayed there for some minutes, with the distance varying from ten feet to no more than an arm's length. Then she zigzagged across the bow a few more times and finally took station about a mile astern and stayed there.

All this time, so far as anyone could see, no one on the destroyer paid any attention to the *Turtle*. There were no rubbernecks topside. No signals were exchanged. Everyone on the bridge just stared straight ahead, except for the OOD who occasionally took a quick peek when they got in close.

In the messroom after the chicken game was over, Webfoot remarked, "You gotta hand it to those guys. They know how to handle that tin can."

"Yeah," agreed Fatso. "But I don't like to have them barging in that close. I want to rig something that will stick out a couple of feet on each side and make 'em stay a little further away from us."

"We could put over a couple of our big cane fenders with a few hand grenades secured on the outboard side of them," suggested Ginsberg, who believed in direct action.

"No-o-o-o," said Fatso. "Them fenders are hard to get. But I want something that will leave a mark on them if they bump us."

"You mean something sticking out like a destroyer's propeller guard?" asked Scuttlebutt.

"Something like that—except I want a good sharp edge on it."

"Hmmmm," said Scuttlebutt. "Hell of a good idea, Cap'n. I'll get to work on it right away."

Scuttlebutt and a couple of helpers got busy with a welding torch, some steel plates, and husky tie rods. In a couple of hours there was a well-braced one-inch steel plate sticking out about three feet from each side of the ship near the bow. The plates were four feet above the water line, faces parallel to the water, and the outer edges had been ground as sharp as a guillotine blade. When Fatso inspected them he remarked, "If you went alongside a dock and nudged a piling with one of those things, you'd cut the top clean off."

"Yup," agreed Scuttlebutt, "that's what they'd do, cut the top clean off, all right. You might say they're sort of a king-sized 'can opener,' " he added, nodding toward the Russian tin can astern.

In the messroom after this job was finished, Fatso briefed the boys on his Op Plan for tomorrow. "I'm going to run in a switch on this chicken game," he said. "If he crowds us again tomorrow, I'm going to nudge him with that—er—paint scraper we just put on and see how he likes it."

"You'll cut him open, sure as hell," declared Scuttlebutt. "Whaddya think he'll do?"

"Well," said Fatso judiciously, "I dunno. And the only way to find out is to try it and see."

Everyone at the table gave sober thought to that statement.

"He's a lot bigger than we are, Cap'n," observed Ginsberg.

"Sure he is. And that's why I ain't gonna nudge him very hard," said Fatso. "You know—one reason why we never get anywhere with the Russians is that we're so damn scared of what they *might* do that we never call their bluff and find out what they *will* do. The only time we ever did was in Cuba, and they pulled their rockets the hell out of there right away."

All heads around the table nodded gravely at this assessment of high-level international policy.

"I don't think this guy will do a damn thing tomorrow," continued Fatso. "He'll be too surprised. These guys do just as they're told, and I don't think his orders cover how to play rough. He'll have to report what happens and ask for instructions. They've been playing this game with our big ships and getting away with it. I think when we change the rules on him, he'll radio his Admiral and say, 'what do I do now?'"

"Hmmmm," said Scuttlebutt, "maybe you're right."

"As soon as I nudge him," continued Fatso, "I want to run up the international signal flags saying 'Do you need assistance?' And I'll send him a blinker message saying, 'Oops—pardon me.' . . . Meantime, there's a couple of other angles I want to work on. . . . I want to make up a canvas dummy and dress it up in a sailor's suit."

"You mean a Charley Noble?" asked Scuttlebutt.

"Yeah," said Fatso. "Except we ain't gonna throw this one overboard."

"Can do, Cap'n," said Scuttlebutt. "Satchmo—you and Webfoot have just volunteered to help me make Charley."

"Now," said Fatso, addressing Judge Frawley, "what is the proper procedure for hanging a sailor at the yard-arm?"

Judge was a bit taken aback by this demand for a legal opinion. "Well, now," he said, stalling for time, "we don't hardly ever do that very much any more. That custom has fallen into disuse in recent years. I don't think you'll find anything in the present Regulation Book about it."

"I know there's nothing in the Book about it," said Fatso. "That's why I'm asking you. I don't want to hold a hanging in a lubberly, unseamanlike manner with our Russian friends looking on. You went to law school. You oughta know the right way to hang a guy."

"Maybe I know more about it than the Judge," said the Professor. "When I was a kid, I read a lot of books about sailing ships. A hanging used to be an all-hands drill. When the Captain decided to hang somebody, they would call all hands aft in their dress blues, and they would put a rope leading up to the yardarm around the guy's neck with a hangman's knot in it—seven turns around the standing part with the bitter end tucked in, pointing up. They'd put about eight guys on the hauling part of the rope, and when everything was all set, the boatswain's mate would blow on his pipe and holler, 'Set taut. Hoist away.' They would run down the deck and swing the guy right up to the yardarm. Enlisted men got hung from the port yardarm—officers from the starboard."

"Didn't they hafta have a trial?" demanded the Judge.

"Sure. It took a general court martial to hang a guy. But that was just a formality. The court always did what the skipper wanted—otherwise, they would of got hung themselves."

"What else did they do?" asked Fatso.

"Well—lemme see. . . . When everybody was on deck in their dress blues they would bring up the guy they wanted to hang, stand him under the yardarm, and read off the sentence to him. He had a right to say some last words, if he wanted to, and then they put a black hood over his head and ran him up. They left him there till sundown and buried him during the night. . . . Oh, yeah, one other thing. When you hang a guy that way it doesn't break his neck like dropping off a trap in the gallows. He

73

strangles to death. So to prevent him from flopping around at the yardarm they used to tie his hands behind his back, and they had a rope from his feet secured to the taffrail."

"Hmmmm," said Fatso. "I think we know enough about it now to put on a pretty good show for our Russian friends tomorrow."

"Who you gonna hang, Cap'n?" asked Jughaid deferentially.

"Charley Noble," said Fatso. "Scuttlebutt, you and your helpers get busy now and make us a good one."

Scuttlebutt broke out a bolt of canvas, a couple of sailmaker's palms and needles, and a pair of heavy shears. He had Jughaid lie down, spread-eagled, on the canvas and carefully cut around him, thus getting a reasonable facsimile of the outside of a man. Meanwhile, Satchmo was pulling the kapok out of a dozen old life jackets to provide the insides for Charley.

As they finished cutting out the second half of the dummy, Jughaid remarked, "I always thought Charley Noble was the name for the galley smoke pipe."

"It is," said Scuttlebutt.

"Why?"

"Search me," said Scuttlebutt. "It's like a lot of other things. Why is the anchor windlass called a wildcat? Nobody knows."

The Professor, who was watching the making of Charley with interest, said "I've read some things about Charley Noble, too. It seems there was an old sailing ship skipper whose name was Charles Noble. He got tired of looking at his crummy sooty galley smoke pipe, so he sheathed it in brass and made the cooks keep it shined. Ever since then, the galley smoke pipe has been called the Charley Noble. I read somewhere that this Charles Noble was one of Admiral Nelson's captains and that he never did anything else that anybody knows about. But nobody can tell you the name of any of Nelson's other captains. Just goes to show that there's all kinds of ways of making a name for yourself in history."

"Then how come we call this here dummy a Charley Noble?" demanded Satchmo.

"I can tell you all about that," said Scuttlebutt, getting a gleam in his eye the way old sailors do when they feel a tale about to unfold. "I was in the *Salem* about three years ago when it happened. You know," he said, "on most ships the man-overboard dummy is just a sort of a scarecrow that floats and looks a little bit like a man. But the *Salem* was a crack ship, and our skipper was on the make for Admiral. Everything on that ship had to be something special, including even the man-overboard dummy. So our sailmaker sewed up a real fancy one. We dressed it up in a regulation uniform, put shoes on it, sewed a white hat to its head, and painted a face with a big grin on it. When we got it finished, it looked more like a real sailor than Jughaid does. We stenciled 'Charley Noble' on his chest, and Charley got dunked and rescued every time we had a man-overboard drill. . . .

"Now, Jughaid," said Scuttlebutt, putting one canvas profile on top of the other, "You sew up one side of this leg, I'll sew up the other, and Satchmo, you keep stuffing it as we go along."

Resuming the narrative, he said, "Pretty soon, along comes dependents' day, when they take the wives and kiddies of the crew out for a day at sea so they can see where their daddy lives and works, and what kind of chow he eats.

"The Captain decided it would be a good idea to have a man-overboard drill to show everybody what good care the Navy takes of their daddy and how safe he is even if he is dumb enough to fall overboard. So they got all the wives and kiddies together, and the skipper got up and explained to them everything that we do in case a man falls overboard. When he got through, they heaved Charley over the side and passed the word, 'Man overboard.'

"At first everything went exactly the way the skipper said it would. They let go the Franklin life buoy, stopped the engines, and swung the stern over so Charley wouldn't get caught in the screws. They manned the whale boat on the double, all hands fell in for muster, and as soon as the ship slowed down enough, they started lowering the boat.

"Then, with all the wives and kiddies watching, the guy on the after fall goofed. He let the fall get away from him, slip off the cleat, and hang the boat straight up and down by the forward fall, dumping the whole boat's crew in the water."

"Laws a mercy," said Satchmo. "I'm glad it wasn't me on that after fall."

"So instead of just having a dummy in the water, we had five real men! It must of took about fifteen minutes to fish those guys out of the water, get the boat hooked on again, lower it, and pick up all the life buoys and stuff that had been thrown overboard for the guys in the water. Meantime, Charley Noble, who floated kind of high in the water, had sailed away down wind and was out of sight. Of course, all this time the skipper's safety valve was stuck wide open, and he damn near blew his main gasket. When they got the boat hoisted in again, he wasn't about to fool around any more looking for Charley. We got the hell out of there and headed back in for Ville France, leaving old Charley adrift.

"Go easy with that kapok, Satchmo," said Scuttlebutt. "If you make Charley too fat, we'll have to ask the skipper for a uniform to fit him."

"So what became of Charley," asked the Professor. "Did you ever hear of him again?"

"Yeah," said Scuttlebutt. "I'm comin' to that. He didn't stay adrift very long. A big French yacht called the *Jeanne d'Arc*, belonging to a duke, picked him up about sunset that day. A couple of weeks later, our skipper gets a letter from Paris on fancy stationery, with a big coat of arms on it. It says, 'Dear Captain: After you sailed off and abandoned me a month ago, I was picked up by the Duke of Richelieu's yacht. The Duke took me down to the cabin, dried me out, and he and his friends were very kind to me. The Duke liked me so much he decided to adopt me as an abandoned urchin. I am now living in his guesthouse on his estate outside Paris. Two good-looking French maids bring me breakfast in bed each morning, with champagne, and are *very* friendly. Please tell my shipmates on the *Salem* that if they really need me —I shall return. If they don't, I would just as soon stay here . . . signed, Charley Noble.' "

All hands were delighted with this yarn, although several frustrated comments were made upon the fact that it had happened to a canvas dummy.

"I can paint a face on this guy if you want it," said Jughaid, as they finished the stuffing and sewing job.

"We don't need no face, because he'll be wearing a

black hood when the Russians see him," said Scuttlebutt. "All we gotta do now is put a uniform and shoes on him."

"I'd like to have seen your skipper's face when he got that letter," observed the Professor.

"The skipper was a pretty good guy," said Scuttlebutt. "He thought it was funnier than hell and published it in the ship's paper."

"Didja ever hear from him again?" asked Jughaid.

"Yeah. A month later, when we were in Palermo, the *Jeanne d'Arc* came in and anchored, and the Duke invited the skipper over to have a drink. He told the skipper that Charley was a damn liar. He wasn't living in the guesthouse with two good-looking French maids. He was behind the bar in the château's recreation room, with one Bunny bartender."

As they were finishing Charley, the Armed Forces Radio news came on.

"Jerusalem: Arab resistance is collapsing on all fronts. Israeli armies have paused to regroup on the east bank of the Suez Canal. Jerusalem has been liberated and our armies have swept on to the west bank of the Jordan. In the north, our tanks scaled almost vertical cliffs and smashed the Syrian Army, which is now fleeing toward Damascus."

Ginsberg grinned from ear to ear like a Halloween punkin.

"Go on and say 'I told you so,'" said Fatso. "You gotta right to."

The radio continued:

"There is a news blackout in Cairo. However, the government radio has been blasting the imperialist warmongers in England and the United States who have been helping the Jews and who plan to establish colonies in Africa. Cairo says our gallant Russian allies will soon come to the aid of the freedom-loving Arabs."

"Too late," said Ginsberg, smugly. "The Russians will help Nasser the same way they helped Castro, when we called their bluff in Cuba. This war is just about over, now —maybe we can visit Israel after all, Cap'n," he said to Fatso. "There will be big doings there about this time next week!"

"Could be," said Fatso.

Chapter Eight

Storm Gathers Some More

WHILE THESE events were transpiring in the Med, utter confusion rained in Washington, almost as bad as the deluge of it that came down in Cairo. When the Israelis finally pulled the plug, the only ones left more flat-footed than the Arabs were our own Joint Chiefs of Staff (and the Kremlin). All top-level officials in Washington and Moscow were caught with their pants down, and there was a mad scramble to get them up.

Everybody went into condition FRANTIC for the next few days. Generals, Admirals, and Cabinet officers rushed from one top-secret briefing to another all day long, learning things at each briefing that they had read about in the morning paper. Lights burned all night in the White House, State Department, Pentagon, and CIA. Perle Mesta threw a big cocktail party for high government officials at which nobody showed up but the gate crashers.

The hot line to the Kremlin was activated in earnest for the first time. The President and Kosygin held several guarded exchanges assuring each other that they knew exactly what was happening on all fronts and there was no cause for alarm. Both had their fists poised over the panic button while they were doing this, ready to sound the Red Alert if the other had said "Boo!" Luckily, these conversations were via teletype, because the air was so tense that neither could have talked on the phone without audible chattering of teeth.

The morning of the fourth day, the Joint Chiefs met early in their inner sanctum of the Pentagon. Red-faced colonels and four-stripe captains were briefing their bosses on the "reasons" for the Arab debacle. Most of the briefers expected to have new jobs in Vietnam by the time the Israelis got to Cairo.

All the chiefs except the Air Force Chief of Staff listened in stony silence with poker faces. The airman grinned happily throughout the briefing and at the end said, "I told you so! . . . Remember, I warned you that whoever got control of the air would overwhelm the other."

The CNO leaned toward the Commandant of the Marines seated next to him and said, out of the corner of his mouth, "What was it you said about the general's aunt, soldier?"

"Balls! . . . Sir," replied the Marine.

"That's what I thought," said the Admiral.

Later that morning the Security Council and Joint Chiefs met in the Cabinet Room of the White House. Everyone was in a serious mood trying to look like a global strategist except the Air Force Chief of Staff. He had a ball, going from one long-faced group to another reminding them how this war proved the effectiveness of air power when properly used.

The Secretary of State and the Secretary of Defense had their heads together over in a corner when he got around to them. The Secretary of Defense saying, "This is a deadly dangerous business no matter what happens. The possibility of an eyeball to eyeball confrontation between the two great nuclear powers hangs over every move we make. A few days ago it looked like the confrontation might come from us trying to save Israel from being wiped out. That crisis didn't last long. But now, things have changed a hundred and eighty degrees, and the confrontation may come over the Russians trying to stop the Israelis from capturing too much Arab territory. So the situation is still dynamite. I've got all my best people watching it constantly, and I keep telling them we've got to be very, very careful."

The SecState nodded approvingly, and the General cleared his throat and said, "Speaking of being careful reminds me of the time right after the war when I was bringing a B-36 into a field down in Texas. They had just put WAACs in the control tower, and a young southern gal was standing her first watch as final approach controller. I heard a B-29 coming in from the east call in for landing instructions. The little gal rattled off all the dope and wound up with—'cleared to land runway 27.' Then I called in for landing instructions, coming in from the west. She ran through the dope again, for me, and said—'cleared to land, runway 9. Runway 9 is 27 in the other direction.' So I called back and said, 'Hey, what's coming off here? I just heard you clear a B-29 in on the same runway in the opposite direction.' She thought that one over for a moment, and then she came back on the air and said, 'Yall be careful!'"

The Secretary of State laughed heartily and said, "It fits this situation almost exactly."

SecDef, whose sense of humor was computerized, regarded the General with a puzzled frown and made a mental note for future reference that the General was too frivolous to be one of the Joint Chiefs.

When the President entered the Cabinet room he was wearing a broad grin. As the meeting came to order he announced, "Gentlemen, I've just come from the war room where I exchanged views with Kosygin on the hot line. As of now, we are in complete agreement on the Near East. He says he will not interfere unless we do. I assured him we have no intention to do so. He was concerned that the Israelis might go too far, and I told him we were too and would try to make them be reasonable."

"Did he say anything about Nasser's charges that our planes have been helping the Israelis?" asked the Secretary of State.

"No. But *I* did. I told him there wasn't a word of truth in it. He said he knew that because their destroyers report every plane that lands or takes off from our carriers. He said we have kept a six-plane fighter patrol over the fleet for the past three days, but that's all."

"He's exactly right about that," observed CNO.

"Now, we've got to be absolutely certain that none of our ships or planes get involved in this," said the President.

"I've already taken care of that," said SecDef. "I've told both the Air Force and the Navy they've got to keep everything outside a four hundred-mile radius from Suez, . . . and my people are monitoring the command circuits to make sure these orders are obeyed."

"I pulled the Sixth Fleet back west of Crete over a week ago on my own initiative," said the CNO, who wasn't at all disgruntled about having SecDef's people kibitzing on how he ran his fleets."

"Okay—that's fine," said the President, "because I told Kosygin we were keeping all our ships and planes well clear of the combat area. Now, gentlemen. . . ."

At this point, a wide-eyed Navy Captain burst into the Cabinet Room and handed the President a four-foot strip of tape right out of one of the decoding machines in the war room. "We just intercepted an urgent message to ComSixthFleet, sir," he said.

The President's face froze as he scanned it. Then he read aloud, "From USS *Liberty*. Am under attack by aircraft and torpedo boats—S.O.S.—S.O.S."

There was a stunned silence for a moment and then CNO demanded, "What the hell is the *Liberty?*"

"It's a communications surveillance vessel, sir," replied the Captain.

"In plain English, that means a spy ship?" said the Secretary of State.

"Those Arabs must be crazy to attack one of our ships," said the President.

"Where was that ship?" demanded CNO of SecDef.

"I should be asking you," replied SecDef. "It's a Navy ship."

"But it's working for *your* people in Defense Intelligence Agency, sir. They bypass command channels all the time, so we never know where their ships are. Arab torpedo boats *can't* be as far out as Crete. I think the *Liberty* must be much closer to Suez than that!"

A lieutenant from the war room burst in with another tape and handed it to the President. The President read, "From ComSixthFleet to the Commander in Chief: UOD am launching planes and sending destroyers to protect *Liberty*. Her position twelve miles offshore from Gaza Strip."

"What the hell does 'UOD' mean?" demanded the President.

"Unless otherwise directed," said CNO. "It means Sixth Fleet has made up his mind, and we've got to act fast if you want to stop him."

"Hell, no! I don't want to stop him. I'm not going to let those crazy Arabs get away with this. . . . But I've got to tell Moscow what we're doing," he added. "This meeting is adjourned to the war room."

In the war room, the President soon had the Kremlin on the teletype. "One of our ships is being attacked," he sent. "Sixth Fleet is now launching planes and sending destroyers to defend it. They will not interfere in the Arab-Israeli war."

In less than a minute the answer came chattering back from Moscow. "We understand. We know about attack on your ship."

"Those bastards must be reading our codes," blurted the head of the CIA.

"Which code was *Liberty*'s message in?" demanded CNO.

"Plain English," replied the duty captain.

"Thank God for that," said CIA and CNO together.

The decoding machine started grinding out tape again. The President read it aloud as it came out. "From *Liberty*. Have been torpedoed and strafed. Many casualties. Am limping west at ten knots. Attacking planes and ships had Israeli markings."

"Good God," said the President. "That must be wrong."

"The Arabs could easily put Israeli markings on their planes and ships," said Ambassador Goldberg.

"Or it could be they *were* Israeli," said the CNO. "Trigger-happy aviators sometimes go off half-cocked, you know."

All doubt about this point was soon removed. The monitors picked up an urgent message to ComSixthFleet from Israeli Naval Headquarters in Tel Aviv: "Regret to inform you our forces have attacked USS *Liberty* near combat zone in Gaza by mistake."

"It seems almost impossible," said the President, while everyone was trying to adjust to this amazing turn of events.

"Of course," said Ambassador Goldberg, "that last message could be a phony put out by the Arabs."

"Impossible," said CNO. "Our direction finders would pinpoint the transmitting station before they got halfway through the message. It was the Israelis, all right. One of those mistakes the flyboys make. This is why I pulled all our combatant ships out of that area," he added, with an accusing glare at SecDef.

"Harumph," observed SecDef and was about to amplify his observation when the President cut in.

"Let's not get into a hassle here about who's to blame for this," he said. "George, you and the Admiral settle it between you and let me know. Meantime, we've got to rescue our ship—if we can."

Chapter Nine

All Hands to Hanging Stations

THAT SAME morning, right after eight bells, the Russian pulled up abeam to starboard, and the chicken game began again. All Fatso's boys were on deck. No one was visible on the Russian ship except the OOD on the port wing of the bridge, staring straight ahead.

Pretty soon the destroyer came sidling over on an almost parallel course until its side was only six feet from the *Turtle*'s. Then it began weaving in and out—out to fifty feet and back in to six. The third time it started in, Fatso tapped the helmsman on the shoulder and said, "I'll take the wheel." The wheel was inside the pilothouse—not visible from the destroyer's bridge.

As the destroyer was steadying at six feet, Fatso suddenly spun his wheel hard over to starboard and flipped his props into neutral. The *Turtle*'s bow swerved to starboard, and there was a rending screech as the "can opener" cut into the destroyer's thin plates. With its props idling, the *Turtle* began dropping aft, slicing the Russian's side as if it were cardboard. After a couple of seconds, Fatso spun his wheel the other way, and his bow swung to port, pulling the blade out of the Russian's side. As they came clear, Fatso threw his engines to full ahead and hauled out to port, leaving the Russian with a neat six-foot gash in his side an inch wide, four feet above the water line.

"Ah cut a bad friend with a razor that way once," observed Satchmo, admiringly.

"Get that signal up while he's still trying to figure out what happened. Call him on the light," yelled Fatso, walking out to the starboard wing of the bridge and putting his glass on the Russian.

Up went the signal flags to the *Turtle*'s yardarm, saying in international code, "Do you need assistance?" The searchlight began blinking, *"Ya ochen ob ztom sogalyu"* —the Professor and the Judge claiming that according to their pocket dictionary this was the Russian version of "sorry about that."

Followed a tense couple of minutes with the two ships steaming along on parallel courses a hundred yards apart. All hands on the *Turtle* watched the Russian respectfully —as a little guy always does right after he draws a bit of blood from a big guy.

"It's nothin' but a scratch," observed Fatso. "I doubt very much they'll try to make a federal case out of it," he said rather dubiously.

An officer and a group of men appeared on deck of the destroyer and leaned over the rail looking at the gash. They were soon joined by their Captain, who peered over the side for a few moments, then straightened up, shrugged his shoulders, and probably said, *"Neechevo."*

The skipper went back to the bridge and soon their searchlight began blinking. It said, "I object. You improperly violating rules of the road."

"Hah!" said Fatso, with a broad grin. "My guess was right. All he's gonna do is squawk."

This opinion was soon confirmed as the Russian dropped aft and resumed his station a mile astern.

"Okay," said Fatso. "Now send him this on your light," and he handed Jughaid the following: "Regret my helmsman's stupid mistake. He will be punished. Signed, Commanding Officer, USS *Turtle.*"

As the Russian blinked his light receipting for the message, Fatso said, "All right now, boys. An hour before sunset I want all hands on deck in dress blues. We're going to have the first official hanging in this Navy since John Paul Jones's day."

"Do you think they'll believe it?" asked Scuttlebutt.

"I think there's a good chance they may," said Fatso. "This will check with what their own propaganda tells them about us all the time. He'll be able to tell his Admiral about it, and say this proves the Americans know they were wrong. It might even be on the front page of *Pravda* tomorrow."

All day long, the Russian kept a respectful distance astern.

An hour before sunset, Satchmo got out his bugle and blew "Assembly." It was amplified by Fatso's hi-fi loudspeakers so it would be clearly audible astern. The boys all assembled on the bridge in their dress-blue uniforms facing aft, and Fatso fired a couple of red Very's stars in the air. The signal gun let out a boom to starboard, the traditional signal of ships at sea to attract the attention of nearby vessels.

Jughaid, with a spyglass on the Russian, soon reported, "There's a half dozen of 'em on the bridge with their binoculars on us."

Then Satchmo, bareheaded, with his hands tied behind him, was led up to the rostrum where Fatso stood. A rope with a noose in it dangled from the port yardarm. The men were called to attention, and Fatso went through the motions of reading a document out loud. What he actually read was an item from the morning radio news saying the Supreme Court had thrown out Danny Escobeda's latest murder rap and ordered him turned loose.

Then Judge Frawley stepped forward and put a black hood over Satchmo's head while two others got the noose and began adjusting it around his neck. In doing this, they obscured Satch from view for a moment. Satch ducked below and Charley Noble was substituted for him.

Soon the noose was in place, and the two who adjusted it took their places alongside Charley, holding him up by his arms. To observers astern, it appeared that the culprit had lost his nerve at the last moment, his knees had given way, and he had to be held up. The others fell out of ranks and manned the hauling part of the rope.

Fatso broke out his bosun's pipe, let out a long blast on it, and the boys ran forward with the rope, two-blocking Charley in a smart, seamanlike manner to the yardarm.

"Let that be a lesson to the rest of you guys," observed Fatso. "Belay that line from his feet to the rail so he won't flop around too much in the wind, and then secure from hanging stations."

Fatso and Scuttlebutt kept their glasses focused on the destroyer astern. "Must be a dozen of 'em on the bridge now, with their glasses on us," observed Scuttlebutt.

"Yeah," said Fatso. "And there's the captain on the big quartermaster's spyglass—talking a blue streak to the guy alongside him, . . . probably the exec."

Pretty soon the destroyer began easing up closer, and

then sheared out and took station two hundred yards abeam.

"You notice he gives us a little more elbow room, now," said Fatso.

"Do you think they're wise to it yet?" asked Scuttlebutt.

"Hell, no," said Fatso. "Even from right here on this bridge, old Charley looks so real it gives me the creeps to look at him. . . . You see, . . . the skipper is going back to his cabin now, shaking his head. I'll betcha he's saying, 'If I hadn't seen it with my own eyes I wouldn't have believed it—even if I read it in Pravda.' "

"There's a guy on the bridge with a movie camera, taking pictures," observed Scuttlebutt.

"They'll probably be featured on TV and in every movie palace in Russia," said Fatso.

"Do you want to send him any signal about this, Cap'n?" asked Jughaid.

"Hell, no. I don't want him to think there's anything special about it. We'll just go on about our business as if we were used to doing this, and let them draw their own conclusions."

On the Russian ship, that's exactly what they *were* doing. The exec was in the skipper's cabin, saying "What do you think, Captain? Do you believe that's a real man?"

"Yes. I think it is," said the skipper. "That Captain is a wild man. He must be crazy to ram a big ship like this with a small craft like that. So he would think nothing of hanging one of his sailors to excuse himself."

"Is it all right to have our crew on deck and take a look?" asked the exec.

"Yes. Of course," said the Captain. "Get the men all together and explain to them that this is the way it used to be in the Navy of the Czars. But no one has been hanged in Russia since the revolution."

"We have movies of the whole thing, Captain," said the exec.

"Good. They will be well pleased with them in Moscow. We may get promoted."

That evening after chow all hands were listening to the Armed Forces radio.

"Jerusalem: Israeli armies continue to drive ahead everywhere almost unopposed. Arab resistance has collapsed on all fronts, and our troops today overwhelmed the Egyptian garrison and reopened the Gulf of Aqaba."

"That sure goes to show something—but I'm not sure what," declared Scuttlebutt, shaking his head sadly.

"It shows that history repeats itself," said Ginsberg. "We ran the Arabs out of the Sinai Peninsula in five days back in '56. They haven't learned a damn thing in the past ten years."

"Rome: There is a news blackout in Cairo, but Nasser hurled more charges against the western nations and claims that planes from the U.S. Sixth Fleet are helping the Israelis. He said our soldiers in the desert are fighting bravely against great odds. Neutral observers think Cairo may be getting ready to ask for a cease fire."

"They shouldn't cease firing till they get to the pyramids," observed Ginsberg.

After the news, there was a lot of dot-dash traffic on the Russian frequency. The Professor and Ginsberg spent an hour listening in and taking radio bearings on the various transmitting stations. They reported to Fatso, "Our friend back there astern sent a couple of long messages, and the station that receipted for them bears northeast of us."

"That's their base back in Greece," said Fatso. "He was prob'ly telling them about getting nudged—and maybe about the hanging."

"There was also a long message from the base, answered by a station bearing due east."

"Hmmmmm," said Fatso. "Israel and Egypt are east of us. They sure as hell ain't asking the Jews if they need any help beating up the Arabs. They must of been passing information to Cairo."

More war news that evening continued to tell an overwhelming victory for the Israelis. The only claim the Egyptians were still making was that their brave soldiers would fight to the death defending Cairo against the com-

bined forces of the United States, England, and the Jews.
Then! The radio loudspeaker produced a shocker.

"Washington: The White House announced that the
USS *Liberty*, a noncombatant naval ship, has been attacked by planes and torpedo boats in international
waters twelve miles off the coast of Israel. A number of
her crew were killed, and many are wounded. The
Liberty is limping west in nearly sinking condition. The
Sixth Fleet is speeding to her rescue. Present reports
indicate that the attack was made by Israeli forces."

There was a stunned silence for a moment. Then Ginsberg said, "Gawd almighty! That's impossible. It must of
been the Arabs."

"Don't be too sure," said Fatso. "This wouldn't be the
first time that trigger-happy flyboys shot up a friendly
ship."

"The Arabs done it—and they'll try to blame it on the
Israelis," insisted Ginsberg.

Later bulletins confirmed that it was, indeed, the Israelis who shot up the *Liberty*. Then, "Washington: President Johnson called the Kremlin on the hot line to inform
them the Sixth Fleet is sending planes and ships to defend
the *Liberty* but denied that they had taken any part in
attacks on the Egyptians."

"Hoo boy!" said Fatso. "This thing might get blown up
into a *real* war."

"Whaddya mean, *real* war?" demanded Ginsberg. "I'll
bet them Arabs think this one they're in is pretty real,
right now."

"Hell, I mean an atomic war between us and Russia,"
said Fatso. "Compared to that, this one here ain't even a
fart in a teapot."

Later. "Jerusalem: The Israeli government has notified
the United States that their forces attacked the *Liberty* by
mistake. It expresses regret for the error."

Everyone around the table looked at each other for a
moment and then said almost as one, "Sorry about that!"

Ginsberg made no comment.

90

That evening the boys held what the Naval War College would call an Estimate of the Situation, except that the phraseology used might have been frowned upon at the War College. Modifying adjectives were often used ascribing to inanimate objects capability possessed only by human beings of opposite sex.

"What do we hear from the *Pillsbury,* Professor?" asked Fatso.

"Not a (modifying adjective) thing," replied the Professor. "I'm checking in with them twice a day, and old Sparky Wright is right on the ball. He answers himself, every time. He says there hasn't been a word about us in any of the FOX schedules."

"Hmmmm," said Fatso. "It's ten days now since the *Alamo* shoved off. Something mighty screwy has happened, and the Sixth Fleet doesn't know we been left behind. If they did, they would certainly have checked up on us by this time. I'll bet that fat-headed ship's clerk on the *Alamo* will probably send ComSixthFleet a letter about us and mail him our records and pay accounts when they get to Vietnam."

"So where does that leave us now, Cap'n," asked Scuttlebutt.

"It leaves us paddling our own little canoe all by ourselves out here in the middle of the Mediterranean. We're abandoned—just about the way the *Salem* abandoned Charley Noble."

"Well, anyway—we ain't as helpless as we look," said the Professor. "We got that marine tank with a 90 mm. gun. That's more than the *Liberty* had. If anyone tries to pick on us, we could surprise the hell out of them with it."

"Yeah. That's something to think about," said Fatso. "You can't see that tank without coming on board. But if we drop the bow ramp, it would give it a pretty good arc of fire—maybe twenty degrees on each bow. What's the range of that piece, Professor?"

"Oh, about seven or eight miles," replied the Professor. "But we couldn't hit anything smaller than a battleship at that range. But it's got a high velocity and a real flat trajectory—out to about a mile, we can't miss with it."

"I don't want to have no trouble with no battleships," observed Fatso. "No use in being pig-headed about a thing like that. What kind of ammo you got?"

"Armor piercing, for use against tanks, and shrapnel. 90 mm. is about three and one quarter inch—and that's a pretty good-sized slug."

"Okay," said Fatso. "Let's move that tank forward so all we'll hafta do to blaze away is drop the bow ramp. Then if somebody anywheres near our size tries to push us around, we can do business with 'em. Professor—you are hereby appointed gunnery officer of this ship of war."

"Aye aye, sir, Cap'n," said the Professor. "I'll wait 'til I can see the whites of their eyes."

"You know, Cap'n," said the Judge, "ComSixthFleet put out an order recently to all ships, telling when our ships and planes are entitled to shoot. They call it the Rules of Engagement. It says. . . ."

"Yeah," interrupted Fatso. "I heard the officers on the *Alamo* talking about it. I'll bet the *Liberty* was still trying to figure out what the hell it meant when they got clobbered. There used to be something in the regulations about repelling boarders. . . ."

"I just looked it up," said the Judge. "It's still in the book. Article 0730. It says you shouldn't allow no foreign ships to board you. It's real emphatic about it."

"Okay—we'll follow the book on that," said Fatso.

"Do you think that Russian is apt to try to board us?" asked Scuttlebutt.

"No-o-o-o. I don't think so," said Fatso, somewhat dubiously. "You notice he's been pretty polite to us since we nudged him," he added, hopefully.

"How about the Israelis?" asked Webfoot.

"They won't mess with us," said Fatso. "After the goof they made on the *Liberty,* they'll be very leery of us."

"The goddam Arabs are the ones I would be worried about," said Ginsberg, "—if they got any ships left."

"You got something there, kid," said Fatso. "The way we took it on the chin in the *Liberty* business without doing a damn thing about it, they might get the idea they can get away with murder. I wouldn't like to see one of their ships show up."

Chapter Ten

"Repel Boarders!"

THE NEXT morning, that's exactly what did come boiling over the horizon—an Egyptian PT boat, making about forty knots. She charged in on the *Turtle* and started circling at high speed one hundred yards away, stirring up a great wake that tossed the *Turtle* around like a cork. She was an evil-looking craft with fifty caliber machine guns mounted on each wing of the bridge and two torpedo tubes on her foredeck. She seemed to have a crew of at least two dozen men, some of whom were standing around with submachine guns.

"That's a hell of a big crew they got, for a PT boat," observed Webfoot.

"Yeah," said Fatso. "I have an idea they may have a prize crew aboard."

"Oh oh!" said Scuttlebutt. "You think they'll try to board us?"

"Could be," said Fatso. "We'll soon see."

The PT boat circled them three times, obviously giving them a close inspection. No weapons were visible on the *Turtle*. After the third circle, the Egyptian ran astern and pulled up close aboard alongside the Russian destroyer.

"He's getting his orders now," observed Fatso. "Those damn Russians are pretty smart cookies. They always get their allies to do their dirty work. This is what that long radio message we heard the other night was all about."

After a few moments, Fatso said, "Professor! I want you to go forward, man that gun, and stand by. If we have any trouble with this guy I'm gonna wait till he gets pretty close before I drop the bow ramp. When I do, I want you to whistle five or six shots past him close aboard. But don't hit him—unless I tell you to. I think he'll head for home like the Egyptian army did as soon as we start shooting. So I don't wanta hit him unless we hafta. Ya unnerstand?"

"Aye aye, sir, Cap'n. Will do."

"Who's going to be helping you on that gun?"

"Ginsberg."

"Get somebody else. I want to have him up here on the wheel where I can see what he's doing. That crazy kid would put the first shell right into them, if he could."

"Aye aye, sir, Cap'n," said the Professor—and went forward to unlimber the *Turtle*'s main battery.

Fatso cocked an eye aloft and noted they were flying the usual small set of steaming colors. "Jughaid," he said, "I want you to bend on the biggest set of colors we got on board, and stand by. If we start shooting—run them up to the main truck. You gotta have your battle ensign flying when you go into action."

"Aye aye, Sir," said Jughaid.

In half an hour, the PT boat hauled clear of the Russian and ran up one hundred yards ahead of the *Turtle*. As she passed abeam only twenty yards away, a dozen sailors could be seen in the stern sheets with submachine guns.

"They're gonna try to board," said Fatso. "Keep your tommy guns handy—but out of sight."

The three ships were forging ahead at ten knots. The Egyptian's searchlight began blinking, "Stop engines or I will fire on you." At the end of the message they fired a burst of fifty caliber over the *Turtle*'s head. The burst hit the water near the Russian astern and ricocheted past him dangerously close aboard.

"All engines stop," yelled Fatso. "Run up signal 'I am stopped.' "

Up fluttered the international signal flags, indicating "I have stopped."

The ships were soon dead in the water, and the Egyptian began backing down toward the *Turtle*.

"Use your engines to hold her pointed right at that guy," said Fatso to Ginsberg, at the wheel.

"Aye aye, sir," sang out Ginsberg, kicking ahead slow on one engine and backing the other.

When the Egyptian got in to fifty yards, a dozen armed men could be seen standing by on the stern. Fatso called coolly to the Professor, "Load your gun. Be ready for a fast burst of six shots."

As the PT boat neared twenty-five yards, Fatso yelled,

"Down bow ramp!" . . . As it flopped open, he sang out, "You may fire when ready, Gridley."

"Wham!" went the ninety mm. gun, and sent a slug whistling past the PT boat close aboard to port. "Don't give up the ship," yelled Fatso. "Wham!" it went again, and sent another screaming past the starboard side.

"Run up that battle ensign," roared Fatso at Jughaid as the boarding party made a wild dive for cover, half of them losing their weapons overboard. In seconds not a soul could be seen topside. The exhaust pipes belched out a burst of smoke, and the boat leaped ahead with the propellers churning up a storm and flinging clouds of spray astern.

PT boats like the Egyptian are only supposed to be good for about forty knots. Fatso and his crew swear that this one made at least sixty, zigzagging frantically to the east. "Don't shave him too close," yelled Fatso at the Professor between WHAM's. "He might zigzag into one."

When she had put a mile of open water between them, the PT boat let out a couple of puffs of powder smoke, one on each bow. There were two big splashes close aboard the fleeing craft, one on each side, and Scuttlebutt yelled, "Torpedoes!"

"Damn the torpedoes—full speed ahead," yelled Fatso. "Right full rudder."

Fatso and Scuttlebutt put their binoculars on the area where the fish had been launched. As the Professor kept pumping three-inch slugs all around the Egyptian, Scuttlebutt yelled, "I see both wakes, Cap'n. They're going to miss us plenty—astern."

"Yup!" confirmed Fatso. "And now that we've pulled out of their way, they're headed right at the Russian!"

Soon great clouds of black smoke began pouring out of both the Russian's stacks, and her propellers churned up a maelstrom astern.

"Holy cow!" said Fatso. "If she gets sunk, the Russians will sure as hell claim we done it."

If the Russian had simply laid to, dead in the water, pointing head on at the torpedoes, they would both have been near misses, one on each side. But as he picked up headway under full left rudder, his bow swung smack into the path of the left-hand fish. There was a terrific explosion and ten feet of the destroyer's bow went up in the air in a great geyser of water and junk, while the other fish passed harmlessly down the starboard side.

"Gawd almighty," said Scuttlebutt. "They sank the poor son-of-a-bitch."

"No -o- o-o," said Fatso judicially, "just—just blew a little piece of his bow off, is all."

A minute later the second fish reached the end of its run and blew itself up some miles astern, erupting another replica of Old Faithful from the sea.

By this time the Egyptian was a mere speck on the horizon, and the paint on the Professor's gun barrel was bubbling into blisters.

"Cease firing," yelled Fatso. "Secure from battle stations . . . and splice the main brace."

This latter order is somewhat unconstitutional in the present-day U.S. Navy, which has been bone dry at sea since 1914. It goes back to the days of sail in the British Navy when, in order to celebrate a victory, the Admiral used to order a special ration of grog issued to all hands. For reasons known only to old sailors, this was called "splicing the main brace."

None of Fatso's lads knew a mizzentop gallant sail from the lee scuppers, but Scuttlebutt produced a bottle of Bacardi rum, and the main brace was spliced in a smart, seamanlike manner.

Meantime, Fatso brought the *Turtle* within hailing distance of the Russian with signal flags flying saying, "Do you need assistance?" The destroyer was down by the bow about five feet and was too busy with other matters to answer the signal. Soon Fatso got on the loud hailer and yelled over, "Do you need any help from us?"

The answer came back, *"Nyet."*

A few minutes later, the Russian skipper got on the horn. "Thank you," he yelled—and then added, "Egyptian iss *zvoloch.*"

"Da," replied Fatso. "Now let's get the hell out of here," he said to Ginsberg. "Come around to northeast and bend on twelve knots."

At dinner that evening the Professor said, "Cap'n, I was real proud of you today. You reminded me of Admirals Dewey, Farragut, and Decatur all rolled into one."

"Aw I'll bet you say that to all the gals," said Fatso with mock modesty.

"I can only think of one famous line you didn't use," said the Professor.

"What was that?" demanded Fatso.

" 'I have not yet begun to fight.' "

"Even if I had thought of it I wouldn't of said it," declared Fatso. "You ain't supposed to say that until you've had the hell beat out of you and are about to sink."

"Some history books say it was that way—others say it came right at the beginning of the battle," said Judge Frawley.

"Anyway," observed Fatso, "It's about the dumbest famous saying that ever got famous. I don't believe John Paul Jones ever said it. What he prob'ly said was, 'You Limey son-of-a-bitch, I'm going to beat the piss out of you'."

"No-o-o," said the Professor judicially. "That's how *you* would of said it, Cap'n. But not John Paul Jones. In them days, officers and gentlemen didn't call each other son of a bitches. There wasn't no such a word then. He would of called him a 'bloody bastard.' That's a bad word in England even now—almost as bad as *zvoloch* in Russia."

Chapter Eleven

Peace Breaks Out

THE DAY after the *Liberty* bombshell, with the Arab armies in full flight everywhere and no Arab airplanes left that could fly anywhere, Nasser threw in his jock strap and asked for a cease fire.

This caught Washington almost as flat-footed as the outbreak of war had. The global strategists, diplomats, cloak-and-dagger types, and press pundits all said nothing but tried to look as if they knew a lot more than that. Everybody had goofed so badly with their inside dope on the war that now not even Drew Pearson was willing to predict what day tomorrow would be.

For five days, the statesmen had lost control of events and the world had teetered on the brink of atomic disaster. The hot line between the White House and Kremlin had chattered away like a stock ticker quoting the changing odds on survival of the western world. Top officials in Washington and Moscow hovered over the teleprinters like brokers during the market crash, wondering what those damned fools at the other end would do next. For days the fate of nations depended on things over which no one had any control.

The *Liberty* affair showed how easily the whole world might be blown up by mistake. A top-level crisis, which might have become atomic, had been brought on by stupid low-level blunders on both sides. The Pentagon Whiz Kids set the stage for it by passing up regular naval command channels when they stuck the *Liberty* out on a limb. The ship was attacked by trigger-happy flyers and naval officers who should have know better. When news of the attack first hit the fan, all responsible officials in Washington jumped to the conclusion that the Arabs—or the Russians—had done it. Some high-level hotheads even favored immediate retaliation.

Several times the Russian snooper-destroyer helped to preserve world peace by confirming what we were telling

Moscow about operations by the Sixth Fleet. But the balloon might have gone up when Sixth Fleet launched the *Liberty* rescue mission, and the snooper warned Moscow that a full-scale strike mission was taking off and heading east. The hot line saved the day there. But a garble on the teleprinter at that point might have blown the world apart.

When peace broke out again in the Near East, the country heaved a sigh of relief and went back to its normal peacetime business. Stokely Carmichael, Rap Brown, and the Student Nonviolent Coordinating Committee resumed planning to burn down Detroit in a nonviolent manner. The Supreme Court decided, five to four, that the police had no right to arrest citizens setting fire to buildings when their lawyers were not present. SecDef said we were winning the Vietnam war so fast that our soldiers would be home by Christmas, and General Hershey announced draft calls would be doubled next month.

Just as everybody was relaxing and getting ready for a short, cool summer, Nasser dropped another block-buster.

He hurled charges over Cairo radio that another U.S. spy ship had made an unprovoked attack on an Egyptian naval craft southeast of Crete. He claimed this proved that the Sixth Fleet had been fighting all along on the side of the Israelis. He demanded that the U.S. apologize for this flagrant violation of the cease fire and punish the pirates who had made this treacherous attack.

This information leaked out in Washington over the AP news ticker at 2 A.M., catching all the Admirals at home in bed. They came scrambling back to the Pentagon as if general quarters had just sounded. By the time CNO got to the war room, the duty captain had already quizzed ComSixthFleet.

"Sixth Fleet has no idea whatever what this is all about," he reported as the bleary-eyed Admiral gulped down a cup of black coffee.

"Probably some more of the Whiz Kids' work," grunted the Admiral, between gulps.

"I've checked with the SecDef's duty officer," said the Captain. "He doesn't know anything about it either."

"That doesn't prove anything," observed the CNO. "The Whiz Kids didn't tell SecDef about the *Liberty* until she got in trouble. Do they have any other ships like the *Liberty* under their op-con?"

"That's the only one we know of, sir," said the Captain.

"How about CIA or the Coast Guard?"

"We're checking with them now, sir."

"Okay," said the Admiral. "Get me ComSixthFleet on the sideband radio phone."

In a minute the duty officer handed the Admiral the shortwave scrambler phone and said, "Admiral Hughes on the line."

"Hello there, Stinkpot," said the Chief of Naval Operations, using the Academy nickname that Admiral Hughes had stamped out among all officers except the few senior to him. "What's this business that Nasser is screaming about Southeast of Crete? Over."

"All we know is what we picked up from Cairo radio," said the Admiral. "It wasn't one of *my* ships. Over."

"Well, you know we looked pretty foolish on that *Liberty* incident," said the CNO. "Are you sure nothing like that is happening again? Over."

"I've made an ironclad check on every Sixth Fleet ship out here. There's nothing east of Crete except a Polaris sub and she's been submerged all the time. Over."

"Okay. Thanks, Stinkpot. Over and Out."

At the Security Council meeting that morning, the CNO led off.

"Mr. President," he said, "I can assure you that no U.S. Navy ship was involved in this thing. We have no idea what it is all about."

"Is this another cloak and dagger job, like the *Liberty?*" asked the President, fixing a stony stare on the head of CIA.

"This has nothing to do with CIA," said our head spy. "But I can't speak for the Defense Intelligence Agency ... The *Liberty* belonged to *them,* you know, not CIA."

"DIA had nothing to do with this," said SecDef frostily.

The CNO and the CIA glanced at each other, raised their eyebrows and shrugged skeptically.

"Well, then, what do you make of this broadcast from Cairo?" demanded the President.

"It could have been an Israeli ship," said SecDef.

"Or it might just be propaganda for local consumption in Cairo, where the news hasn't been very good lately," observed CIA.

"Or a ship belonging to any one of a dozen naval powers in the Med," said the Secretary of State.

"If one of our ships had been involved in an incident like this, it would have been reported by radio immediately," said the CNO.

"So what do we do now?" asked the President. "Should we issue a denial of this?"

"Certainly not, sir," said the Secretary of State. "So far, all we know is what we overheard on Cairo radio. We can't take any official notice of that. If they are serious about this, they will send us a formal diplomatic note about it."

That afternoon the Egyptian Ambassador handed the Secretary of State a blunt note. It said that the USS *Turtle,* a spy ship, had made an unprovoked attack on a small Egyptian naval craft two hundred miles S.E. of Crete, firing several dozen six-inch shells at the Egyptian. The *Turtle,* identifying number U-1, mounted a thirty-foot radar dish, was flying the American flag, and was disguised as a cargo barge. The note demanded an apology, punishment of the pirates, and an indemnity of ten million dollars.

A State Department courier rushed this note to the Pentagon, where a group of flabbergasted Admirals puzzled over it.

"This thing is crazy," said the Vice Chief. "You don't try to disguise a ship and fly your own colors from it. There is no USS *Turtle* and no ship has a number anything like U-1. A ship big enough to carry a thirty-foot radar dish and six-inch guns has to be at least a destroyer. This simply cannot be an American ship."

"We can't find any foreign ships that fit this description either," said the head of Naval Intelligence. "And I can't imagine how you can disguise a big ship to look like a barge."

"Maybe they're seeing little men from Mars," observed CNO. "After what happened to them in the past five days, I don't blame them for thinking anything is possible."

"It could be an Israeli ship," said the Vice Chief.

"I doubt it," said the Chief. "If it had been an Israeli, the Egyptians would have been sunk. The Egyptians just got the wrong address on this note. That's all we can say about it."

The upshot of all this was that after much skeptical cross-checking by the White House with the Navy, Defense Department, and CIA, the State Department answered the Egyptian note simply saying, "This wasn't our ship." By this time Nasser was so busy shooting his generals, sinking ships in the Suez canal, and opening accounts in Swiss banks—that the *Turtle*'s buccaneering was dropped.

Chapter Twelve

USS *Turtle* Joins Flying Dutchman

THE DAY after the cease fire in the Near East found peace and brotherly love rampant all over the world except in Vietnam, Indonesia, China, Africa, parts of South America, and some of the big cities of the United States.

That afternoon the USS *Turtle* was proceeding on duty assigned (in a manner of speaking, that is), alert and ready to defend the maritime interests of the United States against all enemies in the Eastern Med. She was steering course 090 at ten knots, in one thousand fathoms of water, under high scattered clouds, wind NE at three knots.

Since no adversaries were within visual range at this time, the *Turtle* was not actually at battle stations. Satchmo had the wheel, and everyone else was caulking off in the sun on the well deck.

Suddenly Satchmo spun his wheel hard over to port, let out a yell, and pulled the general alarm. The ship swerved sharply to port and took a list to starboard, as all hands scrambled to their feet and over to the side to see what was happening.

"What the hell's coming off here?" yelled Fatso at the bridge.

"A gahdam floating mine, Cap'n!" yelled Satchmo, pointing at the water broad on the starboard bow.

Sure enough, there was the top of a round object about five feet in diameter, floating past about twenty feet to starboard.

This sight produced a unanimous awed comment from all hands: "Son-of-a-BITCH!"

Then a large wedge-shaped head poked itself up out of the water alongside the "mine." Two wise old eyes regarded the USS *Turtle* gravely for a moment. Then the head disappeared, two big clumsy feet came out of the water on the other side, and the "mine" plunged down out of sight.

103

"A great big gahdam TURDDLE," declared Jughaid.

"Yeah. That's what it was, all right," agreed Fatso.

"Mah mistake, Cap'n," called Satchmo, apologetically, spinning his wheel to get back on course.

"Okay, Satch," replied Fatso. "This ain't the first a turtle's been mistook for a mine. I seen old Admiral Halsey himself turn the whole Third Fleet ninety degrees on account of one during the war."

During the usual discussion of world affairs that evening, the subject of turtles came up.

"Some of them turtles get to be over a hundred years old," declared Scuttlebutt.

"Yeah," agreed Webfoot. "When I was in UDT, we had a trained turdle that used to help us find moored mines. Bosco was his name, and he'd come when you called him."

"Even if that was so I wouldn't believe it," declared Scuttlebutt.

"Well, it *is* so," said Webfoot. "But he found one mine too many and got turned into instant turtle soup one day."

"I read in a book one time that turtles travel around the world," said Ginsberg. "It told about a turtle that was banded in the Galapagos Islands and was caught out here in the Med, halfway round the world from where he was born, six months later."

"How did he make the trip," asked Scuttlebutt, "around the Horn or the Cape of Good Hope?"

"How the hell would I know?" asked Ginsberg. "He mighta gone through Suez or Panama easy enough."

"Don't you believe a word of what that book said," advised Fatso. "Turtles spend their whole life right near where they are born."

"How do you know?" demanded Ginsberg.

"When I was in boot camp," said Fatso, getting the story-telling gleam in his eye, "Old Bosun Biggs told us all about turtles. The bosun started out as one of the old-time apprentice boys they used to have back in 1902 when he joined up. They don't have that rate any more. The Navy decided there would never be any more real sailormen like the bosun and abolished it. All us boots figured the bosun must of served with Noah in the Ark. Anyway, he was our instructor in boot camp back in 1940 when I first shipped. He made the cruise with the Great White Fleet in 1907, when old Teddy Roosevelt sent it around the world. He was a seaman second class then, on the *Maine*—not the one that got blowed up in Havana, the next one. The bosun said he went ashore in a swimming party at Pango Pango, and they found this great big turtle asleep in the sand. He musta been damn near a hundred years old. A bunch of them rolled the old boy over on his back and Biggs carved his name and rate on the bottom of his shell. Almost twenty years later, Biggs made the Australian cruise in the *Idaho*. By then he was a chief boatswain. When the fleet stopped in Pango Pango on the way out, he took a swimming party ashore to that same beach and there was a big old turtle asleep in the sand again."

"Was he still on his back?" asked the Professor.

"No," said Fatso indignantly. "They had rolled him back on his belly and let him loose back in '07. But anyway, they rolled this turtle over on its back, and by Gawd it was the same old guy. There was the name and rate carved in his shell. 'J. Biggs, CHIEF BTSN, USN.' "

"I'll be gahdam," commented several listeners.

"So all that stuff about turtles wandering around all over the world is a lot of horse crap," said Fatso.

This discussion was interrupted by the armed forces radio news. Now that peace had reared its bruised and battered head in the Near East, Vietnam was back in the headlines.

"Washington: At a special press conference today, the Secretary of Defense announced that we are making satisfactory progress on all fronts in Vietnam. He said the recent disorders within the city limits of Saigon have been suppressed. Rockets are still falling around the U.S. Embassy and Army HQ, but most of the large organized units of the Vietcong have been driven back to the suburbs. The body count for the past week has been twenty to one in our favor, and our strategic planners say the VC cannot stand such an exchange rate much longer. The Secretary said it is our firm intention to continue gradual escalation of pressure on the enemy until he sues for peace."

(The idea is to just *barely* win the war," observed the Professor.) The broadcast continued:

"In reply to questions by the press about mining Haiphong Harbor, the Secretary pointed out that merchant ships of many of our allies, including England, France, Japan and the Philippines, use this harbor, and we do not wish to jeopardize noncombatant ships of friendly countries by mining it."

"With those kind of friends and allies, we don't need any enemies," observed the Judge.

"But we're sure whopping the hell out of 'em," said Jughaid.

"How do you figure that?" asked the Professor.

"The man said we're beating them twenty to one."

"That don't mean much," observed the Professor. "It all depends on how you set up your computers. How many gooks does it take to make it an even swap for one Marine? I figure the break-even point is about one hundred to one. For ten thousand dead Marines, we oughta kill about a million gooks. But that's a hell of a lot of Marines."

"This reminds me," said Fatso, "of the one Will Rogers used to tell about when the Japs first invaded China. He was on a ship going to Honolulu and had a Chinese waiter at his table who brought him the radio newssheet each morning. The first day, it said ten Japs and two hundred Chinese killed. The next day it was fifty Japs and one thousand Chinese. The third day, one hundred Japs and ten thousand Chinese. Each day the Chinaman had a bigger grin, and Will finally asked him how come? He said, 'Plitty soon no more Japanese.' We got about the same deal now."

While the boys were mulling over that story, Satchmo, who had remained thoughtfully aloof during the news, piped up and said, "Cap'n, there's one thing about that big turtle at Pango Pango that I can't quite figure out."

"What's that, Satch?" asked Fatso.

"How come that turtle knew that Mr. Biggs had been promoted from seaman second to chief bosun?"

"Well, you see," said Fatso, but before he could ex-

106

plain this point the radio loudspeaker came in with more important news.

"Washington: The Egyptian government today sent the United States a formal protest of an alleged attack on an Egyptian naval vessel by the USS *Turtle*, southeast of Crete. The Egyptians say the *Turtle* is a spy ship and made an unprovoked attack on their ship with six-inch guns. The Pentagon states that there is no such ship as the USS *Turtle*, and that no U.S. ships were within two hundred miles of the scene of the alleged attack. The State Department is replying to the note saying this was not an American ship."

For several moments a flake of dandruff falling in the messroom would have made an audible thud. Then all hands said, nearly in one voice, "Holy cow!" and focused their gaze on Fatso.

"Well, now, whaddya know?" observed Fatso, and for some time, nobody claimed to know anything.

Finally the Professor said, "Looks like maybe we better scuttle this bucket tomorrow and enlist in the Foreign Legion."

"Let's not be too hasty about this scuttling business," said Fatso. "But we gotta decommission the *Turtle*—that's for sure. First thing tomorrow morning, we'll dismantle that radar dish and drop it overboard. I want to cut off those pig stickers we got on our bows and paint our right numbers back on."

"How about that tank?" asked Scuttlebutt. "Hadn't we better drop that overboard, too, and get rid of that six-inch gun?"

"Drop a perfectly good tank overboard?" said Fatso, indignantly. "You must be nuts. Them things cost about a hunnert thousand dollars."

"Yeah. But as soon as they're issued to the fleet, the Supply Department scratches them off the books. This one is bought, paid for, and expended now. I think we ought to get rid of it as part of decommissioning the *Turtle*."

"No-o-o!" said Fatso. "We'll hide it under a tarpoleum. It came in damn handy the other day, and the way

107

things are going out here, we may need it again some-time."

"Of course, they're bound to find out sooner or later that we're the *Turtle*—aren't they?" asked the Judge.

"That depends," said Fatso. "Once the U.S. Government sends an official note to another country and says there's no such ship as the USS *Turtle*, there just ain't no such ship, and that's all there is to it. They *would* make us scuttle before they would admit they was wrong about it."

"I dunno," said the Professor. "Remember the U-2? At first, Ike denied that we had any planes flying over Russia. But we had to take it back."

"Well, hell. They shot down our plane and captured the pilot. We had to admit it. But nobody's going to capture us. That's one reason I ain't throwing that gun overboard."

"I'll betcha if we showed up in Washington now," observed the Judge, "and claimed we was the crew of the *Turtle,* they'd burn our records and claim they never heard of any of us."

"I think you're right," said the Professor. "But don't forget those Russians have got pictures of us."

"If they try to use those pictures with Charley Noble at the yardarm," replied Fatso, "everybody will figure the whole business is a phony."

"What could they do to us, even if they did find out that we're the *Turtle?*" demanded Webfoot. "We never done nothing wrong . . . except maybe I put a couple of pounds too much TNT in that booby trap that blew up them three Russians."

"You don't have to do nothing wrong to get hung when you get mixed up in high-level diplomatic stuff," said the Judge. "They can run you up to the yardarm just as easy as we did Charley—and for the same reason, too—to improve our image."

"So—what's our program now, Cap'n?" asked Scuttle-butt.

"We gotta play it by ear as we go along," declared Fatso. "I think we oughta just lay low for a while and give them a chance to forget about this . . . are you still checking with the *Pillsbury* every day?" he asked the Professor.

"Yessir, Cap'n," said the Professor. "Not a word about us on the FOX schedule yet."

"Cap'n," said Ginsberg; "Why not go into Tel Aviv for a week or so? We could all make a good liberty there while we're laying low."

"Hunh?" said Fatso. "We-e-ll now, I dunno. . . . You can't just barge into a foreign port and make yourself at home. You gotta make a lot of diplomatic arrangements ahead of time."

"We didn't make any in Athens," said Ginsberg.

"That's different. Athens is in NATO, and our ships are in and out of there all the time. If the Israelis started asking Washington questions about us, we'd be in trouble."

"Don't worry about the Israelis making any trouble, Cap'n," said Ginsberg eagerly. "After the goof they made on the *Liberty* they'll just fall all over themselves to be nice to us. This would be a sort of good-will visit to improve international relations."

Scuttlebutt was feeling the urge to get ashore again, too. "Cap'n," he said, "We're getting a little low on oil. If we keep cruising around out here, we'll be in trouble pretty soon. We could lay up in Tel Aviv for a week and save a lot of oil."

"And we're going to be short of rations pretty soon, Cap'n," said Satchmo. "If we go into Telly Veeve Ah can replenish our supplies."

"How the hell could we pay for 'em?" demanded Fatso. "I sure as hell ain't going to pay for it out of our own private personal funds."

"We could sell that tank to them," said Ginsberg. "Well—I don't mean really *sell* it," he added, as he saw a look of scorn come across Fatso's face. "But we could swap it to them for food. Our contract with the government calls for three square meals a day. This tank is written off the books as soon as they issue it to us. So far as the U.S. Treasury is concerned, its value is zero. So if we use it to get the grub the government is supposed to furnish us, we would really be saving the government money."

"Abie," said Fatso, "If you ever get out of the Navy and go to work, I predict you'll wind up either as Secretary of the Treasury or doing time in Alcatraz—maybe even both!"

Meanwhile, Washington hadn't heard the last of the *Turtle*, by any means. The day after the Egyptian note had been answered, the Soviet Ambassador had a frosty interview with the Secretary of State and handed him another hot potato. This one protested the way that our Polaris submarines were harassing peaceful Soviet naval vessels in the Med. It said one of these subs had intruded on the Russian naval anchorage in the Gulf of Laconia and had laid mines there, one of which blew the bow off a Russian destroyer. It said the submarine was assisted by the spy ship USS *Turtle*, which had been making a nuisance of itself snooping around the anchorage.

This note was soon being studied incredulously by a group of Admirals in CNO's office.

"It just doesn't make sense, Admiral," said the Deputy for Operations. "We have no mine-laying subs in the Med. We've got two Polaris boats out there, but we keep a rigid check on them all the time, and neither one has been anywhere near the Gulf of Laconia. This job was done by somebody else—not us."

"Well, who else has got subs in the Med?" asked CNO.

"As of this morning, the Russians have got ten. Tito has a couple, and the Egyptians are trying to learn how to run three old ones the Russians gave them. The French and Italians have thirty-two between them. The Turks have got two, and the Israelis three."

"Okay," said CNO. "So it could belong to half a dozen other countries. All we gotta tell the Russians is that it wasn't one of ours. Let them try to sort out which one of the others it was. Now how about this goddam USS *Turtle?*"

"We don't know any more about it now than we did before, Admiral," said the Deputy. "Sixth Fleet claims they have nothing that could possibly be involved. The *Pillsbury* is the only ship they have in that area, and she's been anchored in Athens for a week."

"Well, something damned funny is going on out there," said CNO, "and it's up to Sixth Fleet to find out what it is."

That afternoon the State Department sent the Russians a pleasant little note simply saying that no U.S. submarines had been anywhere near the Gulf of Laconia, there was no such ship as the USS *Turtle,* and United States ships never laid mines in crowded anchorages.

At the same time, CNO sent ComSixthFleet's Admiral Hughes, a "personal top secret, eyes only" message saying, in effect, "What's coming off here? Maybe none of your ships are involved in this but these things are happening in your area. It's up to you to know what the hell goes on in your bailiwick and tell us about it before the Russians and Egyptians do."

This still wasn't the end of the *Turtle*'s saga. That morning, *Pravda* came out with a story about life in the U.S. Navy and the stern measures necessary to maintain discipline among mutinous crews. Alongside the story was a picture of the USS *Turtle* with Charley Noble suspended at the yardarm. The story said that this was the same spy ship that had made a treacherous attack on a peaceful Egyptian ship and which the United States claimed did not exist.

One of CIA's men in Moscow immediately put the story on the facsimile circuit to CIA HQ in Washington. Next morning, the head of CIA gleefully sent the story and picture to CNO by special messenger with a note saying, "recent Supreme Court decisions raise doubt about the constitutionality of such disciplinary measures."

CNO didn't think this was very funny but called in all his experts to examine the picture. They gathered around it with magnifying glasses, inspecting it distastefully, like doctors holding a post-mortem on a mule that has been dead in the hot sun for a week.

"What do you make of it?" asked the CNO.

"Damned if I know," said the Chief of Naval Intelligence. "It sure looks like a man at the yardarm there."

"What the hell," said CNO. "Nobody hangs people at the yardarm today—not even the Russians. It must be a dummy and some sort of a gag. Just the sort of gag that only American sailors would think of, I might add. Now, how about the ship?"

"It's hard to tell from a fuzzy picture like this one," said the head of ONI. "It looks a little bit like one of our LCUs, except it's ass backwards. The pilot house is forward instead of aft."

"Why do you say that?"

111

"Look at this thing sticking out from the side," said the Navy's head gumshoe, pointing to Fatso's can opener. "It's obviously a propeller guard. So this is the stern. The pilothouse is at the other end in the bow. So this can't be an LCU."

"Yeah. You're right about that," said CNO.

"And that great big radar dish means it's a spy ship of some kind. But it sure as hell isn't anything of ours."

"Then who the hell does it belong to?"

"I must admit we're stumped, Admiral," said CNI. "We can't find anything in our files of foreign ships that looks like it. But of course, it's a small craft that wouldn't take too long to build. It could be a new ship that we haven't photographed yet. Maybe this is part of General DeGaulle's *force de frappe.'* "

"Hmmmm," observed CNO. "Okay. Get off a despatch to Sixth Fleet. Tell them I want them to scour the eastern Med till they find that craft and get some good clear pictures of it."

"Aye aye, sir," said the Deputy for Operations.

Next day, Sixth Fleet photo planes combed the eastern Med, searching for the mysterious spy ship. They brought back quite an album of pictures: a dozen Russian destroyers, one limping along down by the head with a piece of its bow missing; a Russian sub which they caught on the surface and photographed from a dozen angles before she crash dived; an Italian tanker pumping bilges and polluting the Med with a huge spreading oil slick astern; a lateen-rigged Turkish craft with a suspicious-looking, odd-shaped sail; and a Dutch tug towing a barge with a twenty-foot spherical oil tank on it. But no *Turtle*. One photo plane flew right over Fatso and his merry men, but by this time they had disposed of their radar dish and the pilot decided it wasn't worthwhile wasting any film on them.

All these photos went to Washington by facsimile as soon as they were developed aboard ship.

"So . . . that's that," said CNO next day, after he and his experts examined those pictures. "Looks like the *Turtle* is a modern version of the Flying Dutchman."

"Well," said CNI, "There's lots of strange things going on in this world today that nobody can explain . . . UFO's, for instance. The Air Force had to set up a special task group to study all the sighting reports they're getting. They've got a file of about a thousand photographs that screwballs all over the country claim are flying saucers."

"Maybe we better set up a file of USO's," observed CNO. "Unidentified Seagoing Objects."

Chapter Thirteen

Computerized Groceries

MEANTIME, the USS *Turtle* had been relieved on station so to speak by LCU 1124, BM/1c Gioninni commanding. The *Turtle* had disappeared like the Flying Dutchman, and LCU 1124 was now operating on detached duty—in the Eastern Med. A council of war was in progress in the messroom to discuss future plans.

"This thing can't go on much longer boys," said Fatso. "They're bound to catch up with us pretty soon."

"Well, I dunno," said the Judge. "It seems to me like they've lost track of us, just like the Army did with that guy we read about in the *Navy Times*. We might go on like this for months."

"Except we gotta eat—and we're running out of grub, and oil, too," observed Fatso.

"Yeah," conceded the Judge. "But I'll betcha we could go back into Malta just like we did last time, draw out everything we need, and there wouldn't be no questions asked. Unless Sixth Fleet has put out some word about us —they'd never think there was anything funny about it. And if any word was out about us, old Sparky Wright on the *Pillsbury* would have let us know. We check with him every day, and he's heard nothing. They just lost track of us—that's all."

"Yeah. It looks that way," conceded Fatso. "But by this time, even the Supply Department in Malta must know the *Alamo* is in Vietnam."

"Okay—they prob'ly do," said the Judge. "But the USS *Turtle* has nothing to do with them, and there's no reason why they should connect us with it. If they get nosy about the *Alamo* we can tell them we're operating under Com-SixthFleet—even though he may not know it!"

"I don't think we got a thing to worry about on this *Turtle* business, Cap'n," said the Professor. "The government has gone plumb overboard saying that there just ain't no such craft. So there ain't—and there never will be. Too many big shots would look stupid now if they had to take back what they said about the *Turtle*. This ain't like the U-2 business. The Russians had us over a barrel there, because they had our plane and pilot. When a blooper is made on a high enough level it becomes a fact of life instead of a mistake, unless you get caught cold at it. With all the talk there's been lately about the credibility gap in Washington, they'd never admit they were wrong on the *Turtle* now. Hell, even if we came into Naples and tried to admit it was us, they'd prob'ly take us out and scuttle us with all hands on board."

"You know, Professor—I think you're right," said Fatso. "I'm going to head for Malta, and if they get curious there, I'll just tell 'em we're operating on secret orders —you can bet your starboard anchor the *Alamo* would back us up on that if anybody ever asked them."

"There's one other angle you'd better think about before we go into Malta," observed Scuttlebutt.

"What's that?"

"The official car and Commodore's gig," said Scuttlebutt. "The minute we show up in Malta, one of those supply types is going to run up and tell his boss how he can fix himself up real good. Here's an official car and a real nice little boat charged up to the *Alamo* out in Vietnam and expended from the books. The Supply Officer Malta will get himself a private car and yacht before we get through tying up to the dock."

"By gawd you're right on that," said Fatso.

"Couldn't we put 'em ashore in a cove somewheres and pick 'em up later?" suggested Ginsberg.

"It wouldn't work," said Fatso sadly. "That chief in the supply office knows all about them. He gave me a spiel about all the fuss the Commodore had made about them last time we were in. So he'll remember. And if we haven't got them on board, the evil-minded old bastard would prob'ly claim we sold them to the Greeks in Athens. But we gotta get fuel and oil, so we'll just have to take our chances on losing the car and gig."

Next morning as LCU 1124 cruised northwest toward Malta, a large ship began poking its upper works over the horizon on the port bow. During an uneventful watch at sea, the appearance of a stranger always brings the boys on deck with glasses to look her over and identify her. The colors of this one and her commission pennant showed she was USN. Soon an array of king posts and booms coming up over the horizon marked her as a supply ship —but not a familiar one.

Fatso lowered his glasses and remarked to Scuttlebutt alongside him, "She's sure a big son of a bitch—and I've never seen such cargo handling gear before."

He called over to Webfoot who was nearest the searchlight, "As soon as her bridge comes in sight exchange calls and find out who she is."

The upper works of a big ship are, of course, visible to a small one long before her bridge comes over the horizon. And by the same token, the signal force on a big ship doesn't see the smaller one at first. Webfoot had been blinking his light for some minutes before anyone on the big ship saw it.

On the big ship the skipper was seated in his leather swivel chair on the starboard wing of the bridge on the level above the signal bridge with nothing to do at that particular time but rubber around the horizon with his eight by thirty Zeiss glasses trying to spot things that others should have seen first. He was the first one to note Webfoot's blinking light, just coming over the horizon, which of course was embarrassing to the OOD, lookouts, and signal force.

He stuck his head over the rail and yelled down at the signal bridge, "Wake up down there! Answer that ship that's calling you."

Signal floozies scrambled all over each other to get to the light and answer while the OOD put the blast on the lookouts, and the skipper smugly told himself he had the sharpest eyes on the ship. (Of course, his added height put his horizon about a mile beyond that of the signal floozies. But they were a dopey lot anyway.)

Soon the signal bridge reported, "She's just exchanging calls, sir."

"What ship is she?" demanded the skipper, who prided himself on his ability to read blinker—sometimes better than the signalmen.

"LCU 1124," came the answer from the signal floozie, who was well aware of the skipper's unfortunate ability to check up.

116

"Humph," grunted the skipper, a little let down that he couldn't air his skill in reading blinker this time.

Over on LCU 1124, Webfoot reported "USS *SANTEE*, Cap'n."

"Hunh," said Fatso. "She's a new one on me. Never heard of her before."

When navy ships talk to each other officially at sea, the messages go, of course, from captain to captain. But on casual passings the signal floozies often exchange unofficial chit chat by blinker. Webfoot blinked back at his pals on the *Santee*, "Never heard of U, when did U guys join Navy?"

The skipper of the *Santee* took in this message. He was in an expansive mood this morning, and this was his first contact with the Sixth Fleet. So he figured that although this was only a little spit kit on the horizon, he would start right here spreading the word that a new era in fleet logistics was about to dawn in the Med. He leaned over the rail and yelled to the signal bridge, "Answer that, official MSG for CO. '*Santee* is Navy's newest logistic ship. Whatever the fleet wants we've got. Our motto is CAN DO. Do you need anything?' "

"Well now," said Fatso, a bit flabbergasted when he got this official message from the *Santee*, "Ain't that somethin'? Maybe we don't hafta go to Malta after all. Answer this, 'We need food and oil.' "

This was a bit more than the skipper of the *Santee* had bargained for. But he wasn't going to let this little spit kit make him eat his CAN DO motto. He yelled down to the signal bridge, "Tell them, 'Come alongside, starboard side at forward king post. How much of what do you need?' "

"Well, now, I'll be dipped in lukewarm gook," observed Fatso, when this reply came back. "I never heard of such service before!"

"They're giving us a blank check, Cap'n," said the Professor. "We oughta ask 'em for frog legs and Alaska King crabs."

"If we was a big carrier, I'd sure do it and call their bluff," observed Fatso. "But little guys like us don't try to get funny with four-stripe skippers like that bucket has. ... Answer him—'Request a month's rations for eight

117

men and two thousand gallons of diesel oil,'" he yelled over at Webfoot.

Over on the *Santee* the skipper had the Supply Officer up on the bridge. "Here comes our first customer," he said, pointing to the LCU maneuvering into a position a mile or so off the starboard bow. "Let's see what kind of service you can give our little friend."

"Yessir," said the S.O. "I doubt if she'll strip us bare. Just what does she want?"

When Fatso's answer came up from the signal bridge he said, "Hunh. That's a kind of irregular sort of a requisition, . . . but we can handle it all right."

He picked up the phone, dialed the supply office, and said, "We got a small craft coming alongside. They want thirty days food for eight men. Give 'em whatever it takes for the same menu we're serving our own people. Make up proper requisitions and invoices and have the whole works in a cargo net at king post number 1 in five minutes."

"I'll bet you can't do it," observed the skipper.

"We'll soon see," said the S.O. "With all the preprogrammed bookkeeping, mechanical brains, and automatic equipment we got, I think we *can*. But I don't carry any oil in stock."

"Yeah—I stand corrected on that," said the skipper. "But hell, the chief engineer can spare two thousand gallons of diesel. We'll give it to them out of our own ship's tanks."

Ten minutes later, when LCU 1124 eased in alongside the *Santee*, a six inch fuel hose was dangling from one boom on king post number one and a large cargo net full of stores from another. Scuttlebutt and Jughaid grappled with the hose and screwed it into the fueling connection while the rest of the boys eased the cargo net down on the well deck.

The contents of the net would have been a John Bunyan sized cartful at even the most super supermarket. It was everything it takes to feed eight hungry sailors the standard Navy balanced menu for thirty days. And despite the traditional gripes that you hear from old soldiers about the grub, the U.S. Navy eats high on the hog. There were meats of all kinds, fowl, eggs, vegetables, fruits, bread, crackers, cookies, condiments, butter, sugar, vinegar, coffee, and canned milk—the quantities all figured out by mechanical brains. On top of the neatly packaged and tagged food was a big manila envelope with a couple of dozen invoices and requisitions all duly filled in by automatic machines with proper Navy stock numbers, quantities, and prices. The only blank places were for the name of the mother ship that would pay the bill and the signature of the recipient skipper.

By the time Fatso got through filling in the *Alamo*'s name and signing the invoices, the net was empty and the oil tanks were full. Not more than five minutes after they came alongside, the oil hose was hauled back aboard the *Santee*, Fatso stuffed the manila envelope into a bag attached to the cargo net, and LCU 1124 hauled clear, full of everything she needed for the next thirty days.

"Boy oh boy!" said Fatso, as they got away. "That was fast service. . . . How the hell does a boatswain's mate send a four-stripe skipper a 'well done'?" he demanded of the Professor.

"Just tell him it's the best goddam replenishment we ever had," suggested the Professor.

"Okay," said Fatso to Webfoot. "Send it out on your light—except leave the goddam out."

The *Santee* disappeared over the horizon with signal flags flying that said, "Good luck," and broad grins on the faces of her skipper, supply officer, and chief engineer.

Chapter Fourteen

On to Israel

As THE *Santee* went on her way, Fatso and his boys gathered in the messroom to discuss future operations.

"So. Where do we go from here, Cap'n?" asked Scuttlebutt.

"That's what I'm trying to figure out," said Fatso. "And there's a lot of angles we got to think about. All the good liberty ports have got an American consul, who might get nosy about why he wasn't notified that we were coming. Most of the places that don't have a consul are too small to be worth going to."

"Of course, we don't have to go right into the harbor," suggested Webfoot. "We could beach ourselves on the coast nearby somewheres. We got our own transportation."

"Yeah," said Fatso. "But that could get us in a hell of a jam. They might say we was smuggling dope or something. That would really make a federal case out of it. Trying to sneak in is no good. Wherever we go we gotta just barge right in as if we had a perfect right to and try to bluff it through."

"Athens is a good liberty port. We could go back there," suggested Jughaid.

"No-o-o-o," said Fatso, judicially. "Our credit rating may not be very good in Athens. The guy from that night club might come aboard with a big fat bill for that dinner we didn't . . . er . . . quite finish there."

"How about Istanbul?" asked the Judge.

"It's a hell of a good liberty port—and I'd like to go there," said Fatso. "But there's lots of Russian navy ships go through there now on their way in and out of the Black Sea. I think we better keep away from the Roosians for a while."

"Cap'n," said Ginsberg, "I think Tel Aviv is the place to go. There's so much big stuff going on there now they won't have time to get nosy about us. And after the

Liberty goof, they won't want to make trouble for us anyways."

"I think you got something there, Abie," said Fatso. "That's where the action is, right now—and I never been there."

"Cap'n," said Ginsberg eagerly, "You just take it from me. They'll fall all over themselves to be nice to us."

"You're prob'ly right," said Fatso. "The game would depend on the first bounce the ball takes when we come in. Two weeks ago we wouldn't of had a chance of getting away with it. But now, catching them unawares while everybody is sobering up from a big binge and their navy is out in left field on account of the *Liberty*, I think we can."

"Cap'n," said the Professor. "On a thing like this, you might as well go for broke. We want our arrival to look real official. Why not come barging up to the entrance and fire a national salute? You can't make your arrival any more official than that. And it will put them on the spot. They won't be expecting anything like that from a little bucket like this, and failure to answer a national salute could stir up an international incident. They'll have to make up their minds fast what to do. Their navy is in the crap house right now, and it's one hundred to one they'll answer the salute. When they do, they'll be committed on a high level right from the start."

Fatso's eyes lighted up and a broad grin spread across his face. This sort of broad strategic thinking and high-level hanky-panky was right up his alley. His long years of naval experience had taught him that the best way to get away with murder was to do it right out in the open, as if the Admiral himself had ordered you to hit the old lady with the ax. The usual reaction was—"he wouldn't dare do a thing like *that* unless he had a right too."

"Hmmmm," observed Fatso. "I'll go for that. . . . Now, how are we gonna fire that salute?"

"No strain," said Webfoot. "Our two 20 mm guns make a perfect saluting battery—all we gotta do is take the bullets out of our ammo."

"Okay," said Fatso. "We gotta fly the Israeli colors at the mast head while we're saluting. How about that?"

"That's easy," said Ginsberg. "I'll draw a sketch of their flag and Webfoot can sew it up for us."

"The only other thing is sounding off with their national anthem," observed the Professor. "And we got a platter that has it. We put that on our loudspeaker, run up their colors, and we can fire just as good a national salute as a battleship."

"Okay," said Fatso, "Let's get the chart and lay out a course for Tel Aviv. . . . Boy oh boy! I'd sure like to see the face of the Captain of the Port while we're blasting away, and he's got half a minute to figure out what he's going to do!"

Since the Professor was practically an MIT graduate, Fatso had appointed him navigator of the LCU 1124. The Professor soon had the chart of the eastern Med laid out on the table and was bent over it with his parallel rulers and dividers. While all hands watched with interest, he laid out various zig zags on the chart from his previous noon position to where they ought to be now.

"You know," he observed, "Our Polaris subs have got mechanized brains to do this for them. All the navigator has gotta do to find out where he is, is to read the latitude and longitude dials."

"They've got the same thing on the big surface ships," said Jughaid. "The Dead Reckoning Tracer. It's connected to the compass and the propeller shafts, and it moves a little bug around on the chart. The navigator don't have to do no figuring at all."

"The hell he don't," said the Professor. "That DRT only tells him where he *oughta* be, if everything is just the way he thinks it is. But usually it ain't. The helmsman always weaves back and forth a few degrees each side of the right course—all you guys know that. Barnacles on the bottom slow you down so the speed ain't what the engineer claims it is. And the wind and currents throw you off course. So the navigator has gotta keep checking his DRT against the stars, by loran, or by satellites. But the Polaris subs have got inertial navigators that can tell whenever you change course or speed the least little bit, no matter whether it's from bum steering, currents, or what have you. Even if you stop your engines and drift, it knows which way you're drifting and how fast."

122

"How about explaining to us poor ignorant sailors how it does that, Professor," asked the Judge.

"It's got things that they call inertial accelerometers that can feel and measure every change of direction or speed. When you're in an elevator, you can't *see* it move, but you can feel it whenever it starts up or down. Or when you're riding in a car, you can feel it when it turns. This is on account of inertia. If you want to know what that is, read Sir Isaac Newton's *Principia*. He got hit on the head by an apple one day and sat down and wrote this book that explains all about inertia. Anyway, Polaris subs have got inertial accelerometers that keep track of exactly where they are all the time. They've gotta know, or else their Polaris missiles wouldn't be any good. There's no use in having a missile that can hit a gnat's ass one thousand miles away unless you know exactly where you're shooting it *from*. A Polaris sub can zigzag around submerged for a week and know where it is to within about a city block."

"I'll be gahdam," observed most of his listeners.

"How about this satellite navigation?" asked the Judge.

"Yeah—that's very accurate, too," said the Professor. "We've got these satellites flying around the world now, like the ones that send TV programs all over the world. We've got others that fly around going *beep-beep-beep*. They go round the world in about an hour and a half, following the same track in space, and the world rotates under them, so there's one or two of them overhead a couple of times a day, no matter where you are. The satellites are pretty near as regular in their orbits as the sun and the moon, so we always know exactly where they are. You tune their beeps into a black box, it measures what they call the Doppler effect, feeds that into a computer, and the computer tells you where you are."

"Uh huh," commented the listeners with grave nods.

"Every now and then a Polaris boat will come up and get a satellite fix to check their inertial navigators. They usually come out only a few hundred yards apart, so then the skipper flips a nickel to see which one he believes."

By this time the Professor had finished working out his dead reckoning for the past day. He took his dividers, made a pinprick in the chart and drew a very small ring around it. Then he took his parallel rulers, drew a line from the pinprick to Tel Aviv, slid the ruler over to the compass, rose, and announced "Course to Tel Aviv 089, Cap'n."

"Okay, Professor," said Fatso. Then turning to the voice tube on the bulkhead, he yelled up to the chart-house, "Steer zero seven nine."

An injured look came across the Professor's face. "What's the matter, Cap'n?" he asked. "Don't you trust my navigation?"

"Don't get your tits in a flutter, pilot," said Fatso. "Didn't you tell me one time that the first thing they teach you about computers at MIT is that the answers you get out are no better than the dope you put in?"

"Yeah. That's what they call the GIGO factor."

"GIGO? What's that?" asked Webfoot.

"Garbage in—garbage out," said the Professor.

"Okay," said Fatso. "That's what I'm allowing for. Zero eight nine is the exact course from that pinhole you got in the chart to the lighthouse at Tel Aviv. But we been zigzagging around out here out of sight of land for over a week. We could be twenty to thirty miles away from your pinhole."

"Sure. But it's the best guess we can make," said the Professor.

"I know. But suppose we steer 089 for a couple of days and when we make our landfall, we find we didn't hit it right on the nose. Which way do we turn—north or south?"

"Yeah. I see what you mean," agreed the Professor.

"This way, I'm heading for a spot that we feel for *sure* is north of Tel Aviv. So when we pick up the coast we just run south along it until we get to Tel Aviv."

"You're exactly right, Cap'n," said the Professor. "And come to think of it, that's how they used to navigate in Columbus's time. Even with all the fancy black boxes we've got today, it's still a pretty good one."

That evening in the messroom the Professor was removing the projectiles from the "saluting ammunition." They were solid slugs with tracers, so this wasn't a danger-ous job. As he removed each slug from the brass shell, he stuffed a little wad of cotton in the open end of the cartridge case. "We'll hafta try a couple of these out tomorrow," he observed, "and see how they sound. We may have to fiddle around with the amount of wadding we put in before they'll make the right kind of a boom."

"You know," observed the Judge, "When I was a kid, I used to think a twenty-one-gun salute meant twenty-one guns fired all at once in a volley."

"Some books say it used to be that way in the early days," said the Professor. "News didn't travel as fast then as it does now. So when a strange sail showed up off the entrance forts, they never knew at first whether it was friendly or hostile. So just as the ship came within range of the fort she was supposed to fire her whole broadside battery—with no shots in it—to prove she was coming in with her guns unloaded and couldn't do any harm."

"Yeah," said the Judge. "And I read somewheres that every now and then a dopey gunner's mate would forget to unload all the guns, and they'd send a few cannon balls bouncing down the main street of the town. The next thing you'd know, a gunner's mate would be swinging from the yardarm just like we had Charley Noble the other day."

"Could be," said the Professor. "Gunner's mate was prob'ly just as dumb in the old days as they are now. Anyway, that's how this national salute business got started—to prove your guns weren't loaded. Reloading them old muzzle loaders was a big job. You had to drag the gun back in on deck, out of the port, and it took quite a while. So when you left your guns out after the salute, they knew you were friendly, or at least, harmless. Later on, they changed it into a sort of a formal ceremony of firing twenty-one guns, one after the other like we do now, . . . and speaking of formal ceremonies, we better be ready to receive official callers."

"On a little spit kit like this?" asked Fatso. "I don't think we'd have any official callers."

"When even a little spit kit comes sailing in firing a national salute, the Captain of the Port will have to put on his frock coat, swabs, fore-and-aft hat, and sword and come out here and pay you an official call. The Israelis won't want to take no chances on creating another international incident."

"Yeah, I guess you're right," conceded Fatso. "And we gotta be sure we receive him the way the Book says to. . . ." Turning to Satchmo, he said, "Get me the Regulation Book out of the bottom drawer of my desk."

As Satch went off to get the book, Fatso remarked, "I've had to look in that book more this past week than I did in the last ten years."

"You're representing the United States, now . . . that's one of the penalties you pay for reaching high command," said the Professor, philosophically.

The book is a volume of a little less than a thousand pages, which tells you as briefly as possible how to run a navy. Almost anything that can happen on a ship has already happened, and it's covered somewhere in the book. Its commandments are based on the experience of our own Navy going back to the time of John Paul Jones, and of the British Navy before that. It contains the distilled wisdom of many years battling with wind, wave, and foreign enemies, corrected up to date as steam replaced sail, flattops took over from battleships, and Polaris missiles took the place of smooth-bore muzzle-loading guns. Some old salts will tell you tolerantly that the book is useful only to feeble-minded sailors who wouldn't know what to do if it wasn't all written down in a book for them. But nine times out of ten, when these old-timers have to look up something in the book, they find it prescribes the most sensible way of doing it—or at least, a way that will work even for old-timers who aren't always as smart as they think they are. It covers just about everything a ship may ever have to do—except how to surrender.

Soon Satchmo was back with the Book and Fatso thumbed through it till he came to the Table of Side Honors. This table lists all the VIPs who are ever apt to come aboard ship, from a reigning monarch down to an ensign. The monarch, of course, gets the works: All hands man the rail, full-dress uniform; eight side boys; full guard and band; twenty-one-gun salute; and the national anthem, followed by martial music while he inspects the honor guard. If by some strange happenstance an ensign ever calls officially, he is entitled to two side boys.

"Captain of the Port isn't listed in the table," said the Professor, as they ran down the list.

"His honors depend on his naval rank," said Fatso. "He'll be either a commander or captain."

"Okay—all he gets, then, is four side boys."

"What are side boys?" asked Jughaid.

The others all looked at him scornfully, and the Professor said, "It's easy to see you've never been in anything but the hooligan navy. Side boys are sailors that stand at the head of the gangway and salute while the boatswain's mate is piping some big shot aboard. It's a custom that goes back to the days of sail. They didn't have gangways then—just rope ladders over the side. When a big shot came alongside in a boat, they'd lower a bosun's chair and hoist him aboard. The side boys used to man the falls and hoist away. According to the old stories, the big shots used to eat pretty well, and the higher their rank, the bigger and fatter they were, so it took more boys to hoist an admiral than it did a lieutenant. They used to teach all about that in boot camp."

"They still do," observed the Professor. "And there's another version of it in some of the old books that they don't tell the boys in boot camp. That is that the side boys were to help the VIP in and out of the bosun's chair. The VIPs were always half full of rum in the old days. The higher their rank, the drunker they were apt to be. So the number of boys it took to help them increased with their rank."

"Now there's one other item we gotta think about on this official call business," said the Professor. "This guy will come aboard in a frock coat, fore-and-aft hat, swabs, and a sword. You oughta be in dress uniform, too."

"All I can do is put on my best suit of tailor-made blues," said Fatso.

"You got about six rows of ribbon you can put on. Have you got the medals that go with them?"

"Yeah—I guess I've still got 'em in my ditty box somewheres."

"Okay. Break 'em out and pin 'em on. That oughta to make an impression on him. We gotta get you a sword, too."

"I can make up a real good sword," said Scuttlebutt. "It prob'ly wouldn't be much good in a fight. But it will *look* real official."

"Okay," said the Professor. "We can receive the Captain of the Port with all due ceremony, just the way the book says."

"You know," said Fatso, "all this stuff about the Captain of the Port reminds me of the time we went into Marseilles on the *Memphis* back in '48."

"Marseilles?" said Scuttlebutt. "That's one of the worst stink holes in the Med. Nothing there but pickpockets, pimps, and whores. Everybody in that town is one or the other."

"Yeah. That's right," agreed Fatso. "So when we anchored there, the skipper was in a hurry to get everything squared away so he could beat it up to Paris. There was some things to be arranged with the Captain of the Port, so the skipper told the young officer of the deck to keep an eye open for him and as soon as he showed up to send him right down to the cabin.

"Well, soon after that a swanky looking launch comes alongside with a Frenchman in the after cockpit, wearing one of those three-cornered hats like Napoleon did and a coat with a lot of gold braid, like a hotel doorman or an admiral. The OOD figured this must be the Captain of the Port, so he sent him down to the cabin. Actually, this guy was the head pimp from the leading whorehouse in town."

"Gawd almighty!" observed the rapt listeners.

"When he comes in the cabin, he hands the skipper a card engraved *Madame le Clair* and the address. The skipper gives him a big hello without looking at the card and sits him down at the table for a cup of coffee. The skipper says, 'I want to be sure everything is arranged so my sailors can go ashore.'

"'We take care of them,' says the Frenchman. 'All of them. We stay open all night.'

"The skipper didn't quite follow that, but he says, 'Okay—that's fine.'

"Then the Frog says, 'Capitaine. Perhaps you like to be with nice young French girl tonight?'

"The skipper still didn't click—so he just says, 'No, I'm going to Paris.'

"Then the Frenchman says, 'Maybe you prefer older lady. We have some very good ones.'

"Then the skipper looked at the card, and it dawned on him what this guy was. He buzzed for his orderly, got up, and said, 'No. Get the hell out of here. I'm not interested in any of your gals. I want the Captain of the Port.'

"The Frenchman looks kind of surprised, and then says, 'The Captain of the Port! ... Eet ees vary deefeecult—but perhaps I can arrange.' "

Chapter Fifteen

Official Visit

NEXT MORNING the boys gathered around the 20 mm. gun on the starboard wing of the bridge to try the saluting charges.

"Should we run up the powder rag at the yardarm, Cap'n?" asked Jughaid.

"Yeah," said Fatso; "I guess you can say we are conducting ordnance tests—run her up."

Jughaid broke out a square red flag and two-blocked it at the yardarm. This officially notified all ships within visual range that experiments with high explosives were in progress and prudent seamen should keep clear.

Webfoot broke out a box of the denatured shells, which now had wads of cotton where the bullets had been.

"Permission to commence scheduled exercise, Cap'n?" he said, loading a shell into the gun.

"Fire away," said Fatso.

Pouf went the gun, emitting a cloud of smoke but not much of a bang.

"Hah!" snorted Ginsberg. "Anybody who got saluted that way would feel insulted."

"Needs more wadding in it," said Webfoot.

They stuffed a little more wadding in the next one and got a little louder *pouf* but still not a very impressive bang.

"Put a big wad in the next one, and ram it down real tight," advised Scuttlebutt.

The third shot produced a sketchy sort of a bang and blew out chunks of burning cotton leaving streaks of smoke behind them.

"Well, there you are," said Webfoot. "It looks like that's about the best we can do, Cap'n."

"It still ain't good enough," said Fatso. "We gotta remember we're representing the United States, and we can't afford to fire no half-assed salutes. Maybe we better skip it."

One of the interested observers at this ordnance test was Satchmo. While everybody was sadly pondering Fatso's command decision, he said, "Cap'n, I think I know how to make that bang a lot louder."

"What the hell do you know about interior ballistics?" demanded Webfoot.

"I don't know nothin' about stuff like that there," admitted Satchmo. "But I do know something about music and how to build up sound."

"What are you gonna do? Try to play the Star Spangled Banner on that goddam gun?" demanded Webfoot.

"What's your idea, Satch?" asked Fatso, who knew from long experience that Satchmo's ideas were usually good.

"We got a small boom because we're shooting with a small barrel," said Satchmo. "We need a sort of an amplifier to magnify the boom. If I took the bell off the end of my horn, all I'd get out of it would be a small squawk, no matter how hard I blowed. But if you made the same kind of a boom we got now inside a big barrel, it would come out a much louder and deeper boom. It's like the pipes of an organ. The high-pitch notes come out of a small pipe. The deep low-pitch notes come out of great big pipes."

"We'll bear that in mind when we install a pipe organ on this bucket," said Webfoot scornfully.

"You're just like every other ordnance expert I've ever seen, Webfoot," said Fatso. "When somebody else comes up with a new idea, the first thing you do is hang out the NOT INVENTED HERE sign. . . . What's your idea, Satch?"

"We got a lot of steel pipe on board, that the marines use for laying pipe lines. The inside diameter is six inches. If you slide a piece of that pipe over the barrel of our little 20 mm. gun, it will act like the pipe of a big organ. It will make a big hollow boom, like a real six-inch gun."

"I think he's nuts," said Webfoot, using the standard Navy argument against any new idea. "You'd blow that pipe into a million pieces and kill everybody on the top side."

"Now wait a minute," said the Professor. "I think Satch has got something. Those blank charges we're using won't hurt the pipe a damn bit. It oughta make a real deep

131

boom, just like Satch says. . . . I think it's worth trying, Cap'n."

"Okay," said Fatso. "Let's try it."

Half an hour later, Scuttlebutt and the boys had completed the job of converting their standard 20 mm. gun into a sixth-inch smooth bore. An eight-foot length of steel pipe had been slid over the barrel of the popgun and jammed in place with wedges. A wooden sleeve around the muzzle of the small gun held the pipe with its center in line with that of the bore. Spot welds to the mount held the pipe in place.

I doubt if the Bureau of Ordnance would have approved this alteration to standard equipment if it had been submitted through official channels. And it would have taken at least two years, anyway, to get an answer out of the Bureau on a technical matter like this.

Fatso inspected the job carefully and said, "Looks okay to me. But I want all hands under cover the first time we shoot it."

A few minutes later, with all hands crouching behind the bulwarks on the port side, Fatso gave the signal to fire, and Webfoot yanked the long firing landyard.

The gun made a great hollow *BOOM*.

All hands let out a respectful "Ah-h-h . . . ," which was suddenly cut short. A swirling mass of smoke erupted from the pipe in the shape of a large doughnut and sailed out, expanding rapidly to the size of a giant tractor tire. It was the most perfect smoke ring that any of them had ever seen. As one man, they all said in awed voices, "Well, I'll be gahdamn!"

"Will it ever do that again?" demanded Fatso, when they recovered from their amazement.

"By gawd I think it will do it every time," said the Professor. "It *has* to."

"We'll soon find out," said Webfoot. He reloaded the gun, they took cover again, and the gun duplicated its spectacular performance.

"It can't help doing it," explained the Professor. "The gases start expanding at the muzzle of the small gun. The pipe holds them in; but the explosion blasts through the center and drags the gases along after it. They've got to come out in a perfect ring every time."

"This is the most important advance in naval ordnance

since the breach-loading gun," said the Judge. "Satchmo will go down in Naval history alongside of Professor Dahlgren."

"Hell, I'd make it stronger than that," said Fatso. "I'd say its the biggest thing since the Chinks invented gunpowder."

Next morning, LCU 1124 made her landfall as planned, twenty miles north of Tel Aviv, ran in to within a mile of the beach, and turned south. An hour later she sighted Yaffo light at Tel Aviv. A big set of U.S. colors fluttered proudly at the gaff, and all hands were in their dress-white uniforms, at their stations for the formal evolution of entering port. When a man o' war does this officially in a foreign port, it is like a duchess entering the throne room to be presented at court. High level protocol is involved, and things must be done exactly by the book. Fatso and his boys had studied the book carefully and were determined to uphold the prestige of the United States.

The Israeli colors were made up in a neat wad and two-blocked at the masthead, with the halyard rigged so that a good jerk from below would stream the colors in the breeze. Ginsberg was standing by to supply the jerk on the first boom of the salute. Webfoot stood by the starboard saluting gun and Jughaid by the port. Satchmo had the wheel, and the rest of the crew (all three of them) lined up in ranks (or rather, one rank) in the bows. Fatso had the conn, of course, and would double in brass as the gunner.

The LCU's approach to the harbor entrance drew only casual interest from the lookouts at the fort. There certainly were no Arab naval craft prowling around in these waters at this time. And from dead ahead, an LCU looks like many other nondescript small craft that inhabits the eastern Med.

When they were about a mile from the fort, Fatso throttled down to slow speed and said "Okay—commence firing."

"BLAM!" went the starboard gun, and a beautiful smoke ring rolled out of the pipe as the Israeli colors broke out at the masthead.

Fatso went into the time-honored gunner's ritual for spacing shots in a salute 5 seconds apart. "If I wasn't a

133

gunner—I wouldn't be here," he intoned. "Port—gun—FIRE!"

"BLAM!" went the port gun, and blew another perfect smoke ring.

"Far from home and my friends so dear . . . star—board—FIRE," continued Fatso.

"BLAM!" went the starboard gun—and so on for twenty-one good solid BLAMS and twenty-one perfect smoke rings.

Ginsberg had predicted that the salute would catch the Israelis with their obis down. It did—even more so than the Israelis had caught the Arabs.

All the high-ranking regular navy officials of Tel Aviv were up in Jerusalem, still trying to explain the *Liberty* fiasco. The only naval officers in Tel Aviv that morning were reservists, of low rank and little experience. The *Liberty* affair had put the Israeli Navy in bad odor at a time when the Army and Air Force were covering themselves with glory. So the senior reserve officer present at the fort this morning wasn't about to make things any worse by failing to answer a national salute perfectly. He didn't fiddle-faddle around with the diplomatic authorities checking on the authority for this visit. He hit the panic button. Bugles blew, drums beat, and boatswains mates bawled, "Man the saluting battery—ON THE DOUBLE!"

It takes only a minute and forty seconds to fire a twenty-one-gun national salute. But within a minute of the last gun, while you could still see some of the smoke rings, the U.S. colors went up on the signal station, and the first answering boom rang out over the harbor.

The crew of LCU 1124 stood at attention with Fatso saluting while the fort banged away twenty-one times. Everybody always counts the number of guns fired in a salute because after all, there isn't much else to do while you are standing there at attention. On the last gun, all hands announced, "Twenty-one!"

"Carry on," said Fatso. "You know," he remarked to Scuttlebutt, "If I had thought of it in time I would of fired twenty-two—like old Joe Fife did one time."

"I've heard a lot of stories about Joe Fife—but not that one," replied Scuttlebutt.

"Joe's ship came in to Plymouth, England, for Queen

Victoria's jubilee, and the dopey gunner lost count and fired twenty-two guns. When the Admiral asked him what the hell was the idea, old Joe said 'Twenty-one guns for Queen Victoria and one for Joe Fife.' . . . I doubt if I'll ever have another chance to fire one for Gioninni."

"Well, anyway.—This makes our arrival here pretty official," observed the Professor.

"Most official arrival I've ever made anywhere," agreed Fatso, "except for the day I was born."

Fatso then kicked her ahead slow, eased in to about one hundred yards from a nice sandy beach, and let go his starboard anchor. "As soon as we can get permission I want to put her in on that beach," he observed. "Keep an eye open for an official boat heading this way," he added, to Jughaid. "The Captain of the Port will send somebody out soon. I want to pipe him aboard as if we did it every day. We'll need two or four side boys depending on his rank, and Satchmo, you take my bosun's call and pipe him over the side. All you gotta do is start a long blast when he gets out of the boat and hold it till he passes through the side boys and salutes."

"Yessir, Cap'n," said Satchmo. "Ah knows how to do it."

Fatso got a reminiscent look in his eye and said, "The last time I piped a VIP aboard I got busted from first to second class."

"How come, Cap'n?" asked Satchmo.

"It was on the *Memphis,* and Bugler Bates was skipper," said Fatso. "The *Memphis* was the damndest spit-and-polish bucket I've ever been on. Old Bugler wasn't much of a seaman—damn near knocked the dock down every time he put us alongside. But he was a flat-bottomed son of a bitch on protocol. Whenever you set foot on the quarter deck you had to act like you was in church. And whenever a VIP came aboard it was like a formal White House reception.

"Well, one day in Hampton Roads I had the watch when a drunk VIP came aboard. He was some big shot Congressman, and he was drunker than a fiddler's bitch. It took him so long to stagger up the gangway I thought I'd blow a gasket keeping my whistle going. When he poured himself aboard and tried to shake hands with the side boys, I busted out laughing. And old Bugler busted *me* two minutes after the guy left!"

"Well, I promise you I won't laugh, no matter what happens, Cap'n," said Satchmo.

"Speaking of old Bugler Bates and side boys," said Scuttlebutt, "reminds me of the wooden side boys we had for a while on the *Missouri*."

"Wooden ones?" said Fatso. "I've seen lots of wooden *headed* side boys, if that's what you mean."

"No. These were all wood. Our skipper was 'Turn-To' Tucker, and he couldn't stand the idea of having eight sailors hanging around near the gangway doing nothing all day but just standing by in case some VIP might show up. So he had eight side boys made up out of plywood, like those traffic cops they set out in the street near a school."

"Not a bad idea, at that," observed Fatso.

"We painted dress blue uniforms on them, and they looked real good. The first few visitors who came aboard got a big kick out of them. We even had a couple of VIP's who never noticed the boys were phony. But then old Bugler Bates came aboard, right after he made Admiral. Boy oh boy!! He got six real live side boys when he left a few minutes later, and the wooden ones had already gone up the flue in the incinerator."

In about ten minutes Jughaid spotted a gig flying an official pennant heading that way. Embarked in the boat was an ensign in the Israeli Navy in full dress uniform, swab epaulettes, cocked hat, and sword, representing the Captain of the Port.

He was brought aboard in a manner that would have satisfied even Bugler Bates. He got two side boys; "attention on deck"; Satchmo did the honors with the bosun's pipe; and Fatso met him at the head of the ramp with a big salute.

"I have come to call on the Captain," said the ensign.

"Yes, SIR!" said Fatso. "That's me."

"Oh?" observed the ensign.

"Yessir," said Fatso. "Would you like to come up to the . . . er . . . wardroom and have a cup of coffee?"

In the "wardroom" the ensign, who was making his first official call on a foreign man o' war, removed his fore-and-aft hat and held it on his lap, but had trouble getting his sword out of the way so he could sit down. When he got himself squared away, he said, "The Captain of the Port is away today. I have been de-sig-nated to rep-re-sent him, to present his com-pli- ments and ask if there is anything we can do to fa-cili-tate your visit."

"Well—yessir," said Fatso. "I would like to run my ship up on the beach instead of anchoring out here."

"Certainly," said the ensign.

"And I have an automobile on board," said Fatso, "That I would like to put ashore while we are here."

"That's all right too," said the ensign. "But it is not necessary. The Israeli navy has assigned an official car and driver for you during your visit."

"Harrumph," said Fatso. "Well, now, that's goddam . . . I mean that's very nice indeed. Thank you."

"Can we do anything else for you," asked the ensign.

"No-o-o; I don't think so," said Fatso. "When should I call on the Captain of the Port and the senior naval officer?"

"It is not necessary," said the ensign. "You can consider this visit to take care of all of-ficial pro-to-col."

After the ensign had been piped ashore, with all due ceremony, Fatso remarked, "Well boys—it's just like we figured. They're going to fall all over themselves to be nice to us."

And—in general—that's exactly what they did.

There is no point in cluttering up this saga with an account of the shoreside activities of Fatso and his brave lads for the next few days. This is a sea story about the hard times, perils, and intrepid deeds of the sailors who defend this country battling wind, wave, and foreign enemies on the briny deep. It is concerned with their feats of derring-do on the seven seas rather than how they kill time ashore while resting up and preparing for their next venture out on the raging main.

On the high seas these men uphold the traditions of John Paul Jones, Farragut, Dewey, Halsey, Nimitz, and all the other great naval heroes. Their conduct in battle is a legitimate field of interest for naval historians. What they do when they go ashore is their own damn business— except when the MPs butt in. It would be a flagrant invasion of privacy to gumshoe around behind them and record in this family journal how they wile away the hours visiting museums, public libraries, and other points of interest in the various seaports of the world. It's really no different from what Eagle Scouts, college professors, or even Supreme Court justices would do if they had the chance, were able, and thought they could get away with it.

And no reader of the current best sellers on life in the U.S.A. today would be interested in even the most uninhibited account of what our sailors do on liberty in foreign ports. Compared to the queer capers in polite society ashore these days, it would be very dull reading indeed. In fact it might hurt recruiting. It could lead adventurous young men of draft age to figure that they can make out better and get more action on any of the college campuses ashore than they can in far-away waterfront bistros.

So the next few days will get only brief mention in this saga.

Fatso and Scuttlebutt shoved off, with the official limousine and driver provided by the Israeli Navy, and spent their time in and around Jerusalem. Jerusalem is, of course, a focal point for three of the world's great religions. It has sacred shrines of the Jews and Arabs, as well as the Christians. Our heros visited all the holy places, and some others too. They had a minor brush with the police when Scuttlebutt accidentally dislocated a citizen's jaw during a discussion of the *Liberty* incident in a barroom. But their driver smoothed that over by explaining to the cops that they were official guests of the Israeli Navy and hence enjoyed diplomatic immunity. Outside of that, their relations with citizens and police were quite pleasant. In fact, as they were driving back to Tel Aviv, Fatso remarked, "Hell, there's no use being an Admiral when they treat ordinary sailors this way."

As soon as Fatso and Scuttlebutt were on their way, Ginsberg and the Professor loaded the commodore's car with cameras and took off for Suez in civilian clothes, posing as *Life* photographers. The rest of the crew took turns standing watches on the ship and participating in the people-to-people program ashore. This program, a brain child of President Kennedy's, is supposed to foster mutual understanding between members of the armed forces and indigenous populations. Since all the local boys of military age were out in the desert fostering better understanding with the Arabs, the contacts of Fatso's lads were mostly with the local girls. Our lads claimed afterwards that because of this, their efforts produced even more mutual benefits and fewer bad reactions than they usually do in foreign ports.

Late in the afternoon of the fourth day, Fatso and Scuttlebutt returned from Jerusalem. By this time, they were bosom pals with their driver, Moe. All three rode in the front seat discussing life on this earth and what ought to be done about it until they reached the outskirts of Tel Aviv. There Moe insisted that his charges get in back, where VIPs are supposed to ride.

Many of the streets in Tel Aviv run right down to the shore. Moe plowed through the sand at the end of one of them to the hard beach and drove right up to LCU 1124. There he popped out and opened the door for his passengers, who disembarked like a couple of Admirals.

Satchmo and Judge looked on proudly from the bridge and the Judge remarked, "We're going to hafta get a red carpet for that ramp if this keeps up."

Fatso invited Moe aboard for dinner. But Moe declined with regret, saying "My old lady would twist my (formal dances) off if I didn't come right home."

"I thought they had women better trained than that, over here," observed Fatso.

"They do," said Moe. "But my old lady is from Brooklyn."

Fatso and Scuttlebutt both offered Moe twenty dollar bills, but he set his jaw firmly and declined, saying "My pleasure. If I can ever be of service to you gentlemen again, just call on me."

His chance to be of service came sooner than they expected. As they were bidding each other goodbye and vowing eternal friendship, they heard the scream of rapidly approaching police sirens. The Commodore's car, heavily caked with mud and dust, burst out of a nearby street and bounced through the sand toward the hard beach, hotly pursued by two motorcycle cops—that is, until the cops hit the soft sand. The car ploughed through the sand, sped along the beach, swerved onto the ramp and drove aboard the LCU with the brakes screaming. The doors opened and out climbed Ginsberg and the Professor, looking as smug as a couple of cats full of canaries *au catnip,* just as the cops finally made it to the ramp, followed by a crowd of excited natives attracted by the sirens.

With the cops momentarily baffled at seeing their quarry take refuge on the visiting American ship, Moe stepped in and took charge.

There was a lot of shouting in Israeli and Yiddish and waving of arms as the cops set forth their alleged complaints. Moe replied in similar dialect, laced with a few emphatic goddams. The cops listened dubiously, then looked at each other and shrugged their shoulders, mounted their motorcycles, and took off.

"What got their ass in an uproar, Moe?" asked Fatso, as the crowd began melting away.

"They claimed they had orders from the Army at Suez to arrest your car. They said your boys also ran through a road block twenty kilometers out of town and they chased them at eighty miles an hour right through the middle of the city."

"What did the Army want them for?"

"They didn't know—something that happened at Suez."

"And what the hell did you tell 'em, to get 'em off our back?"

"I explained that you are guests of the Israeli Navy and have diplomatic immunity. The cops had no idea what that means, but they didn't want to admit it. So they just let the whole thing drop."

"Cops are just as dumb in Tel Aviv as they are in Brooklyn," Moe added, as he got in the limousine and drove off.

As Fatso and Scuttlebutt walked through the well deck on the way to the messroom they noted half a dozen holes in the stern end of the car, about the size of dimes.

In the messroom they were greeted by Ginsberg and the Professor, wearing sheepish grins.

"Well?" said Fatso. "What the hell have you guys been doing?"

"We was down at Suez taking pictures," said Ginsberg. "And boy! We got some lulus—good enough for a big spread in *Life*."

"And just *how* did you get all them holes in the back of the car?"

"Oh-h-h, . . . them *holes?* . . . Uh . . . we got shot at a little bit," said Ginsberg.

"*At,* hell," said Fatso. "You got shot *into*."

"Yeah, that's right," said the Professor. "It was just plain luck nobody got hurt."

"Who shot at you—the Arabs?"

"No. The Israelis."

"Why would *they* shoot at you?"

"Well—there was a sort of a mixup about some movie films we had."

"Movies of what?"

"We got pictures of them executing a couple of Arab spies—real dramatic feature stuff . . . and close ups of them giving 'em the *coop de grass* afterwards—blood, guts, and feathers all over. Beautiful human-interest stuff. They claimed we weren't allowed to take pictures of it, and wanted our films."

"So?"

"Well, it turned out later that the films we gave them was blank—and they got mad about it and tried to take *all* our films away."

"So?"

"So we jumped in our car and beat it."

"And they shot at you, I suppose?"

"No. Not then. That was later, at a checkpoint in the road. When we didn't stop, they took out after us in a tank. But we was outrunning the tank, so they started shooting at us."

"Gawd almighty," said Fatso. "This will land right in the Ambassador's lap. Now we *have* got our ass in a bight."

"Don't worry about that, Cap'n," said the Professor. "They don't know we're in the Navy. They think we were a couple of *Life* photographers."

"Driving a U.S. Navy car?" demanded Fatso.

"By the time we got to Suez, you couldn't tell what

141

kind of a car it was," said Ginsberg. "We had a layer of mud and dust all over us that covered up that U.S. Navy on the side. Nothin' to worry about on that, Cap'n."

"Yeah," said Fatso. "And those cops that chased you right up the ramp—I don't suppose they will suspect you had anything to do with the U.S. Navy? Cops are dumb anywheres in the world—especially traffic cops—but even a Brooklyn cop might get suspicious about that."

At this point, Jughaid and Webfoot returned aboard, having spent the afternoon ashore trying to spread good will and mutual understanding among the local populace. Webfoot had a big black eye and Jughaid a broken nose. Their white uniforms were splattered with red, as if they had been helping to butcher steers.

As they entered the messroom, Fatso shook his head sadly and said, "Oh my gawd! . . . What now?"

"We got into a rhubarb," explained Webfoot.

"Looks like it was a masacree—not a rhubarb," observed Fatso.

"No-o-o—o," said Webfoot judicially, "I think it was about even—at least until the goddam bartender called the cops. After that, things got sort of confused."

"What happened then?"

"Well—everybody started pushing and shoving each other around," said Jughaid, taking over the narrative, "and we sort of nudged two cops off the porch. After that all hell broke loose."

"I don't see nothin' so awful about that," observed Scuttlebutt.

"No-o-o-o," said Jughaid. "Except this was a roof garden joint, and the porch was on the third floor."

"Gawd almighty!" said Fatso. "Did it kill 'em?"

"No. This joint was on the waterfront, and the porch stuck out over the bay—so they hit in the water. While they were dragging the cops out of the water it sort of distracted attention from us for a while, so we shoved off and came back to the ship."

"So now we'll have the mayor down here first thing in the morning with a couple of carloads of cops," said Fatso.

"I don't think it's really that bad," said Scuttlebutt judicially. "Nobody has done nothing real big wrong. Just traffic violations—and disturbing the peace a little bit. I don't think they'll try to make a federal case out of that."

"That's right," said the Judge, putting on his official robes, as it were. "And this ship is U.S. territory. They can't come aboard and take nobody off without going through extradition proceedings in Washington. I think after the *Liberty* business, they will be glad to just drop the whole thing. Maybe the best thing for us to do is to just quietly get the hell out of here and let them forget it."

"The Supreme Court couldn't decide it any better," said Fatso. "Let's see—the next high tide when we can get off this beach is two hours after sunset. Okay . . . We get underway at 9:30 tonight."

But that plan didn't hold up. At two bells of the first watch, half an hour before they were to get underway, a blinker message came in from signal tower at the entrance fort:

FROM SENIOR NAVAL OFFICER:

TO COMMANDING OFFICER:

ADMIRAL REQUESTS YOU CALL ON HIM AT 0930 TOMORROW MORNING. OFFICIAL CAR WILL PICK YOU UP AT 0910.

"Well—there goes the old ball game, boys," said Fatso, as Jughaid handed him the message. "Judge, you better break out your law books and study up on court martial procedure. I'm going to need a good defense counsel soon."

Fatso spent a sleepless night. The two most probable reasons for this summons seemed to be the desert skirmish and the business of the cops falling off the porch. He could think of no plausible explanation for either one of these incidents. It was also possible that certain really harmless things that he and Scuttlebutt had done in Jerusalem, but which could be misinterpreted, had been brought to official attention. And, finally, there was always the chance that the Israeli naval officials had checked up and found out that he really had no damned business in Tel Aviv in the first place.

Fatso had known for years, of course, that rank has its privileges. Now he was learning that rank and command also have their responsibilities. He was beginning to see

143

that the things that drive admirals and captains nuts are not the perils of wind and wave on the open sea but the jams that well-meaning sailors get into ashore. For the first time, the weight of command responsibility bore heavily upon him.

Promptly the next morning, Moe picked up Fatso with the limousine and delivered him at the Israeli naval HQ.

Fatso mounted the steps there with his shoulders back and head up, prepared to accept responsibility, as a captain must, for the conduct of his men, and to defend as best he could the interests of the United States in the premises, whatever they turned out to be.

As the flag lieutenant showed him into the inner sanctum the Admiral rose, shook hands, and motioned Fatso to a chair.

"Have a cigar?" he asked, offering Fatso a box.

"No-thank-you-sir," said Fatso.

The Admiral bit off the end of a cigar, lighted it carefully, and took a few puffs on it. Then he drew in a lungful of smoke, and blew out a fairly good smoke ring.

"I hope I haven't inconvenienced you by asking you to come over," said the Admiral.

"No, SIR," said Fatso.

"I hope your visit here has been pleasant and that our people have been friendly."

"Yes, SIR," said Fatso.

"Have you had any troubles here?"

"Well—nossir—nothing to speak of."

The Admiral puffed on his cigar some more, and blew out some more smoke rings.

"The thing I really want to talk to you about," said the Admiral, "is a matter which I would rather not take up officially. It's a matter which, for various reasons, you may not feel free to explain. If so—I will understand."

"Yes, SIR," said Fatso, thinking to himself, "THIS IS IT. NOW HE LOWERS THE BOOM."

"It's about the salute you fired on entering port," said the Admiral.

"Yessir," said Fatso—certain now that the Admiral had found out that he had no business even being in Tel Aviv, let alone firing national salutes.

The Admiral picked up a photograph from his desk

144

and handed it to Fatso. It showed LCU 1124 blasting away as she entered port with a beautiful array of various-sized smoke rings to port and starboard.

"What I would like to know," said the Admiral, "is how in the world you make those perfect rings? I have asked all my ordnance experts about it and none of them know. Do you mind telling us how you do it?"

"No, *SIR*—not at all, Admiral. It's a pleasure. I'll be glad to," said Fatso, and proceeded to explain the mechanics of the smoke rings.

The Admiral broke into a pleased grin at the simplicity of it all, as Fatso revealed the great secret. When Fatso finished, the Admiral shook his head and said, "Well, there you are. It's just like so many other far-reaching discoveries. After someone has finally made the first wheel, everybody wonders why it took man so long to think of such a simple thing."

"Yessir," said Fatso. "I have some very smart men in my crew. We conducted a lot of tests before we hit on this."

"Well—thank you very much, Captain," said the Admiral, rising and extending his hand. "Next time you come in here, your salute will be answered ring for ring."

Chapter Sixteen

Constitutional Rights

As FATSO returned aboard from his call on the Admiral, Scuttlebutt greeted him at the ramp. "How did you make out, Cap'n?" he asked anxiously.

"Okay," said Fatso. "He just wanted some information, which I was able to give him."

"It wasn't about nothing we did in Jerusalem, was it?"

"No-o-o-o," said Fatso. "It was about sort of technical stuff. We don't have nothing to worry about—yet. . . . Now let's haul up that bow ramp, fire up the engines, and get the hell out of here before we do get something to worry about."

An hour later our heroes were leaning over the rail aft of the bridge comparing notes on their adventures in Israel and watching the shoreline drop below the horizon astern. Sailors get visible proof that the world is round every time they do this. But of course, right after leaving port, they have more important matters to discuss than the shape of the planet on which we live. Since they were leaving a country where all the men had been out in the desert trying to pacify the Arabs, their comments were concerned mostly with the women.

As the top of the Tel Aviv light was dropping below the horizon Ginsberg said to Jughaid, "Where did you find that cute looking little Jewish gal I seen you with the other night?"

"Oh—I met her socially at a party," said Jughaid vaguely.

"Musta been a kiddies' party," said Ginsberg. "She looked too young to be going out with sailors. Did her mother know she was out?"

"Hunh!" said Jughaid; "that gal is older than she looks. She's a widow. And she can take care of herself in any company."

"With her big blue eyes and that red ribbon in her hair

she reminded me of Little Red Riding Hood," said Ginsberg.

"She's more like Annie Oakley than Little Red Riding Hood," observed Jughaid. "She's a WAAC in the Israeli Army reserve and an expert pistol shot. She's got as many medals for pistol shooting as old Shaky Stokes. And she's a top sergeant, too. Her husband was a private in the army."

"Boy oh boy," said the Professor. "Just imagine being a private in the army and coming home every night to a cute dish like that!"

"Yeah!" agreed Scuttlebutt. "And doing what privates are always saying oughta be done to sergeants."

"Her husband was killed by the Arabs I suppose?" asked Ginsberg.

"No. Not exactly," said Jughaid. "I asked her what did he die of, and she said he had very bad luck. Died of gonorrhea."

"Gonorrhea!" whooped all hands incredulously.

"Hell—that ain't a fatal disease," said the Professor.

"That's what I told her," said Jughaid. "She said, 'HUNH! . . . When you give it to *me*, it is.' "

Later, when the boys were gathered in the messroom Scuttlebutt asked, "Where are we heading for now, Cap'n?"

"That's a damn good question," said Fatso. "I'm trying to figure it out myself."

"Don't you think we oughta look in on Naples pretty soon to pick up our mail and—er—see if the HQ there has any news for us?" asked Scuttlebutt.

"Yeah. I suppose we gotta do that pretty soon," said Fatso. "But we gotta do it the way porcupines make love."

"How do you mean?"

"Ver-rry carefully," said Fatso. "I want to just ease into the Amphib Base there without attracting any attention, check in with the chief who has the duty, and then just wait till somebody sends for me."

"What are you worried about, Cap'n," asked the Judge. "You don't think they'll try to say we been AWOL or nothing like that, do you?"

"No-o-o-o," said Fatso. "They can't pin that rap on

147

us. We just carried out our orders as best we could. We checked in with SOPA Athens when we couldn't find the ship, and we been standing by for further orders ever since. So we're okay on that. It's the USS *Turtle* bit that can really get our ass in a bight."

"What did the *Turtle* do that was so awful?" demanded Scuttlebutt.

"It got itself in the newspapers," said Fatso. "Russia and the Arabs both put us on the report, and the Navy went on record officially saying there never was such a ship. If it should leak out now that *we* are the *Turtle* a lot of big wheels will look bad, and there will be hell to pay."

"Well, yeah. I can see how there would be some very red faces in high level circles if they had to admit now that we was the *Turtle*. Maybe half a dozen Admirals would suddenly retire. But what could they do to *us?*" demanded the Judge.

"Hunh!" said Fatso. "Any time low-level guys like us make high-level faces red, some low-level asses get awful red, too."

"Yeah," said the Professor. "The *Turtle* got in the papers, all right. But it got itself officially abolished, too. For that very reason, the Navy wouldn't dare let it come to life again. Too many big shots would be embarrassed."

"Okay," said Fatso; "That's why I say we gotta go into Naples carefully without attracting no attention. If the Navy ever found out that we was the *Turtle* they'd ship us down to Antarctica and keep us on ice there till our enlistments were up. Because if the press ever got hold of the story, all hell would bust loose."

"Well, I see what you mean now, Cap'n," said Scuttlebutt. "We gotta come into Naples as if nothing at all had happened, keep our mouths shut, and just wait till our records and pay accounts catch up with us."

"That's right. I know a chief in the supply department there who can make a routine check with the *Alamo* and remind them about our records and pay accounts. Then they'll find another ship to put us on and that will be that."

At this point Ginsberg, who had been working on his films and taking no part in the critique, let out a whoop.

"Boy oh boy!" he shouted, "You oughta see this film of shooting them Arab spies."

Several of the boys gathered around, and Ginsberg proudly showed a blow-up of his film. "Look at this shot —just before he gets hit—He's saying his last words."

"Gee!" said the group.

Abie flipped the viewer to the next picture and said, "And now the bullet hits him and his eyes are popping as if he seen a ghost."

"There ain't much blood in it," observed the Judge critically.

"That comes later," said Ginsberg, flipping a few frames through the viewer. "There you are. Blood all over, but no brains."

"What do you figure on doing with them pictures?" asked Fatso.

"I'm going to mail 'em to *Life* as soon as we get to Naples."

"I think we better hold them for a while," said Fatso. "It wouldn't be so good for us to make a big splurge in *Life* right now."

"We *can't* hold 'em, Cap'n," said Ginsberg. "These pictures are red hot. Gotta get 'em in right away—air mail. I would of sent them from Tel Aviv, but I was afraid the Israeli censors might get 'em."

"I think we better hold them," said Fatso.

"I wish I could, Cap'n," said Ginsberg. "But stuff like this don't keep. This is a whale of a scoop, and time is very important. Pictures that would make a feature story today may go in the ash can two weeks from now. Even an exclusive scoop like this one can get out of date."

"I said we gotta hold 'em," said Fatso.

"I'd sure like to oblige you, Cap'n," said Ginsberg. "But I just can't do it. This is a cinch to make the cover of *Life*."

"Bring 'em over here and let me have a look at 'em," said Fatso.

Ginsberg gathered up three rolls of movie film, several dozen still pictures, and films and lugged them down to the other end of the messroom. "Look at that print on top, Cap'n," he said. "That's a blow-up from the movie showing the guy's face when he gets hit right in the middle of a word. That's the one you'll see on the cover of *Life*."

"Uh-huh," said Fatso, examining the photo. "Is this *all* you got? The whole works?"

"Yessir, Cap'n," said Ginsberg. "That's the whole package. Negatives, positives, prints, and all."

"Bring your viewer down here so I can look at these films," said Fatso.

As Abie went back to the other end of the messroom to get the viewer, Fatso swept films, negatives, and prints into a bucket, kicked open the door behind him, strode out on deck, and heaved the bucket over the side.

When Ginsberg saw what was happening he let out an agonized scream, and rushed out on deck with his eyes popping like the Arab in the picture.

"Goddam it. You can't *do* that," he yelled at Fatso, as the bucket began drifting astern. "Right full rudder," he howled at Satchmo, who had the wheel. "Keep that bucket in sight. Right full rudder!"

Satchmo held his course and looked quizzically at Fatso.

"Steady as you go," Fatso said.

"Aye aye, sir, Cap'n—steady on two seven zero," replied Satchmo.

Ginsberg ran over to the rail and would have leaped overboard to rescue the bucket if Jughaid and Webfoot hadn't grabbed and restrained him.

Here the stern wave broke over the bucket, engulfed it, and down it went to Davey Jones.

"Oi yoi yoi," moaned Ginsberg, along with a lot of seafaring language which cannot be repeated in this family journal. "You can't *do* that! I got a *constitutional right* —I could of got fifty-thousand bucks for those pictures— I might of got a Pulitzer Prize, you son of a bitch—sir."

"Yeah," said Fatso. "And the rest of us, including you, would of been down in Antarctica for the next year, getting our balls frosted."

While these scenes were being enacted on the former USS *Turtle*, Commander Sixth Fleet was getting his regular daily briefing by his staff on board the flagship in Naples. The Admiral was seated in front of a big vertical chart of the Med, dotted all over with little moveable magnetic markers of various shapes and colors. The shapes told the size and class of various ships; the colors, their nationality. Russian ships had brilliant red markers, which were becoming more numerous every day. The board was kept up to date by a constant stream of position reports from allied ships and by daily photo flights which spotted all the others. By a quick glance at this board the Admiral could tell the current location of all large merchant ships and tankers, and of every naval ship of any nationality in the Mediterranean. (Except, of course, LCU 1124.)

The briefing began with a run-down on the war in Vietnam. The Chief of Staff, thumbing through the top secret dispatches, said, "The White House announced yesterday that we are now winning the war on all fronts, and an enemy collapse is expected soon. The Secretary of Defense, just back from a trip to front lines, declared there is a good chance our troops will be coming home by Christmas. The Associated Press says there was a heavy rocket attack on Saigon yesterday, that two more of the new TFX airplanes are missing, and that a million dollars worth of whiskey has been stolen from the PX by black market operators. Selective Service announced yesterday that draft calls for the next three months will be double as much as previously announced."

"There seems to be a sort of credibility gap," observed the Admiral. "But General Hershey always was a skeptical old curmudgeon. Even if a Pentagon announcement was so, he wouldn't believe it."

Next a sharp young captain read a bulletin from UN Headquarters in New York. "The UN yesterday passed a resolution by a large majority calling on both sides in the Arab-Israeli dispute to arbitrate their differences. It warned that the use of force would be severely condemned by world public opinion and might require the UN to take further action."

"By Gad that will give them something to think about," said the Admiral. "I knew we could depend on the UN when the chips were down. I'll bet that will scare hell out of that one-eyed Jew general—if he ever hears about it."

"Three more Russian submarines and six destroyers came through the Bosphorous yesterday bound for the Med," continued the Captain. "This brings the total of

Russian naval ships in the Med up to forty-eight, half of them now concentrated in Alexandria."

"Hunh!" observed the Admiral. "Ever since the Russo-Japanese war, I've always figured Russian naval officers were sort of stupid on the starboard side. But I must say they are beginning to learn how to use sea power now."

The next briefer was the Public Information officer. "We have a complaint," he said, "from the editors of *Time* against the Captain of the *America*. They say he was uncooperative during the Arab-Israeli crisis and refused to let their man have proper access to the news, despite his clearance from the Defense Department."

"The Captain told me all about that," said the Admiral. "He says all the *Time* man wanted was to take over command of the ship. Some of these reporters think that the major mission of this fleet is to provide them with a grandstand seat, copies of all the top secret despatches, and a radio transmitter. Send *Time* the bedbug letter."

"That concludes the morning briefing, sir," said the COS.

"Okay," said the Admiral. "Now, while we've got everybody here, I want one last run-down on the USS *Turtle* business. I've got the smooth report for CNO on my desk now, ready for signature. It has already been revised twice because the first versions were entirely too sweeping and cocksure. I'm not ready to go on record saying the *Turtle* could not be a U.S. ship. That covers entirely too much ground such as the CIA, DIA, MATS, and even merchant ships. I'm going to confine my disavowal to Sixth Fleet ships under my operational control. I still think I smell a small skunk somewhere in this *Turtle* business. That hanging is just the sort of a thing some smart young American would dream up to booby trap the Russians. But I am ready now, if you all agree, to certify that it definitely was no ship of the Sixth Fleet. So if any of you have any doubts, speak now, or forever hold your peace."

The group of captains and commanders stared straight ahead with what they all hoped were confident expressions on their faces. No one could think of any reasonable way to hedge.

"Can we be sure this is not another *Liberty* affair," demanded the Admiral; "a ship that was actually getting its orders from CIA or DIA without our knowledge but theoretically under our op-con if she got in a jam?"

The Chief of Staff spoke up. "I've checked that from every possible angle, Admiral. That is impossible in this case."

"Okay," said the Admiral. "I'll take your word for that. But there is always the outside chance that some group of long-haired screwballs did this with a chartered U.S. ship that isn't registered anywhere."

"That's a one-in-a-million chance, sir," said the COS. "It's much more likely that if there *is* any such ship as the *Turtle* at all, it belongs to one of a dozen or so Mediterranean sea powers. I don't think the Israelis would hesitate one minute to pull a stunt like that to stir up trouble between us, the Russians, and the Arabs. Or, our adversaries —as the State Department calls them—might just make up the whole bit out of thin air, trying to prove that we really did help the Israelis after all."

"The last one seems the most likely to me—I hope," said the Admiral. "All right. I'm signing that report right after this meeting. After that, we're stuck with it, no matter what. See you tomorrow, gentlemen."

That evening Ginsberg had the wheel watch and Scuttlebutt, Fatso, the Judge, and the Professor were discussing military law in the messroom.

"Ginsberg spent about an hour with me this afternoon," said the Judge, "quizzing me about his constitutional rights."

"Which ones is he having trouble with?" asked Fatso.

"Well, he figured you must of violated most of them when you heaved that bucket overboard."

"Hunh," said Fatso. "Where does the Constitution say anything about heaving buckets overboard? And I ain't heard of the Supreme Court passing any new amendments about buckets—yet."

"He claims it comes under the part about freedom of speech, freedom of the press, due process of law, and several others."

"Well, I dunno much about all that stuff," said Fatso. "The Navy that I grew up in was supposed to defend the United States against foreign invasion. They didn't spend much time explaining about legal rights when I was in boot camp. You had a legal right to three square meals a day, a gun that would shoot straight, and all the ammunition you needed for it. At sea you stood four on and eight off, and in port you got liberty whenever the Captain couldn't think of some reason for not giving it. And it seemed to work out pretty good in World War II—at least I'll betcha the Germans and Japs would say it did."

"There's no doubt about that, Cap'n," said the Judge. "But if you want to get technical about it, I think maybe Ginsberg has a case. You didn't have no legal right to heave his pictures overboard."

"Maybe he didn't have no legal right to take the pictures in the first place," said Fatso.

"Now wait a minute, Cap'n," put in the Professor. "Photographers have got a right to do any goddam thing they want."

"Well—yeah," conceded Fatso. "I dunno about a legal *right,* but we sure as hell let 'em trample all over us. What legal advice did you give him, Judge?"

"I advised him that when we get to Naples, he should go to see the head chaplain and ask him for a sympathy chit and the key to the weep locker."

"Exactly right, counselor," said Fatso. "I couldn't have done any better myself. How does he feel about it now? Is he going to serve out the rest of his enlistment with us, or will he pack up his bag and hammock and quit when we get to Naples?"

"Oh, he'll sweat it out with us," said the Judge. "But he thinks what you did to him was pretty awful. He says not even Hitler would have done a thing like that. He thinks he had it made for a big spread in *Life,* and any photographer figures that's better than getting a Congressional Medal of Honor. It's worth whatever it costs—even a couple of years in Antarctica."

"He shoulda been flogged for even thinking about sending that stuff in," declared Fatso. "You know, abolishing flogging was one of the biggest mistakes this Navy ever made. Hell—we got kids in the Navy now that ain't ever even been spanked by their Old Man. They're as useless as rubber swab handles. But a good flogging might make fine upstanding citizens out of them."

154

"Yeah," agreed Scuttlebutt. "Just like sand and canvas used to clean up the crum bums."

"What do you mean, sand and canvas?" asked the Judge.

"At the start of World War II, we used to have a lot of sand on the big ships for scrubbing down the wooden decks. Every now and then some new guy would come aboard who'd never take a bath. When he got to stinking too much for the other guys to stand it, a bunch of them used to scrub him down with sand, using canvas washrags. The guy would wind up as pink all over as a spanked baby's ass. They never had to do it twice."

"Yeah—them was the good old days," said Fatso. "Before the lawyers took over the Navy."

"How do you mean?" demanded the Judge.

"Before the war the Navy was run by the Articles for the Government of the Navy. They came down to us from the days of sailing ships. Every now and then they had to abolish some that got out of date—like the ones about hanging and flogging. But we won every war we fought under 'em. If you kept your nose clean, you got along okay. If you didn't, the government would wipe it for you whether you liked it or not. But after World War II the lawyers decided that maybe wars would be won quicker if they were fought in a more legal manner and if lawyers had more to say about global strategy. So they abolished the Articles and came up with the Uniform Code of Justice, which made everything uniformly bad for all services."

"Yeah, we learned a little bit about that in law school," said the Judge. "They told us it was a very good thing."

"Sure it was—for the lawyers. It made good jobs for a lot of them that couldn't make a living on the outside. Now we've got lawyers all over in the Navy, wearing captains and commander stripes, who don't know which end of the ship is the bow."

"But aren't your legal rights protected better now than they usedta be?" asked the Judge.

"Balls," said Fatso. "The main thing that's protected under the new system is a lot of good jobs for lawyers. I don't care what kind of a system you cook up for running a navy—it's going to depend in the end on the guys who are running it. If you've got a good skipper, you'll have a good ship, under any system. A bad skipper can figure out ways to get around any rules you write and make a madhouse out of any ship, no matter what the book says, or how many lawyers you got running around wearing gold stripes."

Chapter Seventeen

USS *America*

NEXT MORNING, six hundred miles to the west, a task group of the Sixth Fleet cruised eastward alert and ready to take any action necessary to defend the interests of the United States in that area. In the center spot of the armada was the sixty-thousand-ton carrier *America,* wearing the flag of Rear Admiral Dugan. Around her on circle three, three thousand yards away, were three cruisers with heavy batteries of AA guns and heat-seeking guided missiles. Further out on circle eight, a dozen destroyers formed an antisub screen around the big ships.

On all ships radar dishes swung back and forth searching the sky for strange aircraft. High overhead, jet fighters circled in holding patterns ready to intercept and "frisk" any incoming strangers spotted by the radars below. On the tin cans sonar domes sent beams of probing pings through the water in all directions, searching for submarines. Any unfriendly aircraft or sub approaching the fleet would have gotten a far-out reception and a plain warning to keep clear or be in grave danger.

For reasons understood only by statesmen and diplomats, which this writer will not try to explain, strange surface craft didn't count. It was now accepted as SOP in the Med for each task group to have a Russian snooper. This morning the snooper was a smart-looking little bucket with an array of missiles and radars on her topside. She weaved from one circle to another through the formation, sniffing around the big ships and generally making a nuisance of herself.

Usually she kept out of the way. But when the task group got ready to launch or land planes, she often managed to complicate the maneuver. The fleet must head into the wind to launch or land. By getting itself upwind of the fleet, the Russian could arrange things so she would have the right of way under international rules of the road after the ships got squared away into the wind. This would then produce a chicken game with the Russian having the law on his side.

Among most naval men, ordinary sea manners require an outsider to keep clear of ships maneuvering in formation. But, of course, the sea manners of Russian naval officers are no better than those of their diplomats at the UN. Big ships may have to back and fill several times a day to avoid collisions in which, under admiralty law, they would be at fault.

So all skippers now have to keep one eye on the flagship for signals and the other on the goddam Russian.

On the *America* there was a lull in operations between launches. But a lull on a big carrier is like one in a busy beehive. There's still a lot going on. They fly around the clock these days, so time never hangs heavy on anybody's hands. Each day the crew puts in eight hours on watch, eight hours in the sack, eight hours respotting the deck, servicing planes, hauling bombs and ammunition around, eating, and taking care of their personal affairs. The rest of the time they can do as they please, as long as they keep out of the way on the flight deck.

The *America* is our latest attack carrier, one thousand feet long, sixty thousand tons, thirty-five knots, and able to handle a deckload of supersonic jet planes. This ship and others like her are among the convincing arguments of our statesmen when they get involved in high-level discussions with the communists about international morality, policy, and world peace. Stowed in her magazines are enough atomic bombs to kill more people who disagree with us in five minutes than Hitler's slaughterhouses were able to process in five years.

She is not atomic powered, although all big carriers of the future will be. When the *America* was being built, the Whiz Kids in the Pentagon decided that atomic power was not a paying proposition. Of course no man-of-war has ever been built that put money back in the Treasury. And the Navy claimed that warships are built to defend the country, and atomic powered ships can do it better than oil burners.

But the Whiz Kids set the question up on computers allowing for the costs of everything like material, labor, overhead, advertising, and salaries of computer experts, but not for wind, wave, and a lot of other things that you run into in battles at sea. The answer came out, "oil power is probably good enough." A young naval captain who suggested that, on a cost-effective basis, sails might be even better than oil was sent to duty in Antarctica.

But except for atomic power, the *America* was packed full of all the latest marvels of the jet age. Her radars often told the watch-standers down below in CIC more about what the planes in the air were doing than the pilots knew themselves. Inertial accelerometers and black boxes hooked up by radio to orbiting satellites enabled her to navigate precisely without ever seeing any landmarks or the stars. She had mechanical brains and computers that gave you the right answers to any questions you asked them—and provided you fed the right dope into them in the first place. Even the galley had a black box that told the head cook how many loaves of bread he had to bake each day.

And of course the *America* has the canted deck, steam catapults, and mirror-landing systems. These three new wrinkles are what enable her to fly supersonic aircraft around the clock, moon or no moon, and even in fog. Strangely enough, these three ideas came from the British Navy. Until after World War II, our naval flyers looked upon the limeys as poor country cousins just emerging from the era of sail. Which just goes to show that when you get too far ahead in any game you get smug and are riding for a fall!

This morning the *America* was getting ready for the next flight operation. Purple-shirted gas crews were topping off fuel tanks of the planes. Ordnancemen, wearing red shirts, tinkered (carefully!) with bombs and fuses. Tractors, driven by yellow shirts, towed planes around the deck to their launching spots or parked them on the elevators to go below. The tractor drivers are all frustrated hot rods. When they have those high-priced airplanes in tow, they proceed like old ladies parking a brand-new car in a small space. But when they have nothing in tow they roar around the flight deck like drag racers, skimming the edges of open elevators by margins that would scare the grit out of even a sky diver.

The straight part of the flight deck is always cluttered with airplanes like LaGuardia airport during the tourist season. But the canted part is kept clear to land at all times. When something goes wrong in one of those high-speed jets you can't hang around up in the sky waiting for them to clear the deck for you. You've gotta LAND.

Four and a half acres of flight deck may sound like a lot of room. But it isn't so much when you come slamming into it at one hundred fifty knots in a five million dollar package of machinery that weighs twenty tons! So the canted part of the deck is clear and ready whenever planes are in the air.

Soon after eight bells of the morning watch, a bugle call blared forth from squawk boxes all over the ship that would have brought a gleam to the eyes of General George Patton—*Boots and Saddles.* The Navy has lifted this famous old cavalry call from the Army and uses it for "Flight Quarters," the horses now being the jet propelled monsters on the flight deck.

Plane captains, catapult crews, plane handlers, and taxi directors double-timed to their stations on the huge deck. Pilots and plane crews togged out in their flight gear headed for the ready rooms for their preflight briefing on wind, weather, and general poop.

Each of the four squadrons in the air group has its own readyroom. Pilots and rear-seat men spend nearly as much time in the readyrooms being briefed and debriefed as they do in the air. On each flight they go from there to the planes and back there again when they land.

A readyroom is a sort of squadron office, dressing room, classroom and air crews' clubroom all rolled into one. The bulkheads are covered with squadron insignias, trophies, and bulletin boards. On these boards are posted clippings and cartoons of current interest, the latest word from Patuxent Test Center on the care and feeding of jet engines at high altitude, notices to airmen about the hazards to avigation, and helpful hints about how to avoid high-speed stalls at low altitude, which are regarded as bad luck by jet pilots. In the front of the room are a blackboard and lectern for the briefing officer and a screen with a moving tape, as in a stock brokerage customer's room. This tape puts out the latest dope on ship's course, speed, present location, and where they claim they will be a few hours hence; bearing and distance of nearest land, current and predicted weather, and many other odds and ends of

160

interest to pilots about to venture off into the wild blue yonder.

There are a dozen rows of easy chairs big enough to comfortably seat a pilot wearing his G suit plus all the items of survival gear and housekeeping equipment he likes to take along on overwater flights. And, of course, in the back of the room there are a couple of constantly bubbling coffee urns and a rack for all the private coffee cups, like that for shaving mugs in an old-time barber shop.

Those going out on the next flight get the front seats. They sit there like fighters in their corners before the bell, getting a lot of good advice and planning what they'll do when the bell rings.

This morning Ensign Willy Wigglesworth and his radar man, Joe Blueberry, had the front seats. The squadron intelligence officer was briefing them.

"You'll go off the catapult grossing forty-one thousand five hundred pounds," he said. "You'll be a little heavy rolling off the bow, but we're giving you forty knots of wind over the deck and extra steam on the cat, so you oughta be all right. Climb at max power to angels forty, and then cruise at Mach point eight. Your mission is high-altitude photo, so you just fly to the Israeli coast, jog south fifty miles, and come back, following SOP for photo missions both ways. Bingo fields are Crete and Malta. Tacan is working—and keep your IFF on at all times. Rules of engagement if intercepted are the same as before the *Liberty* business. You're due back overhead at 12:18 with three thousand pounds of fuel. You should be back on board and debriefed by 1300. We'll tell the wardroom to save chow for you. So-o-o—that's it. Just a bowl of cherries."

"Uh huh," said Ensign Wigglesworth, making a few notes on his knee pad.

"Any special instructions for me, sir?" asked Blueberry.

"Yeah," said Willy. "Keep your eyes open back there and keep twisting your neck for other planes—especially in the landing pattern."

"Aye aye, sir," said Blueberry. "Will do."

Up on the flag bridge the Admiral said to the Staff Duty

161

Officer, "Okay—let's get into the wind. Launching course should be about zero two zero."

"Aye Aye, sir," said the D.O. "Zero two zero is correct." He walked over to the rail and yelled down to the chief signalman on the level below, "SIGNALS! Stand by to launch. Turn to course zero two zero."

The chief signalman bawled, "Outboard hoist—Prep; Mabel; Charley—look alive and get 'em up."

Signal floosies scrambled from one end of the flag bag to the other hooking on flags while others heaved around on the halyards, dragging them out of the bag and up to the yardarm as soon as bent on. You might have thought the Old Nick was prodding them in the stern sheets with a red-hot marlin spike.

"Inboard hoist," bawled the Chief. "Pennant zero flag, two flag, zero flag, pennant TURN," and another array of flags shot up to the yardarm on the inboard hoist.

The chief glared balefully at each flag as it emerged from the bag, ready to flay any floosie alive who bent on the wrong flag and tried to louse up the evolution.

On all ships, signal forces leaped into action and similar flags fluttered up to the "dip" (ten feet below the yardarm) showing that the ship had the signal and was checking it in the book. These being simple, well-known signals the hoists were two-blocked almost immediately, indicating "Signal understood. Ship ready to execute."

On the flag bridge, the chief was sweeping the formation with his glass. As the last tin can two-blocked he sang out, "All ships two-blocked"—and then, on a nod from the DO, he bellowed, "EXECUTE!"

On the *America* the signals were snatched down from the yardarm, followed a split second later by those from all the other ships. On all bridges the OOD barked at the helmsmen, "Left standard rudder—new course zero two zero."

"Left standard rudder, new course zero two zero," repeated the helmsmen, spinning their wheels.

All ships slowed a little as the rudders dug in and leaned at first to port, toward the dragging rudders. Then they started swinging left and listing to starboard, leaving creamy curved wakes behind them as they swung together into the wind.

"Pretty good," grunted the Admiral, sweeping his binoculars around. "That tin can in station sixty was a little slow again."

Down in the readyrooms, squawk boxes blared, "Pilots, man your planes!"

Willy and Blueberry donned their hard helmets, gathered up their gear, took a last squint at the moving tape, and trotted off to the escalator that takes heavily laden pilots up to the flight deck.

On deck Willy strode once around his plane, giving it the normal jet jockey's preflight inspection. He noted there was a wing on each side and the tail was all in one piece, gave each of the three tires a sharp kick, and climbed into the cockpit. There he adjusted his seat, squirmed into his shoulder harness, hooked up his G suit and oxygen mask, and plugged in his throat mike. He squeezed his intercom button and said to the after cockpit, "Whaddayou say back there, Blueberry?"

"Set to go," came back the answer.

Willie stuck his fist over the side with his thumb up, indicating to the lad with the starter cart that he was ready.

Soon the flight deck bull horns boomed out the starting ritual: "Now hear this! Check all loose gear about the decks." All the plane handlers and taxi directors glanced around their areas to make sure no swabs, buckets, or coils of wingline were adrift where they could get sucked up into jet intakes. "Check wheel chocks and winglines," continued the bull horns. Plane captains, crouched under their planes, made sure their wheel chocks were in place and the winglines were removed.

"Stand clear of propellers and jet intakes." This is the last warning for rubbernecks to get clear. The penalty for disregarding it is severe and messy.

"Stand by-y-y to start engines. . . ." Starter motors began whining up to speed.

"START ENGINES!" Pilots hit their starter buttons, and the flight deck exploded with a great WHOOMP!

Willie quickly checked his gages, saw they all read okay, ran his engine up to full power, and noted he got proper RPM and his tail-pipe temperature stayed out of the red.

Then he throttled down and gave his taxi director a thumbs up.

The taxi director held both arms straight up in the air with his fists clenched, telling Willy to hold his brakes. Then he bent forward, hauled his arms down, and swept them from side to side. The plane captain yanked the wheel chocks out, scrambled out from under the plane dragging the chocks with him, and dropped off the edge of the deck into the gallery walkway.

The director, arms overhead again, made beckoning motions with his open hands for Willy to come ahead slowly. Pointing at the left wheel with his right hand, telling Willy to hold that brake, and still motioning ahead with his left, the taxi director slewed Willy a bit to the left and then pointed with both hands to the next yellow shirt.

Like nearly everything else on a flight deck, transferring control of a taxying plane from one yellow shirt to another follows a rigid routine. If a pilot gets confused about which traffic director has control, it can cause a jet propelled traffic jam and put dents in expensive vehicles.

The next yellow shirt was pointing at Willy with his right hand and patting himself on the head with his left. As soon as he got a nod from Willy, he stuck both arms in the air and took over control.

As Willy taxied forward, the plane-guard whirlybird stirred up a gale of wind and took off. In the old days, a destroyer used to tag along astern of the carrier to fish bad flyers out of the water. Now, when somebody goes in the drink, the whirlybird is over the crash almost before they get through splashing. If the boys get out of it okay, the whirlybird just lowers a sling and hauls them aboard. If the crew doesn't get out of the crash fast enough, frogmen drop out of the whirlybird and drag them out. Pilots call the whirlybird "the Angel," and it is indeed a guardian angel for everyone in the air group.

After the Angel fluttered off, the first of the returning planes slammed into the arresting gear. In the old days of the straight deck, landing aboard was a much more oopsy business than it is now. True, the planes were smaller and

164

slower then. But you came aboard heading straight at a large bunch of airplanes parked just forward of the barriers. The barriers were a little less than halfway up the deck from the stern and were heavy wire cables stretched across the deck at about the height of your propeller hub. So if your tail hook missed the arresting wires, the barriers would stop you. This meant one washed-out airplane. But you could usually limp away from it.

But if you went through the barriers and into the parked planes, there would be blood, guts, and feathers all over the flight deck; and as often as not, a major fire. So rule number one in those days was, "Never touch your throttle again after you take a cut from the LSO. If you think you're going into the barriers, just brace yourself and go into them. But *never try to go 'round again!*"

Nowadays, with the canted deck, it's different. The rule now is just the opposite of what it used to be: "As soon as your wheels touch the deck, *give her full gun!*"

Then, if you've got a wire, you get pulled up short, and whack off the gun. If you miss the wires, you then become a "bolter." You've got a nice clear deck in front of you, plenty of speed, and a wide-open throttle. You just take a wave-off and go round again. After a little practice your grandmother could do it.

Another jet-age improvement is the mirror-landing system. It used to be that you came aboard following the flag-waving of the Landing Signal Officer. The LSO stood on a platform at the stern facing aft with a pair of signal flags. With those flags he would tell you "go higher—or lower—faster—or slower." As you got to the ramp he gave you either a cut or a wave off. The LSO was the king of the flight deck then, and had as much to do with good or bad landings as the pilot did.

Now, we do it with mirrors. A slick, gyro-stabilized optical system sends a narrow beam of light astern along the correct approach groove. As long as a pilot is near this groove, he sees a ball of light ahead on the deck near the touch-down point. A horizontal line of light splits the ball when he is smack in the groove. If he gets a little high, the ball goes over the line. If he gets low, it goes under. All he has to do is fiddle with his stick and throttle to keep the line splitting the ball—and just sit there till he hits the deck.

The LSO is sill the boss man. When a pilot louses up an approach too bad, he can still wave him off by flashing the lights at him. But the mirror system makes things easier for all concerned.

Coming back now to Willy:

Just forward of the island, the cat crew swarmed around him and took over. They went to work like a pro football team coming out of the huddle on a fourth down and inches to go. They lined Willy up carefully on the catapult, set the heavy towing bridle in place on the hooks on each side of the fuselage, looped it over the shuttle in the catapult track, and fastened the breaking link into the tail hook. Then they took a careful strain with the shuttle, cocking the cat as you do a slingshot. Meantime they raised the big blast deflector plate out of the deck just astern of the plane and checked a few odds and ends such as wing locks in place and control locks removed—which can make quite a difference right after you become airborne if not tended to properly beforehand.

As each member of the crew finished his job he shoved his fist out toward the crew chief with his thumb up and ducked out of the way. The chief turned toward Fly One, the launching officer, stuck his thumb up, and got clear.

Fly One took a last look around, then looked up at Fly Control on the bridge and held up his thumb. In Fly Control, the Air Officer looked forward at the Captain, seated in his chair on the port wing of the bridge, and held *his* thumb up.

(Note: A common expression for a clumsy operator is to say that he is "all thumbs." There's nothing clumsy about air operations on an attack carrier. But they'd have a hell of a time trying to run the show without using their thumbs. It would be as bad as trying to explain what a goatee is without stroking your chin.)

The Captain nodded to the Air Officer, the Air Officer flipped a switch changing the signal light sticking out over the deck from red to green, the bull horns blared "LAUNCH AIRCRAFT"—and the *America* was ready to go.

Down on deck the cat officer raised his right hand over his head holding one finger up and made circular motions. Willy ran his jets up to full power, made a quick check of the gages, throttled back and stuck his thumb up.

The cat officer then held up two fingers. Willy braced his head back against a buffer, shoved his throttle up against the stop with his left hand, and when his RPM reached max, hit the after burner button, saluted briskly with his right hand, and grabbed the stick again. Then he waited patiently for perhaps half a second, as the after burner snarled up to a roar that drowned out even the jet engines.

On deck the cat officer snapped his hand down, pointing forward. At the deck edge a sailor hit a button. Below in the catapult room a light flashed from amber to green. The chief flipped a valve lever, and in the cylinder of the great engine high pressure steam hit the piston.

On deck the bridle took a strain, snapped the hold-back link, and away went Willy and Joe down the catapult track. From a dead stop they were making one hundred fifty knots in little more than a second. As they roared over the bow ramp a doohickey snatched off the tow bridle and whipped it under the deck and out of the way.

Most people think a catapult shot must be an adventure, and in a way it is. But it's a lot easier than a fly-off. When you fly one of those big jets off a carrier, you've got a lot of things to do exactly right. You've got to pour the coal on properly, you've got to hold her straight as you gather speed along the deck, you've got to ease her off at just the right point, and you've got to watch for an air bump at the bow. On a cat shot it's just WHAM, and there you are. All you gotta do is flip up your wheels, milk up your flaps, and you're on your way.

As he cleared the bow Willy went into an easy turn, climbing like a homesick angel. By the time he completed one circle he was at ten thousand feet and flipped open his oxygen valve. It was a beautiful day, just as aerology had guessed it would be, CAVU (clear and unlimited, visibility unrestricted). The task group now looked like pieces on a chessboard. They had completed the launch and turned back to base course, leaving a neat pattern of curved creamy wakes behind them—much more visible than any of the ships.

Willy squeezed his intercom button and said, "How ya doin' back there, Blueberry?"

"Okay, skipper," came the reply. "Cameras are all programmed and ready. All I gotta do is turn 'em on when you tell me we're at point X-ray."

"About ten minutes to go," said Willy. "I'll let you know."

At forty thousand feet on a clear day the horizon is over two hundred miles away. But you can't tell much about what you're seeing that far away, except for an occasional mountain peak sticking up. And even things that are right below you are seven and one-half miles away. Even the *America* looks no bigger than a shoe does at fifty feet. But of course, with pictures taken by modern cameras, photo interpretation experts can just about read the fine print in a loan contract. A reel of such pictures taken by U-2 flights told us more about Russian missiles than any cloak-and-dagger operation could have dug up in years. Taking such pictures on a clear day is just a milk run. The pre-programmed cameras do all the work and most of the thinking.

Willy, like many other jet jockeys, often talked to himself at high altitudes. As he squared away on the outbound leg of this mission he observed to himself, "This is an easier way to make a living than being on relief."

After about an hour they picked up the Israeli coast. Willy jogged south a while and then headed home. He didn't even have to worry much about navigating. There was a black box full of electronic sensors in the plane that had been synchronized with the ship's inertial navigators while they were on the catapult. This box was marking the exact geographic location on every film the camera shot. And as far as finding the ship was concerned, Willy would pick up their radio beacon at about two hundred miles and just home in on it. It was indeed a milk run.

But about halfway back to the ship, some little thing went wrong with Willy's starboard engine. The big jet missed a beat, let out a small burp, and then exploded, tearing off the outer half of the right wing, scattering junk all over the sky, and filling the cockpit with flame and smoke.

In the jet-jockey trade when things like this happen it

is customary to consider that this terminates your contract with the government to fly that airplane. SOP is to get the hell out of there.

Willy didn't diddle around trying to call the ship and explain his troubles to them. He *was* supposed, however, to serve notice on his rear seat man that he was about to leave. He grabbed his intercom mike and yelled, "Bail out! Bail out!"

There was no answer from back aft, and the cockpit was getting hot. Willy yanked his oxygen connection, pulled his feet back off the rudder pedals, sat bolt upright, and hit the eject button. An explosive charge blew the plastic hood off the cockpit and blasted Willy, seat and all, into the wild blue yonder arse over tip.

After three or four somersaults the seat flew apart, and there Willy was at forty thousand feet with no visible means of support except his parachute—which, of course, he didn't dare open up there. The air is too thin to support life and you'd freeze. He had to free fall for almost a minute before he'd get down around fifteen thousand feet, where there's air enough for a man to breathe. However, the Navy thoughtfully attaches a small oxygen flask to its jet jockeys' G suits to keep the boys happy while they're coming down through the thin air. The big danger in high altitude bailouts is explosive decompression—and the G suit takes care of that.

So down Willy came, end over end. When one end was up, he could glimpse the big ball of flame and smoke where his plane had come apart, with many small trails of smoke coming down from it. When the other end was up, all he could see was an empty stretch of salt water below him. Fifty seconds doesn't seem like a very long time, if you're sitting by the fire at home. But when you are free falling five miles or so over the middle of the Med—it's apt to drag out a bit. Willy knew there was a barometric element in his chute that was supposed to pull it at fifteen thousand feet. He was beginning to suspect that maybe it was stuck, when suddenly his seat pack snapped open and out popped the pilot chute—dragging the big chute behind it.

The big chute opened with a crack that shattered the eerie silence like a five-inch gun. Willy was jerked upright

169

and began swinging in big gradually decreasing arcs, like a kid in a playground swing. When he recovered his wits enough to look around him he spotted another chute half a mile or so to the east with a figure swinging below it. "Radarman Blueberry, I presume," he observed to himself.

Chapter Eighteen

Rescue

AT THIS time LCU 1124 was steering course two hundred and seventy at eight knots, two hundred miles west of Tel Aviv bound for Naples. Normal working hours routine was in effect. Webfoot had the watch on the wheel, and everyone else was basking in the sun on deck, caulking off or listening to Fatso and Scuttlebutt trying to outdo each other with yarns about the old days.

Fatso, as was his custom at such times, was holding forth on the U.S. Navy's role in World War II and the impact on it of one John Patrick Gioninni. This impact had been considerable as shown by the array of ribbons Fatso wore on his dress blues. Besides his Navy Cross and gold star he had a couple of Purple Hearts and theater ribbons for all oceans with more combat stars than there was room for. This morning the subject of his critique was naval strategy in the Med in early '42.

"The Germans damn near run us out of the Med altogether," he said. "I was in the *Wasp* then, and we saved Malta after the limeys gave up on it. The Germans had all of North Africa then, and there was Malta sitting halfway between Italy and Libya, smack in the middle of the Med, within easy range of German and Eyetalian air bases and the big wop naval base at Taranto. Malta was having a bad time. The limeys had a couple of whole convoys sunk trying to get supplies to them from Gib. So they finally gave up trying and just wrote Malta off. The Maltese was living on nothing but figs. But they wouldn't give up.

"Mussolini kept sending bombing raids over every day. But they had a couple of squadrons of RAF Spitfires that shot the hell out of the dagoes every time they came over. Of course on every raid they'd lose one or two Spits, and finally they didn't have many left, and it began to look like curtains for them. Spits didn't have enough range to fly in from Gib, and every time a limey carrier stuck its nose in the Med the German subs put a torpedo in its belly. So the limeys said they thought it would be nice if *we* would take a deckload of Spits in on the *Wasp*. So they loaded us up with Spitfires in Gib, and we was supposed to make a high-speed run toward Malta and fly 'em off as soon as they could make it there."

"Like the *Hornet* did on the Doolittle raid?" asked the Professor.

"Yeah. The Doolittle raid was the day we left Gib. Our skipper then was old Black Jack Reeves, and he wasn't about to let the *Hornet* get ahead of the *Wasp*. We snuck out of Gib after dark, ran for twelve hours at thirty-five knots, launched our Spits, and hauled ass back to Gib. Lord Haw Haw claimed on the Berlin radio that they had sunk us. You should of heard the whoop that went up on the *Wasp* when they put that dope out on the squawk boxes! Then we rubbed their nose in it by doing the same goddamn thing again nineteen days later. Altogether we delivered one hundred and twelve Spits, and Malta was a pain in the ass to the Germans until Patton got to Sicily."

"You kind of stuck your neck out on those runs, didn't you?" asked the Professor.

"Old Black Jack didn't think so," said Fatso. "Or at least if he did, you'd never know it. He was a character. He wasn't afraid of anything except getting left out of a good fight. One of the toughest skippers I ever served with —but a good one. He was like Admiral Uncle Ernie King. He used to say, 'Don't expect a medal for doing a good job—that's what you get paid for.' But Gawd help you if you goofed off and loused up a job. He was a hard man to work for. But the Germans thought he was a hard man, too."

"There musta been a lot of characters in the Med in those days," observed the Professor. "I was reading in one of Churchill's books about the two four-star admirals the British had in the Med then. One was in Alexandria and the other in Gib. They used to send each other insulting signals by radio that everybody intercepted and read."

"The one in Gib was Sir John Cunningham," said Fatso. "I was a sideboy one time when he came aboard the *Wasp*."

"Well, anyway," continued the Professor. "The one in Gib had married himself a young wife just before the war started and left her back in London. Nine months later

172

she presents him with a son. So the Admiral in Alexandria sends his pal a radio saying 'Congratulations. Whom do you suspect?' Not long after that the one in Alex took his fleet to sea and beat the hell out of the Eyetalian fleet. He was already a Knight of the Garter, so they made him a Knight of the Bath for winning the battle. So his pal in Gib sends him a radio: 'Congratulations. Twice a knight— and at your age!' "

At this point there was a muffled CRUMP—like big gunfire a long way off.

"What was that?" asked Jughaid.

"Sounded like one of them sonic booms the flyboys make," said Fatso.

As all hands were scanning the sky Satchmo pointed astern and sang out, "I see something, Cap'n . . . over there, and way up high."

There was a scramble for binoculars and soon Fatso yelled, "Yeah! I see it!"

There was a high vapor trail ending in a puff of black smoke about half the size of the sun, with smoke streaks trailing down from it.

"A plane must of blowed up! Right full rudder—ahead full speed," yelled Fatso.

As LCU 1124 swung to head back toward the puff in the sky a trail of black smoke streaked down from it and disappeared just beyond the horizon, sending up a great splash visible "over the hill."

"Head for that spot," yelled Fatso to Webfoot. "She hit about a mile beyond the horizon so we're only six or seven miles from it . . . log the time," he yelled to Scuttlebutt.

"Aye aye Cap'n—steady on course zero seven five," sang out Webfoot.

"Time 1045½," reported Scuttlebutt. "We're making twelve knots—about half an hour to get there."

A minute later Satchmo yelled "Parachute—parachute," and pointed up in the sky about two points on the port bow.

"Come left," yelled Fatso to Webfoot. "Keep your glass on it, Satch, and coach Webfoot on."

Pretty soon Scuttlebutt spotted the other chute, a little lower and further away.

"Okay, Scutt," yelled Fatso. "Keep your glass on that

173

second guy while we're picking up the first one. Matter of fact, the way things look now we may not have to pick him up. He may land right smack on board!"

This prediction was only a quarter of a mile off. It takes about fifteen minutes for a chute to come down fifteen thousand feet, and during this time LCU 1124 covered about three miles. Just a minute after the chute splashed down they eased up to the figure in the water, and eager hands dragged Ensign Willy Wigglesworth aboard over the bow ramp just as he finished inflating his rubber boat.

"There's another guy in the water about a mile ahead," yelled Willy as he scrambled up on deck.

"Okay. We got him in sight," said Fatso. "All engines ahead full."

Five minutes later, radarman Blueberry was hauled aboard.

"Didja get off a MAYDAY?" asked Willy.

"Nossir," said Blueberry. "It didn't seem to me like there was time."

"I didn't think so either," said Willy. "You okay?"

"I guess so," said Blueberry. "But I got a hell of a boot in the ass when that seat ejector fired. Damn near broke my back."

"Yeah," said Willy. "You shouldn't be slouched over when you fire that thing. You gotta be sittin' up straight."

"I found that out, sir," said Blueberry, feeling his back.

"Pretty damned good service you guys give shipwrecked aviators," observed Willy to Fatso. "I was figuring on paddling around out here for a couple of days at least."

"We got a standing order on this bucket," said Fatso. "To always pick up any aviators we see drifting around. Now—where's your ship and we'll take you back there?"

"They're about four hundred miles west of here. You better call them by radio and tell them we're all right. Sometimes they worry if planes don't get back on time."

"Can't do it," said Fatso. "Our transmitter is out."

"Too bad," said Willy. "They'll get nervous pretty soon and put out a search."

"Let's go up to the charthouse," said Fatso, "and we'll lay out a course to intercept them."

In the charthouse Willy flattened out some of his water-soaked files and produced the launching position and predicted noon position of the *America*. "We were due

174

overhead at 1218," he said. "And they'll go into their search routine right away when we don't show up. They'll be looking for us to the east, so I'd say you can plot them coming this way at twenty knots from their noon position."

"Okay," said Fatso, making two pin pricks on the chart. "There they are—and here we are, more or less." He stepped off the distance with his dividers. "Four hundred and fifty miles," he announced. "I wanta be damn sure we don't pass 'em in the dark, so we'll try to meet them about two hours after sunrise—that will be about 0745 tomorrow morning—about twenty hours from now. So we can just poop along at steerage way—maybe even run back east a little at night . . . No strain, sir. We'll have you back on board in time for lunch tomorrow."

Meantime, things were happening on the *America*. Down in CIC the radar had followed Willy on his outbound leg until he went off the screen behind the horizon at two hundred and fifty miles. A sailor behind the big plastic plotting board made a mark where he disappeared and posted the time, writing the numbers backward so they read right on the other side of the board. The CIC watch officer did a bit of figuring and told his plotter where and when Willy should come back on the screen. The plotter marked the spot and wrote "1142" alongside it in red.

At 1143, the CIC officer said to the radar operator, "How about Sugar One? Have you got him on your screen yet?"

"Nossir," said radar. "We've been scanning that bearing for the past two minutes. He hasn't showed yet."

At 1147 the CIC officer called Fly One and told the Air Boss, "We're getting worried about Sugar One. He's five minutes overdue on our screen now."

The Air Boss phoned an order down to Air Ops to stand by for a possible search mission and then passed the news from CIC to the Captain.

"When is he due overhead?" asked the Captain.

"In half an hour, at 1218," said the Air Boss.

"All right," said the skipper; "if you haven't got him in sight by then, scrub your scheduled ops and go into a full-scale search."

"Aye aye, sir," said the Air Boss. "We're laying it on now," he added smugly.

At 1205 word went out from Air Ops to all ready-rooms, "Scrub afternoon schedule. Sugar One is missing. Details coming soon for all-hands search. Stand by."

A quick radio check with the BINGO fields showed that they knew nothing of Sugar One. By 1300, fifty planes had taken off to sweep an area to the east one hundred miles each side of Willy's track home.

Fifty planes is a formidable search armada. One U-2 flying over Russia brings back more detailed dope on missile sites than the cloak and dagger boys can dig up in a couple of years. You might think that it would be able to spot a floating beer bottle adrift in the Med. But an eyeball search from a jet airplane is a lot different from studying high-powered photos with a magnifying glass. The boys were looking for two tiny rafts. Even with dye markers and flashing mirrors it's easy to miss them from the cockpit of a high-speed jet. And in this case, there were no rafts, anyway.

Several search planes passed near LCU 1124. But they had no reason to suspect she might have their friends aboard. Fatso and his boys waved frantically as the planes went by, but all ships wave at low flying aircraft. And jet planes can't take time out to circle and quiz every little spit kit they see on a thousand-mile flight. So all planes came back to the *America* with no news of the missing birdmen.

By 1600 when the last planes were back in the landing pattern a high-level conference was going on in Flag Plot. The Captain, the Admiral, and his staff were gathered around the chart table studying what to do.

"What do you make of it, Captain," asked the Admiral.

"I think he's in the water at least two hundred miles east of us, sir," said the Captain. "We followed him by radar out to two hundred and fifty miles on his outbound leg, and everything was normal. That's the last we saw or heard of him. He's not at any of the BINGO fields. There was no MAYDAY. If he lost his radios he could have navigated back by DR certainly to within fifty miles of us, where we would have seen him on radar. Whatever happened to him happened suddenly, and he had to eject. The fact that our first search didn't find him doesn't prove anything. It's easy to miss a rubber boat on the water. . . . There's no use looking for him at night, but I want to keep combing the area until dark and start in again at first light in the morning."

"Okay," said the Admiral. "Now, Captain, I'm going to go all out on this. As you know, NATO has just put out an Air Sea Rescue plan designed to cover just such a case as this. It brings all NATO naval and air forces in the Med into the picture. It hasn't been used yet, and this is a good time to try it out. I'm going to hit the panic button and ask ComSixthFleet to sound the general alarm."

"Aye aye, Sir—that's fine," said the Captain.

The Admiral wrote the following dispatch:

FROM: COM CAR DIV FOUR

TO: COMMANDER SIXTH FLEET

URGENT

PLANE MISSING IN EASTERN MED. REQUEST NATO AIR SEA RESCUE PLAN BE EXECUTED.

Ten minutes later an orderly brought the following reply to Flag Plot:

FROM: COMMANDER NAVAL FORCES SOUTHERN EUROPE

TO: ALL NATO COMMANDS

URGENT

EXECUTE MY AIR SEA RESCUE PLAN NO. A-1-66. COM CAR DIV 4 IN AMERICA IS

DESIGNATED OPERATIONAL COMMANDER.

"Hunh," observed the Chief of Staff as he read it. "They dump it right back in our lap."

"That's what they should do," said the Admiral. "But they give us a lot of horsepower when they do it. Now—let's cut up the eastern Med into areas and assign them to everybody who can help us, . . . and Captain," he said to the skipper of the *America,* "I'm turning this task group over to you. You do as you like with it. I'll take care of coordinating all the international stuff."

"Aye aye sir," said the skipper. "I'll keep my air search going 'til dark. I'll run east all night and lay it on again at dawn. Meantime, I want to pull all our destroyers on a search line and have them sweep ahead of us. I'll put them ten miles apart, and we can cover a stretch of ocean about one hundred and twenty miles by two hundred during the night."

"Okay," said the Admiral. Then turning to his Chief of Staff he said, "Get out one general dispatch to all NATO commands giving them all the dope we have on this thing. Then we will need about a dozen detailed dispatches to the various commands telling each one specifically what we want them to do."

"Aye aye, sir. . . . we're already working on them," said the COS.

Soon dispatches were cracking out to all corners of the Med to the British, French, Italian, Greek, and Turkish navies. All RAF and U.S. Air Force bases were cut in on the operation too, as well as the many commercial airlines that fly over the Med. Another dispatch went out on the distress frequency asking all merchant ships to keep their eyes open for the downed flyers.

As he released the last dispatch the Admiral remarked, "By gawd, we ought to have the boys spotted by morning with all this talent on the job."

That turned out to be the big trouble that night—too much talent. There were too many eager beavers, and they found too much. From that time on, that night was known in the Sixth Fleet as "The Night of the Gremlins." Before it was over, it seemed that every piece of flotsam and jetsam in the Med had been sighted by somebody and reported as "aircraft wreckage." Merchant ships reported flares, rockets, and lights on the water blinking SOS all the way from Gib to Istanbul. Airline pilots reported many mysterious lights on the water below. Ham radio operators picked up MAYDAYS—probably sent out by other screwball hams. Air force planes dropped flares, which generated a deluge of reports from merchant ships about seeing airplanes explode and fall in flames.

Soon after dark a report came in from a giant Greek tanker. "Have sighted your two flyers flashing a light from a small boat. Am maneuvering to pick them up."

"Well I guess that's it, sir," said the Staff Duty Officer. "Should we get out a dispatch calling off this all-hands search, sir?"

"Hell, no!" said the Admiral. "Not yet. I've been through this sort of thing before. Ask that Greek for his position."

Soon the Greek's position came in. "Hah!" said the Admiral as they plotted it. "Fifty miles east of Gib. That can't possibly be our boys."

An hour later another message came in from the Greek. "Cannot find your boat in darkness. Am proceeding."

(Actually the sighting was a couple of Arabs in a skiff, smuggling opium from Morocco to Spain. They had shown a light to avoid being run down. But they weren't about to be rescued! While the giant tanker was stopping and lowering a boat, they made off in the darkness.)

By midnight the chart in Flag Plot was peppered all over with "sightings" from Gib to Suez and some even well up in the Aegean.

Finally came the dawn, the gremlins went to bed, and left the searchers all gaping at an empty sea.

On LCU 1124 Willy and Joe spent most of the afternoon asleep. You have quite a let down after a high altitude bail-out (no pun!), and, besides, Fatso gave both of them a stiff snifter of medicinal whiskey right after they got aboard. They both took a good nap.

When they were up and around again, Satchmo said to Willy, "Just what would you gennelmen like for dinner this evening, suh?"

Willy was feeling pretty sharp again by now so he said, with tongue in cheek, "Oh—I dunno. I guess Alaska king crab would be nice."

This sally got a good laugh from all hands in the messroom except Satchmo.

"Yes, SIR," said Satchmo. "And just how do you like your king crabs? Boiled with lemon butter—or deviled —or à-la-Newburg?"

"Well now," said Willy, going along with what was obviously a gag, "I guess boiled would be all right."

"Yessir," said Satchmo. "We serve dinner at six."

A little later Satchmo got Fatso aside on the bridge and said, "Cap'n—you know that deep-freeze locker we got aboard in Malta for the Commodore?"

"Sure. I remember," said Fatso. "What about it?"

"Well, they is a nice mess of Alaska king crabs in there. Enough to feed all ten of us. Would it be all right if I serve them tonight?"

"Well now," said Fatso with a grin, "I should think it would be. After all, they won't keep forever. I always say 'give rescued aviators whatever they want for dinner.' I think the Commodore would go along with that, too."

So that evening Satchmo served up boiled Alaska king crab with lemon butter sauce, just as if he did it every day. The eyes of the two flyers popped at this treat. Everyone else had been tipped off, so their only comments were "What the hell? Alaska king crab AGAIN?"

Willy and Blueberry were duly impressed.

Next morning soon after sunrise groups of planes eastbound passed overhead.

"I guess they must of noticed we didn't get back on time," observed Willy.

Half an hour later they met the line of destroyers fifty miles ahead of *America*.

"I'll betcha the ship is following right behind them, Cap'n," said Willy. "We'll prob'ly pick her up dead ahead in another hour or so. Why don't you just keep going and surprise them by going alongside and saying you got passengers for them?"

"The Admiral might not think it was funny," said Fatso. "Webfoot. Get on the blinker light, and tell that tin can we got the two flyers off the *America* aboard. . . . Besides, for various reasons," he added, "we would just as soon keep out of the public eye. We can put you on one of these tin cans and go on about our business without making any whoop-de-do about it."

Evidently the destroyer skipper felt the same way about it. He came boiling over as he was relaying the good news to the *America,* ready to take the flyers aboard.

But the Admiral didn't see it that way. The first thing he did was to crack out a message calling off the search. Then he said, "By gawd, it's funny how things work out. Here we've had all the NATO navies and air forces scouring the whole Med. You'd think they'd be able to find a kid's sailboat. But a little spit kit of an LSU does the job for us! Tell the destroyers to leave the flyers aboard the LSU and escort her back to us. And tell the captain of the *America* I want her welcomed in kings' style when she comes alongside."

So the twelve destroyers escorted LCU 1124 back to *America.* As they were forming a circular screen around her Willy remarked to Fatso, "This is like getting a police escort up Fifth Avenue, Cap'n. I'll bet you'll remember this a long time."

"I'm afraid maybe I will," said Fatso.

When *America* hove up over the horizon, the destroyers scurried off to take their regular stations. As they joined the formation, Webfoot put his glass on the Russian destroyer that was tagging along as usual. "Say," he said, "we've seen that guy before. Isn't that the SOB that almost run us down on the way to Crete? . . . the *Vosnik?*"

"It sure is," said Fatso, focusing his binoculars on her. Then he let out a snort. "Hah! That signal we sent about her to the Russian admiral sure worked. She's got a new skipper already."

"How do you figure that, Cap'n?" asked Scuttlebutt.

"Take a look at the skipper on the bridge," said Fatso, handing him the glasses. "There's a big lanky three-striper up there now. The other guy was a little bit of a short fat fart."

Flying from the *America*'s yardarms on both sides was a "Well Done" signal addressed to the LCU. As soon as Jughaid could read it, the corresponding flags shot up to the yardarm. But instead of executing as soon as the little ship acknowledged, the *America* kept it two-blocked on the yardarm for the whole task group to see and admire.

Fatso brought his ship smartly alongside port side to under the crane just aft of the island. It seemed that the giant carrier could have hoisted the little one aboard bodily had they wished. The *America*'s crew manned the rail as they came alongside to cheer their returning shipmates, and the band sounded off with *When Johnny Comes Marching Home.* Dangling from the *America*'s crane was a deluxe sedan chair with a tassled sunshade, fancy cushions, a small vase of flowers on one arm, an ash tray on the other, and a gilded thunder mug underneath.

As Blueberry was going up in the chair's second trip the staff Duty Officer yelled down through a megaphone, "Commanding Officer report on board to the Admiral."

"Well—here goes the old ball game," observed Fatso again to Scuttlebutt. "You better be ready to take over this bucket. I may wind up in the brig."

Moments later, Fatso was escorted into Flag Plot, getting a big hello from the Admiral and Captain.

"What's your name, Cap'n?" asked the Admiral.

"Gioninni, Boatswain's Mate First Class, sir," said Fatso.

"Well—my hearty congratulations," said the Admiral. "You did a grand job, and I'm going to see that you get proper credit for it."

"Aw—heck, SIR," said Fatso. "Anybody coulda done it."

"We had everybody and his brother out trying to do it—but you're the one who *did*," said the Admiral. "What ship do you belong to?"

"USS *Alamo,* sir."

"*Alamo?* She's an LSD, I suppose—with the amphibious force, HQ at Naples?"

"Er . . . she's in the amphibious force, yessir," said Fatso.

Turning to the COS the Admiral said, "I want you to send a dispatch to Commander Amphibious Force and recommend Gioninni here for a medal."

"Yessir," said the COS. "Commendation ribbon?"

"No. He deserves more than that. Make it a Bronze Star."

"We wuz just very lucky, sir," said Fatso.

"So what?" said the Admiral. "Lot of people get medals for being lucky, and lots of others get hung for being unlucky. It evens up in the end. That's just the way life is on this earth."

"Yessir," said Fatso. "But if you don't mind, sir, I'd rather have you just send a letter to the *Alamo,* sir."

"You're too damn modest about it, young man," said the Admiral. "We had the biggest Air Sea Rescue operation ever seen in the Med going on for the last twenty-four hours—but *you* found our boys for us." Then, addressing the COS, he said, "Let's not deal with small boys on this. Don't send that dispatch to the Amphibious Force—send it right to ComSixthFleet."

"Holy cow," muttered Fatso. "Thank you, sir," he said dubiously.

Soon Fatso was back aboard LCU 1124 and she cast off from the big ship and set course for Naples.

While he had been hobnobbing with the Admiral, the *America*'s crane had delivered the traditional ransom for rescued aviators—fifty gallons of ice cream per head. Then they had thrown in a dozen cases of cigarettes, several gross of Coca Cola, a sack full of the latest magazines and newspapers, and a color TV set.

"Boy oh boy!" remarked Scuttlebutt, as the last cargo net came down. "Any aviator who goes swimming or sailing anywheres near this bucket from now on is gonna get rescued whether he wants to or not!"

Chapter Nineteen

Lost Sheep Returns

AT COMMANDER Sixth Fleet's briefing that morning there were happy smiles on all faces. The news had just come in from *America* that their stray sheep had been found.

"Well," said the Admiral, when this was announced; "our new NATO Air Sea Rescue set-up really produced quick results. Didn't it?"

"Not exactly, sir," said the COS. "It was one of our own amphibious craft that found them—an LCU."

"Well—it was a good drill for everybody, anyway. And it oughta make our young aviators feel pretty good too. They ditch five hundred miles from the ship without even bothering to tell us where. We have 'em back aboard within twenty-four hours. That's damn good work."

"Com Car Div Four has recommended the skipper of the craft that found them for a medal," said the COS.

"Okay. Why not? We had everybody in the whole Med looking for our boys. A little spit kit of an LCU finds them. He deserves a medal."

"Shall I just pass this on to Commander Amphibious Force and tell him to award it?"

"Hell no. I'll do it myself. What's the name of this young officer?"

"The skipper isn't an officer. He's a boatswain's mate . . . Grovino, or something like that. I haven't got the dispatch handy right now, but. . . ."

"Well, his name doesn't matter. But if he's a sailor it's all the more reason to make a fuss over it. I'll pin his medal on him myself."

"Aye aye, sir. His craft is en route to Naples now. I'll bring him up to see you as soon as he gets in."

That afternoon on LCU 1124, Webfoot came into the

messroom with a broad grin and a message blank in his hand.

"Just intercepted this dispatch from *America* to Com-SixthFleet," he said. "They're gonna give you a medal—Bronze Star."

"Yeah?" said Fatso. "I was afraid of that."

"What the hell? Cap'n," said Scuttlebutt. "Ain't you pleased about it? Lots of guys in Vietnam have to get half a dozen Purple Hearts before they get a Bronze Star."

"I already got a medal," said Fatso. "And for a Bronze Star plus fifteen cents you can get a cuppa coffee. The one thing in the world we don't need right now is a lot of publicity."

"You still worrying about the *Turtle* bit, Cap'n?" asked the Judge. "I'd be a lot more worried about eating up the Commodore's crabs, or putting holes in his car—except that he's way the hell and gone out in Vietnam. I think the Medal will take the curse off the *Turtle* caper even if they find out about it."

"Well—maybe so," said Fatso. "And after all, presenting a Bronze Star doesn't call for a fleet review. Maybe they'll just mail it to me . . . I hope! What do you think, Professor?"

"You never can tell about a thing like that," said the Professor judicially. "I read in a book about Napoleon, where one of his generals won a battle by disobeying orders. After the battle Napoleon sends for him and says, "For winning the battle, you get the *Croix de guerre*. For disobeying orders, you're gonna be shot.""

"Holy cow," said Fatso. "I hope this new Admiral in the Sixth Fleet ain't like that. If he was one of our old-time Admirals like Halsey or Nimitz, I wouldn't be worried. They was real sailor men. As long as you stood a good watch and knew how to man your gun, they didn't believe none of the idle rumors they might hear about you from the MP's. But these new admirals are always thinking about their public image. They're scared stiff that Drew Pearson will put their name in his column if one of their sailors lets a loud fart . . . What's this new Admiral's name?"

Nobody around the table knew.

Ginsberg didn't know a thing about him either but saw his chance to make Fatso sweat a little for throwing his films overboard. "I dunno his name," he said. "But I heard a lot about him. He's a hard-assed computerized Captain Bligh—busted a 30-year chief to first class because somebody wrote to a congressman about him. He's a regular square-rigged son of a bitch."

"Boy oh boy," said Fatso. "If this *Turtle* business ever hits the fan the UN and the State Department will be in the act, and half the Admirals in the Navy will get busted to Wave Second Class . . . and I'll probably retire to the Naval Prison Portsmouth instead of to the farm."

"That's exactly why you got nothin' to worry about," said the Judge. "Even if the Admirals found out about it they'd make damn sure nobody else did. Too many big wheels involved. It's like the professor told us in law school—it's easier to beat the rap defending a guy for diddling the government out of ten million bucks than it is for picking pockets. I'd much rather run the *Missouri* aground than get caught swiping a gallon of government alky."

"Maybe so," said Fatso. "It's easy enough for the rest of you guys to laugh it off that way, but *I'm* the guy that's holding the sack. From now on the officers can have jobs like this. That's what they get paid for. I'll just work at being a boatswain's mate."

Next morning they went through the Straits of Messina separating Sicily from the toe of the Italian boot. This is a turbulent stretch of water full of nasty currents and eddies and usually cluttered with fishing boats.

Navigation there is tricky, because you don't always go the way you are heading in those tide rips. So Fatso had the conn, and all hands were on deck kibitzing and enjoying the scenery which featured Mount Etna towering over them to the southwest. Hazy puffs of smoke coming out of the crater showed that though the mountain was asleep at the moment, it was far from dead. In many places on its sides you can see the rivers of now-cold lava that had poured down the slopes during past eruptions, engulfing everything before them. But the volcano's skirts are cluttered with little farms and villages of people who figure it won't happen again in their lifetime.

"Look at that," said Ginsberg, focusing his glass on the slopes. "People living right on the slopes of a volcano that can erupt again anytime. Nobody but a bunch of crazy dagos would do that."

"Oh yeah?" said Fatso, taking up for his ancestors. "How about all them people back home that live on the banks of the Ohio and Mississippi Rivers? Almost every year you see pictures of 'em being rescued off the tops of their houses by boats. But they come right back as soon as the water goes down. Etna only erupts every fifty years or so."

"Ain't this where that city got buried back in the Roman times?" asked Webfoot. "And now they dug it up, and you can see everything just the way it was the day it got buried?"

"Nah. You're thinking of Pompeii," said the Professor. "That's up on the slope of Vesuvius near Naples. And that got buried in dust, not red hot lava."

"I heard a lot about that place," said Jughaid. "I'm gonna take a day and go have a look at it. They say that if you get a good guide, he can show you some stuff that's worth the price of admission. Usedta be a lot of screwing went on there in Roman days," he added with a knowing leer.

"Hunh," said the Professor. "There was no more screwing then than there is now in Peyton Place. But all the dago guides in Pompeii got rich showing popeyed tourists dirty pictures on the walls. It shocks the hell out of these people to see pictures that ain't nothing compared to what their kids see every day at home in girlie and queer magazines. I'll betcha if one of our dirty-book peddlers had tried to set up shop in Pompeii the Romans would of thrun him to the lions in the Colosseum."

"Not if our Supreme Court could stop them," observed the Judge.

"You guys are Fascists," declared Ginsberg. "I'll bet you're in favor of burning books just like you were of throwing my films overboard. Don't you know that the Bible is full of dirty stories? Do you wanta burn that?"

"Yeah," said the Judge. "The smut peddlers always drag in the Bible when they wind up in court. How often do you think a kid sneaks out to the barn with the Bible to read the dirty stories?"

"Well—if you're gonna censor one thing you gotta censor them all."

"Balls," said the Professor. "I wouldn't be found dead trying to peddle dirty books. I'd rather be the head pimp in a high class whorehouse."

"Who the hell wouldn't?" demanded Ginsberg.

At this point the discussion of publishing ethics was interrupted by a hail from a small fishing boat. "What's bothering *him?*" asked Fatso.

"Sounds like he's hollering posta! Posta!" said Scuttlebutt.

"Oh yeah—I forgot about that," said Fatso. "It's too late now, but they want us to throw mail overboard. The stamp collectors in the fleet have got a racket going. Whenever a ship goes through here they put letters and a handful of lira in a tin can with a little marker buoy tied to it. They heave it overboard, the fishermen find it and mail the letters. The post office in Messina puts a special postmark on them."

"Stamp collectors are all nuts," declared Ginsberg.

"Yeah—everybody is nuts—except photographers," said the Professor.

Next morning the ex-*Turtle* made its landfall on the Isle of Capri. A lot of sight-seeing can be done with a pair of binoculars passing that famous spot. In fact, for most mortals that's the closest they can ever get to the millionaires' villas that dot the cliffs. All glasses were exploring the fairyland of castles, chateaux, and villas as they passed the island abeam.

"Some pretty cushy flea bags in that housing development," observed Webfoot.

"Look at that little pad right smack on top of the mountain," exclaimed Jughaid.

"Yeah," said Ginsberg. "That one belongs to a retired movie queen. She got tired of having a lot of nosey neighbors. Nobody but the birds can bother her up there. That 'little pad' cost a couple of million bucks. They claim all the johnnies in it are made outa solid gold."

"Well—you can't take it with you," observed Webfoot. "And I'll bet them solid gold cans don't flush any better than the one we got on here."

An hour later, LCU 1124 stood into the harbor of Naples and headed for the U.S. amphibious base with a signal flying, "Request berth assignment." Soon a light blinked from the tower at the base and said "South Side Pier Four." Satchmo, with Fatso kibitzing, brought her alongside, tied up, and secured the engines.

"Now," said Fatso, "We'll soon find out if we can get back in this U.S. Navy again without answering too damn many nosey questions."

As Fatso walked into the duty shack at the end of the dock, he found an old pal seated behind the OOD's desk, Chief Boatswain's Mate "Hawsepipe" Haley. "Hey, hey, Fatso," exclaimed the Chief. "What are you doing around here?"

"Hi there, Hawsepipe," said Fatso. "Just checking in."

"You mean reporting here for duty?" asked the chief.

"No. I brought in that LCU that just tied up to the pier," said Fatso, "and came up here to request assignment."

"What ship you belong to?" asked the Chief.

"The *Alamo*."

"*Alamo*. Hell—she left for Vietnam three weeks ago. How come you got left behind?"

"They sent me to Malta to get some stuff, and when I got back to Crete they was gone. Been looking for her ever since."

"Hunh," said the chief. "Somebody goofed. They shoulda told us they was leaving you behind. Some long-haired yeoman manning a mechanical brain punched the wrong button, I guess. Well—that's the way it goes these days. This Navy is going to hell in a computerized piss pot. . . . Lemme see . . . um . . . we'll just assign you to the boat pool here at the base till one of the LSD's needs you."

"That'll be fine," said Fatso. "We need some time to work on our engines. And how about reminding the *Alamo* to send us our records and pay accounts."

189

"Okay. I'll get the Commodore to send a dispatch."

"Well, I'd rather you didn't bother the Commodore about this," said Fatso. "Can't you just send the Paymaster of the *Alamo* a routine letter signed by direction?"

"Oh, no," said the chief. "Not in a case like this. When somebody goofs, the Commodore wants to know. I gotta tell him."

"Well—there's another angle to this that you oughta think about. I got a lot of stuff that was meant for the *Alamo* that I gotta get rid of."

"Okay—just turn it in to Supply."

"This is stuff that they're sure as hell not going to ship all the way to Vietnam," said Fatso. "None of it is on charge any more. But it will be again if we turn it in to Supply," he added, with a knowing squint.

Hawsepipe was well aware of the advantages that sometimes accrue to custodians of stuff that isn't on charge. "Yeah?" he said. "What kind of stuff?"

"One item is a black four-door sedan," said Fatso.

"Hmmm," observed Hawsepipe—beginning to see the merit of keeping this business on a low level.

"It's got some holes in the stern end," said Fatso.

"What kind of holes?"

"Bullet holes."

"Oh, . . . bullet holes. . . . Any blood on the upholstery?"

"Nope, . . . and the metalsmith shop can plug up the holes easy enough."

Hawsepipe saw no point in probing into the bullet holes any further. "Well," he said, "I shouldn't think any officers would want to go around in a car with a lot of bullet holes in it. But it would come in handy if I had it to use for official business."

"You can have this one," said Fatso, "if you don't get the Commodore stirred up about this thing."

"Hmmmm. . . . Look, Fatso. We'll just put you in the boat pool here and send the Paymaster of the *Alamo* a routine letter. I don't guess we oughta bother the Commodore about it, after all."

"Okay, Chief," said Fatso. "Your car will be on the dock this afternoon."

When Fatso got back to the ship there was a note there for him from the Staff Duty Officer. "Be on dock at 0900 tomorrow to accompany Commodore out to flagship and receive a medal."

Chapter Twenty

Prodigal Son

NEXT MORNING Fatso, in dress blues with all his ribbons
on his chest and six gold hash marks on his sleeve, met
the Commodore on the dock. Anchored half a mile off
shore was the fleet flagship, the missile cruiser *Memphis*.
She was a sleek, powerful-looking craft of fifteen thousand
tons, her topside covered with rocket launchers and Buck
Rogers arrays of guidance gadgets. The Commodore motioned Fatso into the after cockpit so they could talk on
the way out to the flagship. Fatso embarked first and remained standing till the Commodore seated himself in the
stern sheets facing forward. (By long-standing naval custom juniors get in a boat first and get out last.)

"Now, Gioninni," said the Commodore, "tell me about
this rescue business."

Fatso related how it had happened and wound up his
story by saying, "We wuz very lucky, sir."

"I wouldn't say that," said the Commodore. "I think
the aviators were the lucky ones, to have one of my alert
amphibious craft spot them so quickly. . . . What ship are
you attached to, my man?"

"We're in the boat pool at the amphibious base, sir,"
said Fatso, and held his breath for a moment.

The Commodore was more interested in the forthcom-
ing meeting with the Admiral than he was in the family
history of LCU 1124.

"I haven't met the new Admiral yet," he said. "And
this is a nice way to do it. Better than being hauled up
on the carpet when some of my people goof and do something wrong," he added tolerantly.

"Yes, SIR!" agreed Fatso.

"When we meet the Admiral," continued the Commodore, "you better let me do most of the talking. You
probably aren't as used to talking to Admirals as I am.
But if he asks you any questions, don't be bashful about

answering them. He won't bite you," he said with a chuckle.

"Aye aye, sir," said Fatso.

As they came alongside the rakish looking cruiser, four side boys for the Commodore hustled to their stations at the head of the brass-covered mahogany VIP's gangway, two on each side. The boatswain's mate of the watch took his place next to the after pair, ready to pipe the VIP aboard. The *Memphis'* Captain and the Chief of Staff stood facing the gangway ten feet inboard. The young OOD with a spyglass under his arm stood at the head of the gangway watching the gig come alongside until the bow hook grabbed the guess warp, flipped it over a cleat, and the coxswain began backing down. Then the OOD stepped back on deck just inboard of the forward pair of side boys.

As the gig came alongside the bugler blared "Attention to Starboard," and all hands on the weather decks knocked off whatever they were doing and stood at attention, facing to starboard. The boatswain's mate started a prolonged blast on his pipe, which began when the Commodore's head emerged from the cockpit and had to blast until he got up on deck. The side boys, OOD, Captain and COS all snapped up to salute as the blast began and held it while it lasted.

When the Commodore reached the top of the gangway he faced aft, saluted the colors, then stepped aboard, saluted the OOD, and said, "Permission-to-come-aboard, sir."

"Very well," said the OOD, and the skipper and COS stepped forward and shook hands with their visitor.

Meantime, Fatso had followed up the gangway half a dozen paces behind. He went through the same ritual with the colors and OOD, and exchanged a solemn wink with the boatswain's mate as he passed him.

The bugle sounded "Carry on," and all hands went back to their business as the official party headed aft toward the Admiral's hatch.

"The Admiral is tied up in a briefing now," explained the COS as they marched along the immaculately scrubbed teak deck, dotted with pieces of glistening bright work, with neatly faked down coils of boat falls near the scuppers. A wisp of marline adrift on that quarter deck would have been as conspicuous as a garbage can on the White House steps.

"He'll be through with the briefing soon. We'll wait in the cabin," said the COS, as they went down the hatch adorned with the fancy white line doodads that old-time boatswain's mates love to make.

In the cabin they were met by a Filipino steward in a white high-collared jacket with the ship's coat of arms on the breast pocket and three stars on each sleeve.

"Coffee for me, the Captain, and the Commodore," said the COS.

As the steward bustled off for the coffee, the three Captains seated themselves around the table in the center of the spacious cabin. Fatso, standing just inside the door with the Marine orderly, noted that this was a somewhat plushier layout than his cabin. It took up half the beam of the ship, had overstuffed leather furniture, a carpeted deck, and half a dozen king-sized portholes. At one end was the Admiral's walnut desk, and alongside it a door leading to his bedroom and head. At the other end were the pantry and galley, with sliding panels for passing in the food. There was a big buffet for the Admiral's silver service and plates and on it a handsome silver punch bowl and a set of fancy goblets presented by the Memphis Chamber of Commerce. On the bulkheads were auto-graphed portraits of the President, Secretary of the Navy, and Chief of Naval Operations, as well as a painting of John Paul Jones with a disdainful scowl on his face. He seemed to be saying to himself, "We didn't have all this frippery in *my* day."

While the Captains were having their coffee a couple of sailor photographers and white-hat journalists, accompanied by the Public Information Officer, entered and lined up next to Fatso and the Marine. The Admiral's Flag Lieutenant, with gold aguilettes circling his left shoulder, came in carrying a black leather case with a Bronze Star medal and the citation that goes with it. Addressing the PubInfo Officer he said, "Your people can shoot pictures while the ceremony is going on. You can get all you want of Gioninni afterwards. I'll give you a handout from the Admiral about it, and you can interview Gioninni if you want to."

Turning to Fatso the Flag Lieutenant said, "When the

Admiral comes in, you just wait here until I motion you to come front and center. Then you take three steps forward and stand at attention while the Admiral reads the citation. Then you step forward so he can pin the medal on you and shake hands. That's all there is to it. Okay?"

"Aye aye, sir," said Fatso.

The Lieutenant placed the medal and citation on a rostrum which an orderly set up near the Admiral's desk and glanced piercingly around the cabin to make sure everything was shipshape.

Meantime, the PubInfo Officer had spotted Fatso's Navy Cross with the Gold Star in it and said to Fatso, "My people will want to see you afterwards and talk about those two Navy Crosses you got. . . . Might be a nice little story in this."

"Aye aye, Sir," said Fatso.

Soon the door at the far end of the cabin opened, a Marine barked "TEN-SHUN!" and the Admiral and a half dozen staff officers strode in.

When Fatso saw the Admiral, his eyes almost popped out of his head. But he stood fast.

The Admiral nodded to the three Captains, said "Good morning, gentlemen," and walked over to his desk. There he fiddled with some papers in his incoming basket while everyone bustled to their places for the ceremony.

When the Flag Lieutenant said that things were ready, the Admiral went to the rostrum, picked up the citation, and started glancing through it. Suddenly he did a double take and looked up, just as Fatso stepped front and center. His eyes popped even further than Fatso's had.

"Well I'll be gah . . . , Fatso!" he exclaimed.

"Yes, SIR," said Fatso, standing at a rigid attention.

The Admiral strode out from behind the rostrum, stuck out his hand and said, "How the hell have you been, Fatso? Glad to see you."

He grabbed Fatso's hand and pumped it up and down, reaching out with his other hand and mussing Fatso's hair up. By now, all eyes in the cabin were popping—as were also the photographers' flash bulbs.

The Admiral turned to the astonished spectators, put his arm around Fatso's shoulder and said, "Gentlemen, this is John Patrick Gioninni—otherwise known as Fatso. He's responsible for me being here today. He saved my life when the *Lexington* got sunk. He got one of those Navy Crosses for doing it . . . and if any of you gentlemen who now have the misfortune of serving on my staff think that was laying it on a bit thick—you're entitled to your own opinion about it."

Polite laughter greeted this sally, followed by a round of applause as the Admiral returned to the rostrum, assumed a stern scowl, and said "Attention to orders." He then read the citation, pinned the medal on Fatso, and posed for more photographs.

Then he said, "Okay, gentlemen. That's all. Now, Boatswain's Mate Gioninni and I want a few minutes together to talk about—matters of mutual interest."

As the others filed out the COS said "Don't forget, sir, you've got to meet the Italian Chief of Naval Operations ashore in half an hour."

"Okay," said the Admiral. "If I'm a little late, he'll wait, . . . Orlando!" he yelled at the pantry. "Two cups of coffee."

The two old friends sat down at the table together, and the Admiral said, "Well, Fatso—it's grand to see you again. . . . I'll never forget some of the jams I had to bail you out of when you had that incinerator job on the *Guadalcanal*. That's where most of the gray hairs I've got now came from. . . . What kind of a racket are you working now?"

"Well, Cap'n—I mean Admiral—right now I've got this LCU." (Old sailors always have trouble addressing a former skipper as anything but Captain—no matter how much higher he goes.)

"What ship?" asked the Admiral.

"Well . . . er . . . no particular ship, right now. We're in the boat pool over here at the Amphib Base."

"How come you're not attached to some LSD? I thought those LCU's always were."

"Uh . . . yessir. Usually they are."

"Why aren't you?"

"Well, I suppose in a way, I am, sir," conceded Fatso.

"And what does that mean?"

"Our status is a little unusual at this moment, sir."

"As I remember it, your status always has been unusual —ever since I've known you. So there's nothing unusual about that."

"Nossir."

"Well—are you going to take me into your confidence —or do I have to pry it out of you?"

"Well, Cap'n—that is Admiral, sir—this is a touchy subject. It's something you really ought to know about— but not officially."

"Here we go again," said the Admiral. "This reminds me of the conferences we used to have in my cabin on the *Guadalcanal* when you got involved in high crimes and misdemeanors . . . all right, let's have it. What kind of skullduggery are you mixed up in now?"

"Right now, in nothing, sir. But we really belong to the *Alamo*."

"So—why don't you rejoin her?"

"The trouble is she's out in Vietnam."

"Vietnam?" said the Admiral. "Then what the hell are you doing here?"

"She went off and left me."

"Now wait a minute," said the Admiral. "There must be more to it than that. I'll admit I was tempted to do that several times on the *Guadalcanal*. But unfortunately, we're not allowed to maroon people any more. Some of those fine old customs, like that and keelhauling, should have been retained."

"You see, sir—they sent me to Malta to pick up some stores. When I got back to Crete they were gone. They were supposed to go to Athens after Crete, so I went up there. I tried to report in to SOPA there, like the Regulations say, but I didn't get anywhere." He then explained as diplomatically as he could about the brush-off by the irate, bleary-eyed Lieutenant Commander.

"Well—that wasn't your fault," said the Admiral. "I'll have that young skipper on the mat first time I get a chance."

"After that we looked around the eastern Med for the *Alamo*, and when we couldn't find them, we came up here and reported in."

"I don't see why you have to be bashful about that," said the Admiral. "You haven't told me anything wrong so far."

"No, SIR!" said Fatso.

"But it seems strange *Alamo* didn't leave any orders for you. Are you sure they didn't?"

"We check the FOX schedule every day for radio orders. There were no orders in Athens—and none here."

"Hmmm," said the Admiral. "This *is* strange. It looks like the *Alamo* goofed, and the skipper should get a crack over his knuckles for it. . . . I'm going to send him a sharp dispatch," he said, reaching for the buzzer that hung over the table.

"Just a minute please, Admiral," said Fatso. "I think it might be better not to do that."

"Hunh!" snorted the Admiral. "It's all very well to stand up for your skipper. I understand an old-time sailor man doing that. And I approve of it. But we just can't tolerate gross carelessness and slackness."

"Nossir, Admiral," agreed Fatso. "But there's more to it than that."

"There always is, in anything you're mixed up in," said the Admiral, shaking his head. "All right—let's have it."

"There were a couple of things happened that maybe you wouldn't really want to know about."

"By gawd I might have known it," said the Admiral. "Just like old times. But whatever hanky-panky you had going there, the *Alamo* is out in the Far East now, and you're here. So you've got nothing to worry about."

"Nossir. But this really has nothing to do with the *Alamo*."

The Admiral scowled, squinted one eye, and pondered this statement for a moment. Then a light began to dawn —a red light.

"You've been up to some kind of mischief since leaving the *Alamo*?" he stated.

"I wouldn't really say we done nothing," said Fatso. "But it all depends on how you want to look at it, sir."

The red light was flashing now, and the Admiral could almost hear an alarm-bell ringing. Admirals often are nowhere near as dumb as they look. "Where were you around the time of the *Liberty* incident?" he demanded.

"Lemme see," said Fatso. "We were south of Crete— off the coast of Africa."

"Oh migawd," said the Admiral. "The Egyptian coast?"

"Yessir. But way outside of territorial waters."

The Admiral weighed his next question for some moments and then asked, "Would you by any chance know anything about the USS *Turtle*?"

"Well, yessir, . . . quite a bit."

"So now we've found the skunk at the lawn party," said the Admiral. "Gioninni—I've said this before, and I say it again. One of the biggest mistakes I ever made in my life was letting you rescue me. Things would have been much simpler if I had just gone down with the ship."

"Yessir—I mean nossir. I wouldn't say *that*."

"Now I've got real trouble on my hands," said the Admiral.

"Not yet, Sir. Depends on who else hears about this."

The Admiral buzzed for the orderly. "Tell the Chief of Staff to come in," he said.

The COS entered looking anxiously at his watch and said, "We have to be leaving pretty soon, sir."

"Our Italian friends will have to wait," said the Admiral. "We've got a top-level international problem to consider here. Sit down, Captain."

The COS sat down.

"Joe," said the Admiral, "You are of course cleared for Top Secret, and I suppose have a Q clearance, too, from CIA and the Atomic Energy Commission?"

"Yessir. I have."

"Well, I'm giving you a higher clearance now. A special one held only by the three of us seated at this table."

The COS looked puzzled.

"You are about to hear something that could embarrass a lot of Very Important People. It's something you have a right to know as Chief of Staff and on which I want the benefit of your advice. But I don't want a word of it to go outside this cabin."

"Yessir."

"This man and his LCU were left behind by the *Alamo* when she went to Vietnam. There was a snafu somewhere, and the *Alamo* never notified us. He's been on his own in the eastern Med for the past three weeks, unbeknownst to any of us. . . . All right now, Gioninni—tell us about the *Turtle*."

So Fatso related the saga of the *Turtle*, beginning with its birth the day they sent the signal to the Russian Admiral about the destroyer that had almost run them down. He told about their visit with the Russian fleet in the Gulf of Laconia and their hasty departure when the Russian motorboat blew itself up. He recounted their chicken game with the Russian destroyer, the hanging of Charley Noble, and finally, the repelling of the Egyptian boarders.

At the start of this narrative the Admiral's face was stern, and the COS's face soon assumed a look of shocked horror. As the tale went on the Admiral had to struggle suppressing a grin that kept trying to break out. When the Russian boat blew itself up, the grin finally forced itself loose. The chicken game and hanging were just too much for even the Admiral's strong will, and he burst into uproarious laughter.

Meantime, the look of horror on the COS's face was deepening, and by the time Fatso finished, he looked like a man about to ascend the gallows and get hung.

"Well, Captain," said the Admiral. "What is your advice in this matter?"

"Migawd," said the COS. "This is awful."

"Is that all the advice I'm going to get from my Chief of Staff in this important matter?" demanded the Admiral.

The COS did not remain flabbergasted long. After all, he was a battle-seasoned veteran with medals to show for his quick thinking and bravery, had been a brilliant student at Naval War College senior course, and could whip out a sound estimate of a situation with the best of them. "This thing could have very high-level repercussions," he said. "We have gone on record officially several times saying the *Turtle* was no U.S. Navy ship. The Navy Department has assured the President that it wasn't. The State Department has sent official diplomatic notes denying that what the Russians and Egyptians said was true. This has to be handled *very carefully.*"

"Now wait a minute," said the Admiral. "Let's walk back the cat a little on that. We did *not* go on record saying it was no U.S. Navy ship. We said it was no ship in the Sixth Fleet under our op con. I insisted on that. Remember?"

"Right you are, sir. I stand corrected."

"So we haven't made any incorrect report. The *Turtle* was never under our op con. She still belongs to the *Alamo*, and the *Alamo* is out in the Far East in Skinny Jones's Seventh Fleet. If this is anybody's headache it's *his* —not ours."

"Hmmm," said the COS. "I suppose, in a way, that's right, sir."

"In a way, hell! This craft belongs to the *Alamo,* until we get a proper set of orders for her, records, and pay accounts. She's *Alamo*'s responsibility and that's that. We haven't done anything wrong so far. Now, the question is, where do we go from here?"

"I see what you mean, sir," said the COS. "I think maybe the smartest place to go is nowhere. After all, the United States has done nothing really wrong in this matter. The . . . er . . . *Turtle* had some provocation for the things she did. It would be very embarrassing for our government to back track now on what it has said about the matter. Even if we made a full report to the Navy Department now, the President and State Department might prefer to suppress it rather than admit to the whole world they had made a blooper. The case has been closed, and it's probably best to leave it that way. I recommend that we do nothing."

"A very shrewd suggestion," said the Admiral. "I wish I had thought of it myself," he added, with a wink at Fatso.

"Of course we do have to get this craft properly transferred to us, and get the records and pay accounts of her men," said the COS.

"I think that is being taken care of, sir," said Fatso. "The Supply Department here has sent a reminder card about it to the *Alamo.*"

"Good. That keeps it on a low, routine level," said the Admiral.

"By George," said the COS, "I think maybe I know what happened here. The *America* lost a helicopter about a month ago."

"Yes, I remember that," said the Admiral. "We had to ground all the whirlybirds and make a fix on the rotors. What's that got to do with it?"

"When that accident happened the whirlybird was returning to *America* from Crete, with mail from the Amphibious Force. The papers from the *Alamo* about this craft were probably in that mail."

"Of course!" said the Admiral. "And the *Alamo* never found out that mail went to the bottom, so we can't hold anything against her. . . . Now—what does the Commodore know about all this, Gioninni?"

"Nothing, sir."

"Fine. That's all he needs to know about it. . . . Now get my boat alongside, Captain—I don't want to keep that Italian Admiral waiting."

"Aye aye, sir," said the COS, buzzing for the orderly.

"And—oh yes, one more thing," said the Admiral. "Tell that young Public Information Officer I want to see the negatives of all pictures taken this morning before any prints are made. Some of the shots may be a bit —too informal."

"Well—yessir," said the COS. "But they are fine human-interest stuff. They would project a good public image."

"The hell with the public image," said the Admiral. "I'm not running for office. And God knows we don't want the public to think that the safety of this country depends on Admirals and boatswain's mates like me and Gioninni in our relaxed moments."

When the COS left, the Admiral said, "Well, Fatso— that pays off another installment on what I owe you. For gawd's sake take it easy for a while now."

"Aye aye, sir, Cap'n," said Fatso.

"I would have given a month's leave to have been there when you hung Charley Noble and to see the face of that Russian skipper."

"His eyes bugged out like a tromped-on toad," said Fatso.

"And when you made that Egyptian gunboat haul ass. . . ."

"Most fun I've had with my clothes on since the day the Master at Arms fell down the forward elevator!"

"Well—I gotta go," said the Admiral, getting up and sticking out his hand. "God bless you, Fatso—and keep your nose clean—if you can!"

On deck the journalists plied Fatso with questions about how he saved the Admiral's life. Fatso tried to beg off by pointing out they were holding up the Commodore. But the Commodore waved this aside. "No hurry at all—take all the time you need," he said tolerantly.

Going back ashore in the gig, the Commodore was no

longer mildly condescending as he had been coming out. It would be an exaggeration to say he was respectful. But deferential comes close to being the right word.

"I guess you and the Admiral had a lot of old touches to cut up," he said.

"Yessir. We been shipmates a couple of times. He was my skipper here in the Med for a year in the *Guadalcanal*."

"He seems to think quite a lot of you—naturally."

"We get along pretty good, sir. Finest skipper I ever served with."

The Commodore pondered for a few moments and decided that a man of Fatso's obvious talents and high-level connections might be more useful to the Amphibious Force (and its commander) in some other job than running an LCU in the boat pool. Employment on a somewhat higher level seemed to be indicated.

"Gioninni," he said, "I need a new coxswain for my gig. How would you like the job?"

Coxswain of the Commodore's gig is a sort of chairman-of-the-board job. It involves few command responsibilities and, in fact, he is usually defrauding the government when he draws his pay. But it is a nice status symbol and gives you elbowroom for outside activities. "Why . . . uh . . . yessir," said Fatso. "That would be fine."

"Okay. You'll hear from my office soon."

So—in due course Fatso turned over command of LCU 1124 to Scuttlebutt, duplicate records and pay accounts came in from the *Alamo*, and Fatso became a hard-working, regulation sailor setting a fine example for young recruits just out of boot camp. The Russian fleet retired from the Med to the Black Sea and never bothered us again. The Arabs and Israelis quit picking on each other —and we all lived happily ever after.

CLEAR THE DECKS

"One of the best adventure tales of the war."
—Time Magazine

"A book you don't want to put down once you start reading it." *—Our Navy*

"Clear The Decks . . . has an authentic, briny tang to it. And the climax, the tale of Admiral Gallery's brilliant capture of a German U-Boat, is breath-taking. . . . Anyone who wants to know the real reason why our Navy wins wars ought to read this book." *—Herman Wouk*

(64-411, 75¢)

EIGHT BELLS

"Delightful reading." *—America*

"Dan Gallery is an admirable admiral."
—Cleveland Plain Dealer

"Eight Bells is the story of Gallery's life in the Navy. The things that happened to him were enough for three careers. With his brash and breezy writing style, his rapid-fire quips and irreverent comments, he has produced a book which will not disappoint those who have come to expect high-spirited, rollicking entertainment from him." *—Navy News*

(54-659, 75¢)

You Will Also Want To Read . . .

THE SANDTRAP COMMANDOS
By Jack Lewis

They were the oldest, oddest, dirtiest, screwiest bunch of gyrenes ever assembled on one tiny island. There was Private Farrington, the flower power Buddhist who threatened to blow the military mind to smithereens. There was Shamley, fresh from a career as a rent-a-grave frozen corpse salesman. There was Lt. Crowd, who considered golf an affair of honor. And there was the sneak who replaced TV with a blue movie.

They're wild and wonderfully unpredictable! Move over Mr. Roberts, here come—THE SANDTRAP COMMANDOS!

(65-329, 95¢)

YOU'RE STEPPING ON MY CLOAK AND DAGGER
By Roger Hall

"The funniest record (unofficial, that is) of rugged adventure in the O.S.S."　　　　*—New York Times*

"Hilarious . . . the irreverent Mr. Hall takes us backstage into that incredible world of wartime espionage with a light heart and a raised eyebrow."
　　　　　　　　　　　　—Pittsfield Advertiser

"A terrifically humorous book about a dangerous assignment . . . We enjoyed it thoroughly."
　　　　　　　　　　　　—Berkeley Gazette

(64-263, 75¢)